For Melana, On your upcoming Wedding --
With Very Best Wishes,
(married) Marlene Cunningham
PS (Don't use this book as a primer.)
2011

In the Houses of Men

MARLENE CUNNINGHAM

authorHOUSE®

AuthorHouse™
1663 Liberty Drive
Bloomington, IN 47403
www.authorhouse.com
Phone: 1-800-839-8640

First published by AuthorHouse 10/5/2009

ISBN: 978-1-4490-1758-3 (e)
ISBN: 978-1-4490-1760-6 (sc)
ISBN: 978-1-4490-1759-0 (hc)

Printed in the United States of America
Bloomington, Indiana

This book is printed on acid-free paper.

1.

'What are they?!'

I was alone on the street.

From afar, I thought it was a field of flowers, like something from 'The Wizard of Oz'— Mom had just taken me to see my first movie, down on State Street.

But as I neared home, I saw that they were what I now know as caterpillars; fat cigars, sprinkled with brightly colored dots.

'I've never seen anything like these before!'

They covered the tree-lined street, blanketed the lawns, and crawled along over the red-brick sidewalk.

I climbed the concrete steps leading up to my house, stepping gingerly, so as not to squish them: I would ask my parents what they were.

Suddenly, my father appeared, a scowl on his face, nearly knocking me over as he brushed by me on the steps.

'Dad—?!'

He stormed off. Didn't answer me.

As I rounded the house to the side where we lived, I saw my mother coming onto the porch holding a clean white cloth up to her face, her bright red blood splotching through it, as she leaned up against the porch railing.

Her apron. . . The blue sky behind her.

I can see her frail figure still.

He must have broken her nose—it never looked quite the same to me, after that. And neither did he.

Though I have traveled many roads since then, this was my first taste of unease in my world, and in their Land of Oz.

A heavy, cold rain washed the filth down the sewers in Greenwich Village and sabotaged Jack Connelly's new camel hair overcoat, the night that he waited for Ellen to appear. His wide-brim hat did nothing but propel the water down inside his collar and soon, the blue suit was soaked, too.

'Jesus Christ!,' he told his watch, 'It's eight-thirty! She's half an hour late!' The idea, the very idea, occurring about the same time: 'She—! Stood me *up*? *Nah!*— That *bitch!*'

He lowered his head, plowing up the street and away, through the puddles and toward the Fourteenth Street Subway, while behind the gritty safety of the Jane Street Tavern window, Ellen watched. As Jack passed by, she downed her vodka-straight, and then she smiled.

Ellen Sipola, my mother, first laid eyes on Jack ('The Face') Connelly on a trip to New York, after strolling into a bar on Eighth Avenue with some friends. She was wearing her brown leather jacket, and a '30's beret pulled rakishly down, almost over one eye. It didn't quite hide her sharp nose or her purity of plainness.

There was The Face, a double for the handsome actor Tyrone Power (or Regis Philbin in his later-life), regaling the throng at the end of the bar with stories of how he could arm-wrestle anybody, and pick up 50-lb bags of sugar—with his teeth.

'I didn't get my High School diploma, but I know a Napolean Complex when I see one!'

'Yeah,' agreed her pal Liz, 'but he's nice looking. And it looks like he knows how to pick up *girls*, too.'

'Well, *I'm* not interested,' she said, turning away—but just not fast enough. Because at that moment, Jack made a bet with his friend, Crawford, that he could make a date with any girl in the place. And Crawfie, pointing out the blonde-browed Finn said, 'What about her?'

'Her? That one? He scoffed. 'Boy, it's *her* lucky day!'

So of course, Laverne 'Crawfie' Crawford (who always hedged his bets) told The Finn what The Face had just said, and ultimately, The Finn left The Face on that corner in the rain. Stood up. Begging for more.

'Funny,' he said, snapping the water off the brim of his hat, and waiting for his uptown train, 'She didn't seem to be the type of dame to do that.'

So he cajoled, persuaded, and eventually, even followed the enigmatic Finn back to her hometown: 'I can find work in the Erie Shipyards,' he told her.

He did. And she stayed with him, and overlooked his tantrums. Ellen never complained; Finns never complain. They sigh a lot, they mop a helluva lot of floors, but they never complain.

And that lasted for a while, until New York called him home again, with all the perversions and enticements its cavernous soul could offer an ex-Christian Brother, his now-wife and some still-pending progeny. That's how Maura, Cassie and Tim came about.

All so easy. All so hard. What would become of us?

I am Maura.

Brown. It was a brown, fitted dress I wore my first night as a hostess. I felt like a wren in the dress, but soon, under the pinks and the greens; the neon glow of the vertical USO sign outside of the window; the Christmas decorations; amid the bubble of laughter, I began to glow, too. A self-glorified goodwill permeated me.

There was this big USO somewhere in mid-Manhattan, catering to the enlisted men, the sailors and soldiers, all who served their country; it provided some soft lights, soft drinks, soft music and soft flesh in the form of 'hostesses,' to smile and dance with these out-of-towners. I volunteered. Maybe it was out of a weak sense of altruism, but mainly, it was to meet men and escape my unbearable home life.

I was nineteen now, rapidly attaining my peak of prettiness, and looking to do some damage. Typing and office activities had occupied my time for long enough, ever since I was fifteen and was graduated from high school. Nature was now calling me to do some genetic 'typing.'

I looked over the lame group of servicemen stuck like barnacles to the walls, clinging together or slumped in club-chairs, some in uniform, some, not all, looking morose. Dancing with one or two dorks, I had a pretty inflated opinion of myself, thinking, 'I really am doing something for my country!' Then, a truer moment: 'This will definitely be my last night here.'

But I saw one young blonde fellow, sitting off by himself, soft and vulnerable in a pullover sweater, looking kind of like a fuzzy blonde duckling.

'Hi,' I said, going over, dutifully extending my hand. My name is Maura Connelly. What's yours?' He looked up rather cautiously. For a fleeting second—as his eyes raced up the brown dress to my face—the duck morphed to fox, then back to duckling.

'Dick,' he said, reaching up for my hand, 'Dick Earhart.'

'May I sit down?'

'Oh! Sure,' he said, making a space next to him on the couch. '. .You a 'New Yorker?' . . . 'Yes.' He smiled and shook his head. 'I just can't believe that.' . . . 'Why not?'. . . 'you're so nice. New Yorkers aren't supposed to be like that.'

I laughed. 'They're not?! Why do you say that?'

'That's what I heard.'

'That's a misconception. They're—We're people, just like anybody else. Where are *you* from?'

'A little town in Wisconsin. Grantsburg. And Minnesota.

'Well, do they dance in Grantsburg?'

The song on the juke box was 'All The Way,' which we later called 'ours.'

Whether it was the softness of his sweater against my stomach, or the Minnesota accent or the blond-shyness that got to me first, I don't know; maybe it was my genetic code seeking that particular moment to kick in, but under the Holiday spell, I felt a burst of maternal protection toward this golden gosling, this poor, alien soul. I volunteered to show the Coast Guardsman the city.

Soon, after a few soft kisses and blood-pounding dates, we shared the mesmerizing sex of those newly installed in the Kingdom. It is always the best place to be, even though the Kingdom is a ratty hotel room. It was also the place where I got my first introduction to hangovers: how it feels, when a bed spins around of its own volition . . . how to crawl all the way across the room to the yawning sanctum of the porcelain bowl.

What an induction! What an initiation!

For those who newly discover it, whether it is a Garden or a Kingdom, it is bliss. We explored it together.

'I want you to elope with me to Elkton, Maryland. A lot of people do it there.'

'Are you crazy? No! I couldn't. We've only known each other a couple of months!'

'I'm shipping out to Gitmo Bay in three months. If you don't marry me, I know I'll lose you!'

His voice, soft as wind-chimes, entreating, coaxing, convincing me. . .'Yes, but!'. . .

'Don't you *love* me?!'. . . 'I *do* love you!'

It was a way out for me, a way to escape my past, I thought; I hoped. And he was physically as unlike my father as he could be, a good thing, to me.

So in three months, it was done. The super-salesman, from a long line of salesmen, had won. He had sold aluminum cookware and he had sold me. Played a mean trumpet, too. His gleaming smile was mine, mine, alone. Or so I supposed.

Two days before we were to elope, I was at the Taft Hotel, taking a shower and shaving my legs. One leg was propped up against the inside of the tub when I made a half-turn and slipped—just as I drew the razor up.

A six-inch gap slowly opened up like a portfolio on the inside of my calf, and parted like the Red Sea. My scalp tingled in horror, and I called out in a choking murmur for Dick—even though I knew he had gone out for sandwiches.

I tied my calf back together in two places with rags and awaited his return.

'I'm sick to my stomach! I think I have to go for stitches.' He looked down gravely through his yellow eyelashes and then back up at me.

'Nah. It'll be okay.' The coldness in his face shocked me.

That look and a long white scar is all that remains of that hideous night—a night that should have been a warning for me. Had I cut my wrists, I might have emerged in better shape.

Dick (and he was) Earhart was related through his grandpa to that famous female flier who disappeared, apparently a trait shared by that entire small clan. He, too, disappeared, as had his father before him. My eloper and I lasted a while, he pursuing a career in the Navy and a sideline unbeknownst to me, of lifting wallets from his shipmates. 'Transfers' followed: from Boston, and a third floor loft in Allston-Brighton over a lovely three-generation Italian-American family—(Mary: *'Fahgive my fatha fah nat speakin' English—he's only been in America fah fahty yeahs!'*)—to, finally, New Bedford, Mass.

I knew things were wrong, but not that he had had a frisky stable of women and an extensive personal library on con-artistry. I was older than he (chronologically, anyway) so it was I who cosigned on the Corvettes he totaled; that was only fair—to Dick, anyway.

'What happened to the rent money!?!'

'I don't know: I put it in an envelope in the bureau, like I always do! Is it gone?'

Dick nodded grimly: 'You must have spent it, and you forgot.'
'No. No, I didn't! I would have remembered!'

Soon after, I discovered, with a trembling, sinking heart, that
the casket-cut ruby ring my mother had given me for my eighteenth
birthday was gone, too. A tiny light went on. Sadly, it stayed on.

That I had an appalling lack of taste in men can be traced back
to hatred for my father for the things he had done to me. But for the
confusion, no, I mean, the *blindness!*—I cannot forgive myself.

Discovery was almost funny; almost funny. . . The way I checked
my account balance at a store in Boston one day. I was working in the
Motor Mart Garage in Park Square in Boston for Hertz Rent-A-Car,
and I dropped into the Shawmut TV store, just downstairs from my
office, and leaned casually up against the counter.

'Say, what's the balance on my portable TV?—I think I have one
more payment left on it.'
'Five thousand six hundred and seventy five dollars,' the clerk
replied.
'You must be mistaken!' I gasped. 'Please check again!'
He shrugged. 'There's only one *Earhart.*'
'Well—! Can you tell me what it's *for?*'
'Stereophonic sound system; television. You know—for the
summer house—? In Mattapoisett?'
Luckily, I was hanging onto the counter: I might have fallen
down—and I was two weeks pregnant.
Dick had furnished an entire summer home, stereo—the works—
on my lame-assed credit. George, one of his fleeced shipmates, let
me know that he shared the house with a few ladies—two of whom
he was 'engaged' to. It floored me.

I did have a baby. I did have a lawyer. I did have some wonderful
friends.

And he did disappear. And he did come back. And I had *another* bun in the oven! Even now, I hit my forehead in amazement. I loved him, whatever that was.

Yes, the blows kept on coming, and the ho's, too. He knew that I knew, and there was no fun in that for either one of us.

So Dick laid down his exit strategy.

'If you raise these kids,' he said, clearing the gravel from his throat and gazing levelly at me with his Billy Graham-look, 'bring them up, the way a good mother should until they are of college age, I—I—! will see to it that they get a college education!' He took my two hands in his and actually waited for a reply. There was none.

'I *said*, I—will pay for their college—' My burst of insane laughter stopped him. I stood up. I said nothing.

He left, taking cameras, money and anything else worth cash with him, piling it all up before leaving on top of the wash machine in the kitchen. Something fell on the floor that I wanted; he reached for it and I stepped as hard as I could on his trumpet-playing hand. He backed me against a door with a steak knife pressed against my throat. 'My knees are weak,' I said. He put the knife back on the stove. It was the next to the last time I would see him.

'Good riddance!' one would think, but every now and then, I would press my face into a couple of shirts he had left behind in the back of our closet and remember his scent, and cry. Then I stopped sniffing them altogether—something like giving up drugs, I guess.

Mystery had surrounded him like a newborn's membrane. It intrigued me, it captivated me and ultimately, it nearly ruined me. I fell under his Draconian influence. Poor goose.

An FBI guy came looking for him one day over some missing government calculators that had been traced to Yeoman Dick by their serial numbers, and now that he had been discharged from the Coast Guard, they wanted to know if I knew where Dick was.

'I'm filing for divorce by desertion,' I told him, 'I have no idea where he is.'

'Did you know that he had a nose-job when he was sixteen?' he asked, looking up from his notebook.

'Oh! I always loved his cute little nose!'

'And he has a sister, Nancy, who tells us he physically stepped over his mother, who died just inside the doorway, and did the *'Mr. Clean'* bit on her house, too, taking away all of her last worldly possessions. Did you know that?'

'No,' I nodded dumbly, 'I'd only known him for a few months.'

'This fella was born in Grantsburg, Wisconsin,' the FBI agent said, looking up from his notes, 'in case you didn't know that. . . if you're trying to find him. . . The 'Cheese' State. . . Hmm. Not surprising.'

'What d'you mean?'

'Given his character,' he said dryly, 'he must'a just <u>loved</u> cheese!'

'I sure can pick 'em!'

The FBI guy stood up and looked appraisingly at me, screwing the top back onto his fountain pen, and putting away his notes. 'Often, there are reasons why we do that.'

'Do what?'

'Pick the wrong person. You look like a pretty smart girl. You should take stock. Ask yourself, 'What made me pick a character like this?' He nodded, as if he were chewing over a secret. 'Maybe something in your past?

'—Because you don't want to make a *habit* out of picking wrong, Miss.'

In the beginning, the *very* beginning, there were butterflies and golden sun, and no hint whatever of the abject darkness to come my way.

2.

The plan was that I, as the oldest, would accompany Dad on the train to New York, where I would stay with his mother and sister, Kathleen. He would stay with friends until he could find a job, and an apartment for our family.

'We'll get a sandwich and drink on the train,' he said.

So began the trip and its residual memories of endless fence posts, clusters of black and white and cows, the stiff plush on the armrests and the unforgiving rash it bestowed upon my elbows, the stale smell of the train; the clickety-click of the conductor's ticket-punch and the strange names of passing towns he called out, and dozing in between, and then the same thing all over again for five hundred miles.

And the man in a white jacket, hawking food from a basket: 'One quarter!. . . Only a quarter!'

Two pieces of dry white bread and a slice of American between, washed down with a tepid orange liquid of unknown origin, so that it wouldn't stick in your throat—even while it was being laminated in your memory.

A burst of steam and the clang of wheels heralded our arrival in Grand Central and as we rose in the crush of the crowd to the street, under a still-intact memory of blue sky, I recall inhaling deeply.

'What is that—smell?'

'What? Oh. That. You'll get used to it,' Dad said.

A passing bus belched fumes in my face, and I was sworn in as an official New Yorker.

'Where're your *brains*?!? What d'you <u>mean</u> walking this poor child all over town—in *new shoes*! You ought to be <u>ashamed</u> of yourself!'

As Grandma put cooling liniment on the souls of my burning feet, she scolded Dad, and he stayed silent. I'd never heard anyone speak to my father that way before.

The day after we arrived, he'd taken me on a tour of the city, of marvelous marble-topped soda fountains and department stores and newsstands with tons more comic books than Jimmy Enstrom back in Erie owned.

By the time we got to the Empire State Building, I learned both that I had a fear of heights—and never to wear new shoes sightseeing.

This would be my home until Dad got a new job. In the world of Grandma and Aunt Kathleen, all was calm and order. I felt happy and safe here. My father couldn't rant and scream and drink. I almost forgot that he drank!

Grandma Connelly had blue eyes, too; we all did. And even though her cheeks crinkled up to meet them when she laughed, they contained a deep sorrow that you couldn't quite fathom.

She was a stately Irish woman from Roscommon, which made her—maybe, five-two? Her black hair, streaked with gray and worn banked high up off the forehead like a Gibson Girl, show-cased a startling blue gaze, the regal aspect severely undercut by a common pug nose.

11

She and my Aunt Katie lived on the third floor of a huge, brownstone apartment building that squatted on the corner of ninety-third and Columbus, a massive place with wings reachable down marbled hallways on the ground floor to apartments upward, on magically spiraling dark polished-wood staircases.

A Maintenance Codger named Mr. Taber, who wore a corn-cob pipe clenched MacArthur-like in his teeth at all times, striped blue-and-white railroad overalls and matching railroad hat, constantly scanned the distant hallways for trains, trouble or dust—a General, supervising the landing of unseen troops.

In an unexpected cubicle at the front of the building, I fell upon Dottie, a one-armed switchboard operator, manning her two-position plug-board like a machine-gunner. The ash from the cigarette in her mouth lengthened, drooped and fell, gently drifting across her stump: I gasped. I could not speak, awed by her obvious sophistication.

She glanced up at me, her brown eyes flashing, and grunted. I squeaked back a reply, and ran away.

I knew she was a real New Yorker.

As if this were not heaven in and of itself, what of the iced orangeade and bottled milk that appeared early each morning at the door of 3-A? Nearly frozen! So delicious! Add to that, the fact that everything I said, Grandma Connelly thought was funny. (I could tell, even though her brogue was a bit bewildering.)

My bed was the daybed by the bow window, overlooking a steady stream of busses and cars on Columbus Avenue. Beautiful Aunt Kathleen had her own little room, big as a Dutch shelf-bed, and festooned with rosaries and other religious replicas.

When I walked with her on the street, men turned and stared at her. Her long black hair was fluffed out around her cupie-doll face in the 'forties movie star fashion; her electric-blue eyes and black lashes stopped them cold—and when she wore her fox fur and ankle strap champagne heels, they were dead in the water.

Phil Grogan— 'Portly Phil,' they called him—was a roomer, as was Barney Sweeney, 'in construction,' and both of them 'dacent men!' Grandma stiffly proclaimed.

Choice as they are, all fairy tales come to an end, especially the one where the ogre pretends to be a prince. My idyll at Grandma's house where I was protected and loved, ended in two months, when Dad found work and sent for the rest of the family.

The five of us settled into a railroad flat up on 102nd and Columbus, purported, according to my Dad, to be 'about the finest place anyone could possibly want!' But it was about as far away from Erie, Pennsylvania as anyone could possibly get.

Flocks of butterflies gave way to gangs of fresh, freckly-faced Irish boys who sneered and yelled, 'Fuck You!' as you passed by them, or Spanish teens who in their macho way presented to we three childish imports a more ominous threat, gang-jacketed, serene in their solidarity. Whether it was all facade or not, it worked. I was terrified.

When I walked around the corner to go to the A&P, I did as I'd been told, staring straight ahead, ignoring the crude and raucous, cursing, stick-ball wielding street-toughs and bringing home the bread, the milk; the occasional tumor-bellied alley-cat, preferably blind in one eye. My parents kept the milk and the bread, gently releasing the other.

Two identical flats to each floor. . . We shared the top floor, the fifth, with Mrs. Wynn (who, oddly, looked a lot and *sounded* a lot like Ed Wynn, the 'Cowardly Lion.') She smelled like carrion, maybe due to liver trouble; I don't know. But that odor was pervasive in the hot summers.

The tarpaper roof over us made it a certainty that we would melt in the summer and freeze in winter. It sloped downward toward the courtyard, and doubled as our play yard: we were not allowed to play on the street. The roof just ended abruptly. Not even a lip at the edge: ball playing at your own risk—peril, in my case.

Railroad flats, or rabbit-runs, as they call them in Boston, are simply rooms in a straight line with an entrance at each end. The 'front room' had the living room furniture in it and was always so freezing-cold in the winter that the rumbling, sliding door that was supposed to seal it off from the next room actually *did* seal it off until the Spring came.

The 'master bedroom' was followed by two smaller rooms, usually used as bedrooms, too, with a large kitchen at the other end of the flat. This was the main family room. It contained a closeted dumbwaiter—to send the garbage and commuter roaches down by a pulley-rope; a sink, and a large bathtub on legs with a white chipped enamel lid covering it, for use as a kitchen work surface, drying dishes or food preparation. Clothes were washed in the tub. The toilet, a suspended tank and a pull-chain type (think, *'Godfather's'* restaurant-execution scene) stood off behind a door.

Airshafts were all that separated the row of adjoined tenement buildings on the block from each other; you could jump from roof to roof.

While Cassie and I wiped the dinner dishes, we talked to each other, during *'Superman'* station-breaks over our roach-filled radio. 'Yeah,' Cassie muttered, dangerously close to being overheard by the main bread-winner, 'The Connelly's are living in the lap of luxury!'
'Shh!,' I whispered cravenly, 'Dad will hear you!'

It is no secret to tenement dwellers that the roaches are Kings of The Hill and that it is we who are encroaching on their turf.

It sat in the middle of our kitchen; creaky, durable, second-hand. It had a green Formica top and a grooved metal border, hiding its dark and secret underpinnings; we ate all our meals at this table. It was the one place where we could momentarily relax; where, if

Dad thought of it, we had the *Question of the Day*, a poser each of us was required to provide to 'increase our store of knowledge.' If we missed our turn, we had to put a nickel in a jar for some future family 'trip'—an outing that, now that I think of it, somehow never materialized.

Anyway, Tim never took his turn, never provided a question such as, 'What is a large branch of bananas called?' or 'How many feet in a mile?' and somebody else was obliged to come up with one.

'Who was the third President of the United States?,' Dad asked as Tim got up to put his nickel fine in the jar. We all heard its sullen plunk.

'Tim, you never have a Question of the Day!' Cassie remonstrated, cutting into her Spam. We were having Spam, mashed potatoes and pork 'n beans, my favorite dinner. I had cooked it. Mom smiled, pouring me out a tall glass of milk.

'Then think how much money we'll have in the jar for later,' Cassie said.

'Yes, I prattled happily, 'Tim, wouldn't it be easier just to come up with a question—any old question?!' I curled my fingers comfortingly under the rim of the table, about to dig into my dinner.

'Does *anybody* know who the third President was—!?!'

Instantly, I became aware that the feeling in my palm was something more than conviviality.

It was large. It tickled. It had legs. I looked down—and opened my hand.

It—was the biggest roach I had ever seen. I flung it.

'Aggh!' I screeched and leapt to my feet, knocking back my chair and spilling my milk.

'What's the matter?! . . . 'For Christ's Sakes!. . . What's wrong!?! Are you having a *fit*?!'

'It—It—was a *roach!* . . in. . . in my *hand*!' Slowly, I held up my hand as partial evidence.

Everyone was busy mopping up milk and picking up chairs. Across from me, Timmy was laughing his silent '*Muttley The Dog*' laugh.

'Are you <u>crazy?!</u>,' Dad yelled.

'I don't blame her one bit,' my mother said, using a towel on the floor. 'I hate them! If I could touch them, I'd—rip them to pieces!'

'Yep,' Dad agreed. 'Some of 'em are so big, you could practically throw a saddle on 'em and ride 'em off into the Sunset.'

Time flies, but roaches remain. (Hello, to all you computer roaches. I know you're in there somewhere, cutting, pasting, editing, eating.)

Some weeks later, while checking the trip fund jar (maybe for bus fare?) Dad discovered that Tim had been putting metal slugs in the jar instead of nickels for his forfeit fines.

'And they're exactly the same size and weight as a nickel!' Dad marveled, holding one in his hand. We were all properly amazed as we examined it. A wry grin spread on his face: 'Maybe he isn't so dumb, after all!'

The makings of a cop. . .

Sadly, this was one of the few times I ever saw Dad proud of his son.

Dad's Aunt Nell, a pretty white-haired old woman, lived on the floor below us with her daughter Sarah, who once played the 'evil queen' in Snow White, and never stopped, and her husband, Nick, the small and long-suffering; once a prince, now a toad.

On a hot summer night with our windows open, you could hear Sally's threatening snarl, nagging at poor Nick with such venom that eventually, it drove him to suicide. Nell sometimes escaped her daughter, taking a quiet smoke up on the rooftop, contemplating distant chimneys, holding a cigarette between her fingers like a stolen codfish.

Nell's other daughter, Mary, The Sweet & Good, lived next door to them with her 'sickly' house-husband, Frank Farringate, who jocundly manifested the voice and witticisms of the late 'Arfur Garfur,' as he called him, and said things like, 'you dirty cow-yard,' and 'I'll commit sewer-pipes.'

He taught us to lip-synch *'You suffer much!'* which translated into *'You S.O.B!'* across a crowded school lunchroom—much to our delight—which many would argue, he truly was. . . While Frank tanned himself on the rooftop, Mary slaved at the Telephone Company to pay the bills.

One day, rushing home from work to fix her beloved 'Bunny' dinner, she died of a heart attack. . . Yes, he remarried—a month after. And yes, Mary gave credence to Billy Joel singing, *'Only The Good Die Young!'*

On the floor beneath Dad's relatives, on the right, lived a bookie never seen, never heard, while across the hall on the left, Bart was *often* seen, wearing an apron and cleaning house for his Italian mother and brother—but never good enough to suit them.

In a last act of defiance, he (emulating Nick upstairs) swallowed two big bottles of aspirin and was laid out, in the accepted practice, in the front room.

'You go in first!,' said Carmen Fernandez, shoving me in ahead of her.

'No! *You!*,' I hissed back at her, but it was too late: I stood in front of the coffin, staring at Bart's powdered remains, his folded dishpan hands, motionless at last. His brother sat nearby, bored and expressionless, picking his teeth.

I made the mistake of looking over at Carmen and we burst out laughing and ran out. I glanced back as we raced down the stairs, but the brother still sat there, picking things out of his teeth.

'It must be strange to leave behind your skin and bones, when you die . . ?'

'. . . it must be like the tenant has left the building,' Carmen finished, as we shuddered together.

The second floor was rented and re-rented so often that it was a 'Mystery Floor.'

Mrs. Mack, the Super on the ground floor, kept an amazingly clean, 'erl'-clothed apartment, and shared that floor with her buddy, Mrs. Houlihan, a genial Irish haystack of a woman, across the way.

All crumbless; all separate we stood, but all united, against our one common foe, The Roach. Our weapon of choice? *'Raid's'* forefather, The Flit Gun, kept loaded with DDT.

During the winter, the three small windows in a half-circle around our side of the airshaft stayed sealed up, so there was nothing to see across the way in the next door tenement, but winter or summer, no one in the building wanted to look down into that airshaft sinkhole, filled with garbage, paper and unknowable debris at the bottom of the pit. Rotten smells sometimes wafted up to us on the fourth, and it was amazing to me how those on the first floor withstood the hot stinky summer.

The kitchen window overlooked the courtyard five stories below the fire escape—which was not only a clothesline pulley hook-up, but an improvised icebox in the winter. Or a cool resting place on a hot summer night, if you weren't afraid of dozing and falling off.

'I know of some man who did just that—and fell to his death,' Mom said. 'But maybe it was just a *story!*' I said.

'Maybe,' she shrugged.

Our fire escape connected with the kitchen of the people who lived across the airshaft. There was a big dark-haired woman named Josie and her two homely daughters, Dottie and Johanna. Josie and Dottie were prostitutes (we later learned), while the other daughter, Johanna aspired to the opera, a slightly higher calling. On summer nights, her screechy high notes assaulted our eardrums.

'There's no hope for success with *that* one, with Rudolf Bing,' my father groaned, 'or *whoever's* in charge at the Met!—Unless it's Helen Keller.'

Occasionally, Josie gave great fun-sounding parties and their bathtub was filled up with ice and small bottles of Mission Orange and cans of beer. She good-naturedly offered chilled sodas to Cassie,

Tim and I when, hearing the laughter and music and envying the fun, we inched our way over on the fire-escape.

It was then that we learned forcibly from our father, about Josie and Company's 'negative life-style,' as it might be called today, and were forbidden to socialize ever again at her kitchen window. It was kind of a shame, because we had grown to like black, crippled Artie, their friend—or, perhaps, 'business associate.' He was always at the ready with a cold bottle of pop, a chuckle and a funny remark.

'Joe' sold ice to the Connelly's in the summer and coal to others in the winter, carrying it all up with a smile, and a sack on his back.

'All the icemen are named 'Joe,' but not all of them smile half so nice as ours,' Dad pointed out, and in the same blanket endorsement added grandly, 'And our *apartment* is one of the good ones! Mrs. Mac keeps it very clean and we get oil delivered right on the spot!'

With appalling timing, we had moved to New York for the winter of 1947, and the biggest snowstorm of the century, thereby providing ample opportunity to test the oil deliveries. It was always freezing so wearing two or three sweaters in the house was a necessity, even for vain little Cassie, who disliked the 'bulky look.' Tim, on the other hand, said nothing, his hands disappearing into his sweater sleeves like tiny hermit crabs. His response was to wet the bed. It soon became a ritual response.

One day, when Tim came in from school trudging through to his little room in the middle, he discovered that every raincoat and umbrella in the house had been placed strategically all over his bed.

'What's all this junk on my bed?! This—stuff?!' came the plaintive cry. My sister and I exchanged knowing glances, as we sat doing our homework on our pull-out studio bed.

'What stuff?' Dad inquired innocently, walking past us and into the Rainforest.

'This—! This stuff!'

'Well, the *roof* leaked last night, so I—'

'—Grrr! Rrrr!'

We heard the animal-like growls of anger and the sound of raincoats and umbrellas being pitched onto the floor, the sound of Dad's hideous laughter and Tim's angry tears. So much for child psychology.

Mrs. Mac, to the credit of our building, really did do her best, and was ever seen with mop-and-pail in hand and hair-on-chin, 'the wicked witch of the West Side,' as Dad called her. She had a strong New York accent—plus, she lisped.

As I walked in one day from the armed camp that was my school, I entered the foyer and heard Mrs. Mac in the back, by the Boiler Room, talking to the Oil Delivery Man, whose name, purely by chance, happened to be Earl.

'*Oil*,' she yelled, 'Youse can put the '*erle*' in the back!'

They all laughed when I got upstairs and told them the story, so I repeated it. We had no telephone, and no television, so— 'Everybody loves a good story,' Dad smiled.

—'Is that why the roaches live in the radio?'

Cassie always asked the best questions, and she never ever cracked a smile. She was a pretty good actress even then.

But there *was* always 'a fly in the ointment.' That fly was my father's temper. We all lived in dread of it. In later life, he copped a plea for his temper, drinking and wrongful acts, blaming them on. . . 'the death of my father, when I was just five.'

(I found his story then and now amazingly self-serving and, not surprisingly, the subject of child abuse never came up. Not surprisingly, I can barely talk about it, much less write about it. But yes, fire burns, Hell is reputedly hot, so here goes.)

. . .'I remember being called into the bedroom (*he said*) and walking up to my father in bed; kissing him goodbye on his forehead. His eyes followed me all the way back across the room,' he shuddered, 'I can still see those eyes!

'And then, after that, after he died, my mother had a breakdown and they sent me away to live with my Aunt Mary in upstate New

York. It must have been for some time, anyhow, because I can remember thinking, 'Nobody wants me!' I wanted to die. I found a rope, but I couldn't figure out how to hang myself: I was only five!

'And things got worse when I was sent away to seminarian school, as the oldest Irish boy was meant to do in those days, for the hoped-for attainment of purity. In the priesthood.'

(He sighed and shook his head, and in the pause that followed, Cassie said, '*Must have been terrible.*')

'Oh, there were some funny times when I—at my life at St. Mary's and then, the Christian Brothers!'

('*Like what?*' Tim ventured gravely.)

'...Wal, there was this one big horse on the farm at St. Mary's that we were warned about, that bit everybody. One day, this great big red-haired Irish novice was out on the farm working, and I guess he bent over to pick up a tool, or an apple from one of th' apple trees, and this horse took a bite out of his behind!

'He let out a roar, straightened up and punched the horse between the eyes, and knocked him out cold. That horse never bit anybody again. Cured him!'

Well, somebody or something 'took a bite out' of my father because he could be like a demon from hell.

For a while, things proceeded in what most would call a fairly normal fashion. Dad landed a job with Dowd Sprinkler & Maintenance as an Inspector. He carried a badge, wore Adler's 'Elevator Shoes,' and regaled us with stories of climbing up ladders to reach those old wooden water towers to inspect their water levels— the storage tanks on stilts that still stand atop many city buildings.

'Cedar is the best! They don't last as long as the metal tanks do, but the water has a better flavor.'

'How he can even get *up* those ladders is a miracle!' Mom confided to us disgustedly, 'Each one of his shoes has to weigh at *least* ten pounds!'

(The actor Alan Ladd and Dad had more in common than a pretty face. Dad would've had to stand on a box for *his* romantic scenes, too.)

People liked my Dad. He was handsome and he was also gregarious, though 'Teflon-guarded' (before it came into the vernacular) and he wore the politician's shield of invulnerability.

Had he more confidence rather than braggadocio, he could have tried modeling or acting, or with his word skills, a career in advertising (his younger brother was a Veep with the Associated Press for quite a while.) He could have parlayed his languages, English, Latin and French; his mathematics, and his seminarian experiences into a teaching job and done quite well. He could have. Anyhow, he never did.

People often thought he was a City Fire Inspector when he flashed his badge at them; thus, he frequently brought home canned goods, framed pictures or whatever was on hand or in the barrel at the factory he was inspecting. Fire hazards and water levels were something he took seriously: he took what goods they pressed on him, but never compromised his values by accepting a cash bribe, or looking the other way at any safety infraction or violation of a code. . . In retrospect, this ethic seems a little strange to me.

He seemed contented with his vainglorious position, probably taking home, maybe forty a week, and he kept the job all his life, still going in to work a few days a month, well into retirement.

'Your father is a nice man,' people would tell us, or a friend might say enthusiastically, 'Gee, your Dad is so nice!' Other than with a quiet laugh, neither Cassie nor Tim nor I ever responded.
We couldn't.

Sociability all but vanished inside the home. He had a quirky penchant for playing fast music on the radio, like polkas or mazurkas, so we would work faster dusting and cleaning, but he was tyrannical.

We lived in fear of upsetting his equilibrium, or there could be all hell to pay. One of those 'Adler's' would come flying at us and hit us right in the stomach or the head. The Italians call it, 'Street Angel/House Devil.'

But it was more than that. Drunk or sober, there was a dark uncertainty lurking within him, a side that we all sensed he could not control. It was just beneath the surface, hiding behind the half-smile, lurking; waiting to erupt.

There was a cold potato salad-smell that doorway delis used to have. Pungent pigs' feet lay behind glass casement windows in the display case, along with the salads, as eight-cent loaves of Silvercup, Bond and Wonder bread presided over them, on top; overall, the aroma of fresh rolls, the rarest of roast beef and somehow, the ubiquitous fragrance of beer, Rheingold or Ruppert, managed to permeate these stores in an olfactory brew, a magical scent never to be forgotten.

The one downstairs next to us was run by a quiet, auburn-haired man with immaculately clean hands. He wore a white apron and spoke in a gentle, low voice that commanded a certain respect. I could not imagine anyone cheating him.

There was a wooden refrigerator packing case in our room upstairs that served as closet space for Cassie and I. A dime lay wedged deep but visible, in a crack along its top edge. Mom had fifteen cents and we needed one more dime to get a container of milk, just a quart, just one more dime.

'Let me try!,' I said, 'I have smaller hands'. . .
'Use a knitting needle. . . Try a steak knife!'
Mom stood behind us, a bemused and sad smile playing on her face.
It took us well over an hour, but finally, the dime was retrieved and someone went down for the milk.

It sure wasn't Dad: it was Friday night. He was out spending it. So that forty bucks a week that he made didn't go far. Not for *us*.

Maybe the Deli Man knew that, too. Because more than once, he would overlook my fiercely blushing face and forgive the two or three cents I was short, lean over the counter and hand me the white-wrapped spiced ham; the quarter pound of roast beef.

So Mom kept her 'Day Job' as a chambermaid, and Dad had his 'Day' and his 'Night Job', chasing 'skirts.'

As an off-shoot, today I can't throw away a crust of bread, but Cassie can toss out party loaves without a twinge. But what has that to do with the price of potato salad—? Plenty, if you cite the disparate subject of Psychology, and nothing, if you argue that Cassie is an actress and makes plenty of 'bread.'

The medieval mausoleum known as P.S. 102 that masqueraded as a school, stood uptown. Not unlike a prison fortress, its crumbling ruins were held back within a courtyard that was surrounded by tall black iron gates, manacled together and spiked—against all hope of escape for the inmate/pupils.

Except for my brother, silent Tim.

One lunch period, he ran in desperation across the packed courtyard toward The Gates and somehow surreptitiously scaled their Gothic heights to freedom, making a bee-line for home and mother. Only she was at work as a chamber-maid at the Hotel Marcy on 95th and West End. When the school finally located her after they found him missing, the lady from the Attendance Office informed her grimly, 'No one has ever escaped from here before! *Ever!*'

'Something like 'The Rock,' Mom told us wearily.

The hint of a smile creased the corner of Tim's little lips, hinting at the possibility of future corruption.

I started the third grade in that crumbling dump. My teacher, Mrs. Shaffner, had square glasses, a glow and a beautiful smile.

But I sat terrified at that brown desk, aged smooth as satin; ink-welled and ink spattered, terrified—because everyone was much bigger than I! We were about to have our first test, a spelling test, and as I passed back the paper we were to use—narrow white strips of blue-lined paper—I fretted and stewed internally, knowing I was about to disgrace myself.

Mrs. Shaffner cleared her throat. I clutched my pencil.
'The first word is . . . CAT. . . . Cat,' she repeated gently. 'What?!,' I whispered in disbelief.
She smiled down at me gently, in the first seat there, and said softly, 'Cat.'

I exhaled with relief and wrote it down.
'Da-<u>Aw</u>-Gah!. . . Dog,' was the next word, followed by 'A' and 'The' and '*Is*.' I 'aced' the test, while a big boy next to me nervously chewed the stub of his pencil and tried to look at my paper.
It wasn't till the term was half over that someone discovered I was in a 'retarded' class.

Mrs. Shaffner called me to the back of the room by the Cloak Room and, smelling like Cashmere Bouquet powder, put her soft arm around my shoulder. (Somehow, I sensed what was coming: I wasn't that retarded.)
'Dear,' she said, 'We're going to have to put you in another class.'
'No, Mrs. Shaffner! I love you!' I started to cry. I was the star of that class! 'I don't *want* to go!'
'You'll learn more. You'll like it much better.'
She lied.

It's obvious that parents didn't go to school much those days. Mine never did.
School enrollment was by district, and pupil's address and was strictly enforced. I transferred to a 'better' school, P.S. 93, using Grandma's address and walking to her house for lunch sometimes. My sister, Cassie, was already enrolled there and already a grade *ahead* of me, even though I was two years older. Don't ask me how that happened, but it did.

Cassie had made friends with another slim, quiet girl named Lily Shimamoto and together they inflexibly ruled their 'Special -in-a-Good-Way' Fourth Grade Class; I was put in a regular dopey fourth grade class and as it turned out, was later comically promoted—into the *same* fifth grade class as my sister and her stalwarts!

Horror of horrors. Clunky me, and cookie-times alone, while Cassie and Lily broke peanut-chips together, and happily washing them down with two-cent cartons of milk. . . Wherefore art thou, Mrs. Shaffner!?!

They skipped me out of there, nearly prompting a belief in God in me, to Mrs. Taylor and the Sixth Grade—a normal Sixth Grade—with two weeks left in that term. Mrs. Taylor, a gracious old sot, very generously awarded me for absolutely nothing, with a perfect report card, all A's and 100's. . .My father carried it to work in his wallet and showed it to everybody, though all the marks were unearned.

Maybe she just liked me. So much, for fame and injustice.

From thence, I went to what they'd call a Magnet School these days; brand new Joan of Arc, half a block from Grandma's, and skipped from seventh to ninth grade, completing high school at fifteen in Julia Richman Country Girl's School; then on to an illustrious career as secretary and coffee-carrier.

Progressive Education was in its first bloom, so educators based many of their opinions on intuition and I.Q. tests; one such test had me at 112 points, another, at 149. An Assistant Principal named Dr. Birnbaum called me down to his office. As I never even scratched my head without a pass, I couldn't imagine what I had done wrong.

He eyed me appraisingly as I entered his office, and I asked him the obvious—that is, for the nature of my offense.

'Nothing,' he answered. I just wanted to see what a person who tests at a fourth-year college vocabulary level and a Fourth-Grade Math level, *looks* like.'

Perhaps I should have referred him to Mrs. Taylor for that, though I'm sure she couldn't take all the blame for that differential. Nor for the fact that if I left school by the 'wrong' door, I was irretrievably lost, no matter how long I went to any school. Even college. A sense of direction, like math ability, must be built-in. A sense of fear can be acquired. . .

Once in a while it happened in the day. She was on her knees scrubbing the floor, when the 'Building Inspector' came home. Whether he wanted lunch or she moaned a complaint about having to do floors before going on to her chambermaid job that day, we never knew. More likely, someone had made light of his authority that morning, or some woman had turned him down. Something.

He hit her, kicking over the bucket of water before he stomped off 'to get a *sandwich* somewhere!'

Cassie and I ran to her.

'Why don't you *leave* him? . . . Why don't you hit him with a *mop!* That's what I would've done! . . .

'Throw him out! . . . Throw him out!,' went the chorus.

'I've tried to leave him! I *have!* When we lived at Scapetti's, I put his suitcases outside the door, but he climbed in a window from the roof!' This was the 'clincher' told after every argument they had; dragged out quite fondly like a favorite doll, as if to say, 'See? There you are! He couldn't leave because he *loves* me. What can I *do* about it?!'

'I've *tried!*' came the plaintive refrain, as Timmy dried her tears and Cassie and I scowled and sopped up the water. As much as we scolded, '*Get off your knees and head for the hills,*' the harder she silently scrubbed. We were beginning to learn the score of an operetta entitled, *'The Sadist & the Martyr.'*

Only Cassie was seemingly unafraid of Dad, seeming to regard him with a patient contempt, like a little Japanese General held Prisoner of War—her eyes, blue and slanting—as if she realized his evilness was to her, only a temporary inconvenience. Sometimes she even stood up to him as he yelled at her, spit flying; when he turned in a huff to go, she would murmur sullenly, 'S'Long, Stumpy.'

Back he would come.

'WHAT did you say? *WHAT did you say to me?!?*' She only stared.

He turned away: Same thing! He returned, nearly hysterical with fury, raising his entire arm to her and threatening to kill her, if she called him that again. . . fearfully, we muzzled her.

No fear of roof-tops, no fear of Dad, no fear of the world. I admired her composure and wondered how it could be. But undoubtedly, she felt the pressure, too: she *had* to have.

One night, after a particularly bad week, after we'd finished our chores, going from kitchen to bedroom to do our homework, everything was the same—but something had changed. There was a desperate silence between the parents.

Dad's anger remained a black and brooding cloud, given to clashes of lightning. Mom's dreams of love had been given a terrible drubbing and lay now and forever in soft strips of sadness all over her face, veiling her Nordic beauty; they had gradually hardened into a plaster cast of betrayal. She wore it proudly, but imprudently, because even though it antagonized my father, it contaminated every aspect of her being: all part of the 'Passive/Aggressive Package' in her tour of the Garden of Love.

Whether it was propriety, fear or a deep and bitter-rooted stubbornness that held her there, I cannot say; probably all of those. She still exuded peace and comfort for us, but it was not enough:

'Let's run away.'

Who said it first? Who knows?

'Timmie,' the little warrior Cassie said, marching staunchly into his lair in the middle room, 'We're running away.' He raised his eyes from his comic book.

'To—where?'

'We don't know yet. But we're packing and leaving. Are you coming with us?'

'I—don't know. If you don't know where you're *going*—'

'C'mon,' I elbowed her briskly. 'We have no time for this! Let's pack.'

'We need socks,' she said efficiently, putting white anklets into a paper bag. 'More than that!. . . and underwear' . . .Don't forget shoes!'. . . 'We're <u>wearing</u> those!'. . . 'Oh, right. And some blouses! And'. . .and . . .'

Misery was our motivator. Escape was the answer. About school? We never gave a thought. Of lodging? Destination? Un-uh. No. Maybe a half-baked notion of staying at Grandma's briefly, but only that. We had to 'hit the road' that night, before we lost our nerve.

Timmie cautiously poked his head around the doorway. 'Are you going?'

Quick nods. He favored us with a peculiar look. 'You two are crazy,' he muttered before retracting his head back into his shell.

Mom was walking past us to her room and stopped short. 'What's all this?'

My heart was beating wildly. 'We're running away.'

She gaped at the twenty-five or thirty brown paper bags of varying sizes, cram-packed with clothes on our bed—and burst out laughing.

'Jack! Jack, come here.'

Enter Dad, looking quizzical.

'They're—running away!' she gasped, pointing to the bags— and the two of them laughed until the tears streamed down their faces, and as the tears rolled down our cheeks, we yelled, 'Stop *laughing*!

'What are you <u>laughing</u> about?! We hate you! We hate it here! . . . 'All right,' my father said, wiping his face, 'but how are you going to *carry* all that?'

As we gazed at all the wrinkly paper bags, the realization sunk in and the absurdity of our plan dawned on us.

'Look, if you really want to go, that's okay.' Dad added almost gently, 'Why don't you get a good night's sleep and go first thing in the morning?' Cassie and I looked at each other, confronted the enemy—and capitulated.

'Good,' said Mom, 'you don't want to go when it's dark out.'

'And,' Tim called out from his room, 'It might rain!'

'Oh,' my father said with wide-eyed innocence, 'Tim _knows_ about _rain!_'

Tim appeared suddenly in the doorway and the burning look he leveled at Dad was almost worth staying home for.

'Well, you <u>do</u>,' Dad said to him, 'Don't you?'

Snap! Back into his shell, and gone. Memories. . .and hermits, are made of these. Also, 'New York's Finest.' Tim did all right, despite the extra baggage, and my sister and I folded up all the paper bags and went to bed.

The sense of foreboding I felt loomed larger.

Cassie was sixteen when finally she did run away.

3.

We always heard him first, never her; loud, like a clarion call. It was usually late at night. Somewhere beyond the blur of sleep, the words came to us in a roar: 'WHAT lipstick?!'

A barely audible reply. We were now fully awake, dreading his response.

'Well, if it IS lipstick—By God, Ellen, it must be yours, because I don't know how ELSE it got there. It must be yours!' The faint reply, then louder, 'It's GOT to be!!'

That's the kind of argument that never de-escalates. If you're an adult, it's merely annoying and sleep-disturbing. When it is punctuated by the sound of slaps or furniture being knocked over, there is always the question of whether or not, or when, to call the police. But if you are two children just off a kitchen, and there *is* no phone, you are gripped in fear, a terror that is icy and immobilizing, too scared even to cling together; twin statues, listening and wondering if the younger brother in the middle room hears it, too.

If Dad's Aunt Nell or his cousins downstairs heard it (and they must have) they never called the police. In those days, it wasn't done.

Anyway, it was a 'family matter,' wasn't it? My mother had soft skin, soft as a dove. . .They must have seen the bruises.

We had a cat called '*H*' (because she had that letter in white on her head.) She used to answer our bell to let the people downstairs into the building.

'My arms were *filled* with packages, and you only rang a little bit! What were you trying to *pull*?!'

'Well, why didn't you ring the bell?'

'Of *course*, I rang the bell: I *did* ring the bell! But you never answered it, only like—a little *teaser!*'

'You're crazy. Why would I do that?'

'You're full of crap! I hate you!'

This kind of thing went on for a while until one day, the downstairs bell rang and I saw 'H' streak out to the kitchen, hop up on a chair below the bell, and with her right front paw stretched way up, 'answer it.'

Dad complained that Tim never closed the doors between the rooms before he left for school, to save the heat in the winter.

Tim swore that he did. Nobody really believed him, until he missed school because of asthma one day. Tim was home alone in bed, when he saw the doorknob jiggle and gently turn.

He began to sweat, figuring that maybe some desperate 'dope fiend' had hit our apartment for cash (*he must have been desperate!)* but exhaled, rallying his nerve, and peeked around the door, as it slowly opened —to find the cat, leaning out over the pillows on our daybed, and jiggling the knob with her two tiny paws. She seemed every bit as shocked to find Tim home alone, as the school authorities would have been. Riddles? Solved! Small cat, big brain.

But her big brain did not save her, any more than mine saved me: my parents made me call the ASPCA to get rid of 'H.'

I suppose she was just more trouble than she was worth. She was truly a beautiful cat, and I put on a hard-hearted manner and called them up. A big man in overalls came, and when he threw her in the crate he carried, I knew her fate. Really, I knew before he got there.

I just didn't let myself think about it. But underneath it all, I still haven't forgiven myself.

Something terrible happened to me soon after. My mother disappeared.

We were told that she had gone to Erie for a visit, and that she had become very sick while there. (Much later, we learned that she had been the victim of a botched abortion and had nearly died of Peritonitis.)

My father remained his surly self, working, drinking more than ever, playing the polka music on Saturdays so we cleaned faster. We were on our own most of the time and were used to the latch-key business. The entry doors at each end opened with a simple skeleton key, not that we had anything worth taking. Other than a huge stumbling drunk once mistaking our flat for his, we were not robbed or invaded.

Now Dad was confined in his off-hours 'caring' for us, and as he learned Mom grew increasingly ill, he drank even more heavily.

I came home from school that cold rainy day, my socks and shoes wet, and strangely, a kindness I never expected transpired: Dad removed my socks, sitting me on the bed, rubbing my feet to restore the warmth to them. He pulled the covers around the both of us, continuing to rub my feet, my ankles; my calves. His hand moved up my leg. His fingers had a hot, distressing feel to them and anxiously, I began to pull away.

Suddenly, he reached into my underpants and forced his fingers into them, and began rubbing himself against me.

Instantly, I was inflamed and appalled; heard the blood pounding in waves in my ears; felt my cheeks burning scarlet; my mind refusing to come to terms with what was happening. Today it is called 'inappropriate touching.' How innocuous a term is that!

Today, then and tomorrow, molestation is the nightmare that perches like a vulture on the shoulder of every child who falls prey to it, observing everything you do, participating in every relationship you have at every level, until the day you die.

Yes, it is 'inappropriate,' visiting at night, when you know your parents are together in bed as, to still the pounding in your ears at each creak of their bed, you clamp a pillow over your ears in desperation.

In later life, different agonies await your choice of a partner who will surely betray you in some way and being, ironically, successful at this choice—ironic because this might well be the only success you will ever achieve—if the Vulture, ever there, ever malcontented, has anything to say about it! Oh, yes, 'inappropriate,' if ever anything was.

At once, that day, I was aware of my brother and sister pounding on the door, returned from school, saving me. Abashed, I turned to the pale wall. My father went to answer the door. I heard him tell them I was 'asleep,' but this crushing, sinking disaster descending upon me had put me closer to death than sleep.

One or two similar incidents or near incidents followed, so that I was cloaked in a dreadful apprehension every moment I spent in his proximity. The prospect of being alone with him was terrifying. I avoided it at all costs.

It changed all that had come before and all that was to come after. That dreary tenement interior, those dark, tallow-colored halls, the acrid smell of D.D.T. at each landing had always depressed me; now, however, they filled me with an overwhelming shame and despair, as, gripping the railing, I dragged myself up the stairs, as if everyone on each landing knew what had happened to me. It seeped through my pores!

When Mrs. Mac passed me by in the hall, an alarm bell clanged within me, as if she could see what had gone on. And perhaps she could.

In looking back at old, creased black and white photos of those days, taken on the roof or with the family gamely dressed for Easter, I see the weary look of disgust etched on that young face, changed forever from my earlier, laughing poses; shrinking away from the father's hand, draped casually about the group; changed forever, changed from youthful hope to sardonic fear of discovery and a self-loathing that was unimaginable.

What right?! Ah, but wrong—wrong is everywhere, and who can deny it? The victim stands alone; here, revealed beneath her Easter finery; reviled, under the studied gaze of the world; alone and ever confused. My perspective had been marred, skewed and irreparably screwed—though thankfully, not in the actual sense of the word. I was nine years old.

After some months when finally my mother came home, she was skin and bones, weighing eighty pounds. She stood in the kitchen, leaning against a chair, fine-tooth combing our hair, weakly pulling out nits. We were all lousy, having contracted head lice in school that had evolved into monumental colonies: when I lay down at night, I could envision them scurrying here and there, playing on swings, on the bustling itching playground that was my scalp. I was so grateful for her soft touch even at such an odious task, that I beamed with gratitude.

'Oooh,' Cassie said, coming up and putting her small child's arms around my mother's aproned skeleton, 'Why are you so skinny, Mom?'

'I was very sick, honey,' came the same sweet voice, 'but I'm glad to be home again.' She took off her apron, put away the combs and went to get the bug shampoo for us.

'I had bad dreams all the time I was sick,' she sighed.

'What bad dreams, Mom?' I asked, following her anxiously into their bedroom. She looked down at me, as if from a great distance, leaning back against her bureau, while I perched on the edge of the bed, reveling in the sight of her sweet face: I had missed her so much.

'. . . In a dream that I had all the time, I was clawing my way up the side of a steep cliff, until my hands and nails were bleeding. And the winds—!' she cleared her throat of her tears carefully, swallowing hard—'the winds were howling, trying to blow me off, down to the rocks below. I was nearly to the top, and my arms and hands were all scratched—And then giant birds came; vicious, swooping down like eagles, pecking at my hands and face and my eyes—so that I almost fell. But I still hung on, exhausted and bloody. Finally, I pulled myself up and onto the top of the cliff, and lay there, panting: I made it. That was when I knew that I would live.'

'What a horrible dream!'

She nodded. 'In between that dream, I kept seeing you,' she said, a puzzled frown creasing her brow. 'You were sitting here on this bed, and your arms were stretched out and you were calling for me. . . You were crying.'

That was an awful moment for me. I was as still as death. As she was turning away, about to walk from the room, I choked out, 'Mom!'

'Yes?'

'It was real, Mom. I was calling you!'

Great sobs engulfed me. First, she held me gently in her arms, but she fell back in silent horror as I recounted the incidents with Dad. She made me tell her precisely what occurred and though now I'm sure that many of her dreams for the future ended right there, at that moment, she said, 'Never be afraid to come to me about anything. I promise you that this will never happen to you again.'

'What are you going to do?'

'I don't know,' she answered, hugging me tightly, tears still burning her haggard cheeks, 'I don't know.'

'I'm afraid. Do you—still love me, Mom?' She was nodding and crying into my hair at the same time.

It never happened again. They stayed together, whether for love or lust or habit or hopelessness, I cannot say. But sadly for me, for the betrayed mother and the never-pardoned guilty one, it had indeed happened. It shouldn't be that way, but it is; nor should babies have Cancer or people starve to death, but they do and it is, and it does happen. I feel sorry for a lot of people.

The loss of self-worth that should be the perpetrator's burden alone, is companion to children who bear this relentless secret, indoctrinating them into a silent society that is sure— it shows.

'They must read it in my eyes. Maybe they do. Maybe they do, and don't say anything. . . ! What could they say. . !?'

It never occurred to me back then, that this debasement had happened to anybody else. The backboard of my life had been shattered, yet I had to face a world of Wholesome Others; they would not know—they must not know—this shameful secret. . .

There was school, and my friends there. There was family.

No one must know.

Painting her would have to be accomplished with a soft brush. Palliative colors—perhaps pastels? But oil, to give her the golden glow of resolution; but full-figure—to portray hope! But, no. It cannot be done. Some people believe in angels appearing when all is darkest, to light the way. One such came my way a bit later in the form of a tiny young English teacher, Miss Elizabeth Colucci.

And there she stood, before our English class, this ever-immaculately groomed bird of a woman; a tilt to her head, black eyes twinkling, a wondrous smile and a cruel twist of a nose—a flaw soon forgiven and forgotten. She embraced us, each one of us, as future statesmen, with intent of purpose, kindness and stressing what might be accomplished in our lives: I thought she was talking to me.

At a time when I plodded to school, each day a dirge, her gentle voice soothed my soul, so parched for approbation. I yearned for her esteem, for her approval.

An essay assignment about our families prompted me to write an amusing story, far from the crux of my pain. I laid the humor on thick.

'Delightful!' she chirped, looking directly into my heart.

'Maura, you are a *writer*. This is a gift that you must cultivate.'

Delightful. . .! I scarcely heard a word beyond that. I strove hard in that class to maintain and deserve her faith in me. Today, if not the talent, there remains her smile of encouragement.

She was not by any means beautiful, but her face is with me still.

A sense of theater, we children did have. This came to early fruition on Thanksgiving and Christmas holidays, and, for me, it was a form of salvation. I could temporarily be someone else.

Dad's relatives and friends assembled at Grandma's for Thanksgiving dinner—many-vegetabled affairs that started out with half a chicken floating in soup bowls around the dining room table, huge helpings of brown and crisp turkey and stuffing and heaps of mashed potatoes and gravy, and came to a groaning conclusion with two or three kinds of pie.

Later, Aunt Katie tootled on the piano in the living room, where we had all adjourned, singing her reedy issues of 'I'll Take You Home Again, Kathleen' and 'White Christmas,' and culminating—culminating! . . . in we three children putting on our play.

Our audience: Prosperous Uncle Tom and Aunt Marge, she, of the leopard jacket; drunken Johnnie O'Connor, or whatever 'Drunk o' the Month' Grandma had invited; Uncle Frank, Barney Sweeney, the kindly monkey; our parents; sundry—all left, for a few moments, the cool confines of the living room, highballs or a ginger ale in hand, while we went 'into rehearsal.' Only one of us was reluctant.

'Tim, why do you eat Thanksgiving Dinner under the kitchen table?' Cassie was impatiently fitting 'prison clothes' on him.

He shrugged, as she pulled at him: he was going to be electrocuted, anyway.

'Yeah, that's stupid. Everybody is eating at the dining room table and you're all by yourself out there,' I added, 'in the kitchen. 'Under the table!'

'I'm not doing this play.' He wriggled his arms out of his gray sweater, which we were trying to button backwards onto him. 'Stop that! That's your *uniform*. Hold still, you stupid thing!'

'I'm not doing the stupid play. It's your idea, not mine.'

'Don't start this,' I said, 'You do this every year.'

'All right,' said Cassie smoothly, looking at me and transitioning into the Good Cop, 'This is the last year he has to do it, okay?' 'Right. Last time!'

He thought this over. 'Okay. But I'm not getting electrocuted. One of you can get torched.'

'But it's not funny if one of *us* gets it . . . !'

Well, little Timmy burned, and the audience died. It was our crowning performance. We killed. Uncle Tom's eyes teared over with laughter—a family trait—nearly spitting out his drink, as I asked the prisoner, 'Have you any last words?' and Tim replied, impassively as only he could, *'Pull the plug.'*

Uncle Frank wasn't always my Uncle. At first, he was just a tall, skinny soldier dating my Aunt Katie. He had an 'Adam's Apple' that stuck out like a sharp rebuke and an ability to make us laugh when he did the 'Miles Shoes' commercial 'dance:'

> *'Mi-els Shoes! Are the—shoes to wear/Why don't you go out'n—get a pair?*
> *Millions and millions buy their shoes, I said—For TOP shoe values, Miles er'—*
> *MILES ahead; THAT'S what I said—Miles Ahead!'*

Frank clapped his hands and with his long arms flailing, did an elaborately exaggerated 'soft shoe' dance, so funny, you could marvel or die. All for our amusement; all for the love of Katie.

He became a pharmacist and was graduated from Columbia University and though nobody could 'see it,' he became a part of her life. Marrying Frank Havelock was the smartest thing she ever did. And the luckiest thing for us kids:

'Tell us about the *landing*, Uncle Frank!'

'Well, all the guys were nervous, you know, and as the landing barge got nearer to the shore, we could hear the big guns going off, you know, getting louder; feel them rattling our helmets. Some of us were praying; some of the guys were throwing up.'

'What did <u>you</u> do?,' Timmy whispered.

'Me? I ate a baloney sandwich and read a comic book. What else was there to do?' He laughed that nervous, bubbly laugh he had, full of air and love, his Adam's Apple taking its crazy ride. 'One fellow got mad at me because I kept reading and eating, while he was throwing up!' Frank had one of those clear nasal tenor voices that tall, thin guys sometimes have.

'. . . Sure, I was scared. But what could ya do? You had to hit the beach. You didn't have a choice!'

He must've been scared; he lost half his stomach to an ulcer operation after the war ended. Yet he still could eat three helpings of turkey dinner at Grandma Kate's table—before stretching back and delivering the classic (pre-fast food) line, 'Anyone want to run out for a burger? I'm buyin'. C'mon!'

'Lucky for us you only have half a stomach, Frank,' Grandma sniffed, 'or, sure none of us would have a wing and a prayer!'

Eating was important to a man who had grown up with ten or eleven siblings. (One of them, Cathie Downs, was an actress in the 'forties, briefly married to the boxer, Barney Ross.)

And with all those brothers and sisters, so was an audience. . . 'My parents were Quakers—thee and thou; ye and thee, y'know—And My Dad was bald 'n had a long white beard.

'One night, we were all clamoring and pushing around the table for dessert, while he was cutting this huge pie,' he said, making his arms into a circle to describe it.

'Anyway, I was whining that my brother's piece was larger than mine. He told me to be quiet, but I kept it up, yelling how it wasn't fair and why should *Jim* have more than I?

'Finally, he looked across the table at me, and he said, 'Ye want the pie, ye shall *have* the pie!' And he let me have it—right in the face.'

We gasped: 'The whole <u>thing</u>?!'

Uncle Frank nodded. "And it was a <u>big</u> one. . . I fell over backwards, chair and all!'

'Were you hurt?!'

He chuckled, remembering it. 'I was sitting on the floor crying and while I was crying, I was eating the pie off my face!'

Gawky Frank and Beautiful Kathleen had three sons together, and plenty of pie to go around.

He was faithful to my Aunt Katie until she died, always bringing her candy and little presents from the drugstore at 86th Street where he worked, always feeling a little guilty that maybe The Iron Horse of the New York Yankees, Lou Gehrig, was really the *second* 'luckiest man alive!' Frank was an 'Iron Horse' of a different color, and how we loved him.

Bus fares, bread and the cost of living in the city was rising rapidly in the late fifties. It took more than a nickel now to move that heavy wooden subway turnstile.

Our rent had gone from a modest twenty a month, including utilities, to a cost-prohibitive twenty-five, and then to an unheard of thirty dollars a month.

'There's no reason I can't put that, plus what you're makin', Ellen, wit' it, on a house. Both of us working,' he added earnestly,' while we kids listened from our beds off the kitchen, late at night, 'an the kids'll have somewhere to play, other than the roof! An' they won't have to deal with the *low-lives* around here anymore!'

'Yes. But how'll we get the Down Payment? We have no money. . !'

Cassie and I drifted off to sleep, listening to their kitchen plotting, sensing that a plan was being hatched.

Grandma Connelly always had the same curious detachment from others that my father had, one blue eye gazing slightly off, as if from a great distance, creating for herself an other-worldliness. Her inner-self, well-guarded, was as far away as was any hope of ever getting to assay her true feelings.

To be sure, it wasn't warmth or maternal nature that was lacking, it was just—say, information? A nineteenth-century reserve in the twentieth century; Irish or Old-World rigidity—I suppose these might explain that 'cordoned-off' persona.

Anyway, persona, be damned. She loved her son and his 'half-breed' children as much as any alligator loves its eggs. And she provided, whether she kept it in the 'bank' tucked in the top of her tan cotton stocking, or in a bank account; or, whether more likely, she cashed in her life insurance policy to get it: she came up with the Down Payment.

The Matriarch provides!

We all drove out to Queens in our new-old Buick to look at the parents' final choice, a semi-attached brick Tudor style, bought from a widowed Italian lady, the original owner. Grandma was ensconced regally in the front seat, black hat and dress-coat; the money-bringer.

She was in her early sixties and at that very moment, in the fast lane to Alzheimer's, but we thought she was just happy.

'It's wunderful, Johnnie, for the children! A home in the suburbs!'

The ethnic mix was changing so much now, that half of New York City got Grandma's indignant raised eyebrow and the curt warning to her grandkids, 'Thim's not your kinda people!,' followed by a sniff. I was not so happy to escape 'thim,' as much as the personal torments that the house on Columbus Avenue held for me: I could never again look Dad in the face. I didn't know the dread would move right along with me.

What a surprise.

The Queens Village house stood right off a corner and down a block from Hillside Avenue.

'Look at all the big trees!' Cassie exulted. 'They're perfect,' smiled Mom.

After the first big rainstorm, we soon found out that perfection is quite a limited commodity. Water poured down from Hillside Avenue, overflowing the shallow catch basins and flooding our finished basement until it was truly finished. The far-reaching roots of the huge trees lining the block wrecked our plumbing and heaved up the sidewalks.

To help meet the mortgage, Mom got a job as a junior underwriter at a downtown Manhattan insurance company.

Two weeks later, I, at fifteen, joined her at National Surety as a junior secretary in a deadly daily three-hour commute by bus and subway, to be then set adrift on a vast sea of clattering typewriters; only one or two electric typewriters dotted the horizon. I handed over half my weekly pay 'toward the house.'

'Sucker!' Cassie sneered.

'How much are you going to give?' I asked her, in my usual state of confusion.

'Ten.'

'Ten Dollars?'

'Maybe. Maybe I'll throw them ten dollars once in a while, and that's it!'

It wasn't long before her exasperation got the better of her, and she went to live with a dentist's family as a live-in maid. Of course, no one thought she would stay with that. Cassie was industrious, but nobody told her what to do for long. Eventually, she married an importer, got a few walk-ons on television and then steady work on two consecutive 'soaps,' first playing the beautiful bitch, and then later, much later, the aging beautiful bitch, Cassandra Winters.

'I quit when they wanted me for the grandmother!'

Nobody fucked with Cassie. She stayed home in a new role, managing her kids, their kids and their lives—and doing it almost too well.

Once, Tim—retired from the cops to sip beer and trim trees—took a sip and asked: 'Hmmph! How *is* 'Rose Kennedy' doing these days?' He called her that. Or the Little Manager.

'Oh, she's doing fine. Though I don't hear that much from her. Let me know if you do.'

'Hmph.'

Cassie was my beautiful bull-dog, an oxymoron, I know, but about the best way I can describe her. After she left home, my unease grew exponentially. I worked all day, but the dread I felt when home became too much for me.

Tim was in his early teens and in Queens Village, like the set-up on Columbus Avenue, he had the small bedroom between my parents' bedroom and the bedroom Cassie and I shared.

But the space, the time, the universe, would never be wide enough to quell my anxiety.

The subconscious hunt for a mate probably began when I was eighteen. I changed jobs. (Today, you would say, *I upgraded my position.*) There were plenty of secretarial jobs in the late '50's. I would circle five a day in the Times, and be offered four of them that same day. I had been working now for three years and was a pretty good typist, about eighty to one hundred wpm, with plenty of errors. But I dressed well, was attractive and people seemed to like me. So I worked—primarily, in advertising.

And on weekends, I went to Spanish dances (Tito Puente) in the city for rumba, samba or meringue, alone, or with friends, hunting; maybe at Manhattan Center, to bag a cop or a firemen. But face to face, I was fearful of these Irish or Italian guys, and thus, unsuccessful in my quest.

*Some*body told me *some*thing about a pre-Christmas Dance being held at the USO: It was December the Seventh.

That night at *that Dance* (that for *some* reason I had to attend) led me to crossing a new threshold in New Bedford, Massachusetts; led me, in light of what the FBI guy advised me, to try to rethink my past and future choices.

But credit Dick Earhart with two children, both model-pretty, both soon fatherless.

After Dick fled, we got by without him, and though I was always 'looking,' hoping a Substitute Daddy would (*some*how!) appear, I felt we would be all right.

Friends in Boston bailed me out—'Lynn-from Lynn-who-took-me-in,' despite the burden of her own children, and Frank, a Transportation Lawyer, who not only staved off many a car and that appliance creditor for me—but also made me believe the world owed *me* a living, and that I would stay helpable and attractive for many years.

'Hell,' he said, brushing the few hairs back on his scalp, 'You're lucky!'

'*Lucky?!*'

'*Sure* you are! Would any of this be happening to you if you were *ugly?*! Some mothers would give *anything* for a guy to ask their daughter out on a real date! You're *lucky*!

'And if it weren't for that bum, you might be married to some nice guy today, and live in a duplex and own the *Twin Towers!*'

Though the Towers are gone and Frank is gone, with those few good friends, I still stand tall, and it has not been unassisted.

Oh, but it has been a long while since New Bedford, which is where I spent many a good, good morning.

4.

New Bedford is a coastal town, a fishing nook once bustling with whalers, and when I landed there in the 'sixties, (friendless but not childless) it's gentle streets were peopled with the nicest sorts, French, 'Port-gese,' and the affiliated Cape Verdeans, all calling out a cheerful 'Good morning!'

The Wagon Wheel and other brawling sailor bars were there downtown, where the fishing boats fringe the Harbor. That was all fine, too. Chair-bashing and red noses are not without a certain picturesque charm, so long as one isn't too intimately involved.

We lived on genteel South Sixth, in the old McCulloch Mansion, a brick building facing on a Temple, thus, converted into apartments for eleven old Jewish ladies. And me. Baby Kay and I had the basement apartment: before Dick took off for good, there was a Baby Jay 'in waiting.'

Yet calling it a basement apartment was a misnomer: it was a slow-winding wood-paneled 'S' shaped pad, with a bedroom at each end of the 'S.'

I was the 'trafe' light/TV turner-on for everybody: the old ladies liked their television on a Friday evening, but didn't want to break the Sabbath, so I'd switch off the lights (their candles being already lit)and turn on 'Gunsmoke' for everybody.

All unique they were, from the very beautiful ninety-year old Mrs. Alpert, to the staunch and sturdy Mrs. Miller, and the 'kvetching' Mrs. Serading, who made me potato latkes—but who can say it all? All, all were wonderful to me and though at the time I thought I was the most unhappy young woman, sitting alone, or among them, under the oak tree in the big yard doing my mending, I wore a crown of gold. Truly, conversely, these were the happiest days. God help me, I learned. And they helped me.

One day I got a pencil-scrawled note in the mail from Dick. My hands trembled as I opened it.

> *'I'm in Providence at this address. Come and meet me. Everything is okay. I miss you, Dick.'*

It contained a twenty dollar bill. I spent the money on groceries. But woman does not live on bread alone, especially one in her early twenties.

That night, when I tossed alone in bed, how I remembered the feel of that guy's hands on me! The sound of his voice was electroplated in my brain. At last, finally, somewhere between three and four in the morning, I picked up the phone and called him.

'Hello?' his voice answered sleepily.

'Oh, Dick,' I burst out, 'I love you, I love you! I miss you so much! I got your letter. I—I wanted to tell—I wanted to *call* you <u>so</u> many times—to tell you—that I love you. That's all. I love you!'

'I love <u>you</u>, too, honey.' But a raucous peal of feminine laughter accompanied this message into the mouthpiece. I clearly envisioned some woman's head on his shoulder, listening and laughing at me. I winced and silently hung up the phone.

Consecutive flaming blushes kept me company for the rest of that night.

The Great Being provides. Posie was the other goyem at South Sixth: at 54, a buxom Cannuck waitress of steel-gray hair and corn-flower blue eyes. She worked at Mickey's Luncheonette downtown.

Ratta-Tat-Tat, on my door: 'Come on. I have the afternoon off. We'll take a ride out to see the pumpkins.'

'No, Posie, I can't. I have these *cans*, and this surplus food to put away. I have too much to—' The light blue eyes flashed at me, the little mouth pursing into a frown: 'Don't you ever tell me that again! If someone is nice enough to come to you on a sunny day to take the kid to pick *pumpkins*, don't refuse. 'Do you think someone is going to put, *'She swept the floor'* on your tombstone? Do you!?'

I still have that picture of little Kim sitting atop a huge pumpkin, the sky, dark blue behind her. . . I was never that good about floors, anyway, but I was always great at picking friends. And pumpkins.

One day, I heard a scuffle or a rustle at the door, a noise so slight I thought I'd imagined it. When finally I thought to open the door, there was a large cardboard box, like a coat box, leaning up against it. I looked around, but no one was there. I took it inside.

No name, no address on it. 'Someone's made a mistake,' I murmured, ' I probably shouldn't open it,' I said, even though I knew I would.

There were several layers of white tissue to unwrap and when I did, a billowy aqua chiffon dress flowed out; a cummerbund embroidered in fishnet-threaded rhinestones circled the waist and an attached scarf drifted back from the neck, Grecian style. I lifted it up and pressed into it, inhaling its newness. 'It can't be for me!,' I whispered. 'But it's beautiful. . . And—it's my size!'

And it was definitely my color. So whether or not it was for me—voila! It was for me.

I couldn't wait for Posie to stop by my door after work, as she always did. She didn't even have a chance to rap on the door!

After examining the Cinderella dress, Posie peered off to some unseen vantage point. A smile played on her lips: 'I think I know who left this here.'

'You do! Who?!'

'Well, hier soir, I was talking to him about you and he—'

'He, *who*?!!'

'Mon cousin, Renaud. Je pense qu'il est Renaud.'

I stopped to think. Posie had a cousin named Reynaud Robitaille. We had met briefly not too long ago; she had introduced us. Rey had an oil burner business in nearby Fairhaven. Instantly, I recalled the sleek fat face of the portly Reynaud smiling at me; eyes twinkly; black wavy hair slicked back.

His wife ran off years ago, leaving him with a red-haired daughter and a blond-haired son, now handsome teenagers; oddly, neither of them remotely resembling Rey. Yet he was a great father to them.

'Does he have a girlfriend?'

'One he sees off and on, for years.' . 'La Meme fille?. . . 'Oui. Same one: Gracie. They call her *Grande Titons*! . . . Ah, Big—?! . . . Yes. . . But you should keep the dress.

'I suppose he wanted you to have it; the dress. Bien sur, he meant you to wear it and think nothing of it. You know, he has beaucoup d'argent!'

'Oh, but I *couldn't.*'

'Oh, but you *must!*'

So, of course, I *did*. And it would not have cost me a thing, especially since R.R. already had a live-in lady-friend. But fair is fair, and since he was so very nice, tres suave and kind, we had dinner together at the Fairhaven Manor and (bien sur) I was tres horny.

I sank back into the luxury of Rey's large, well-upholstered car, glancing sideways at him, as we tooled back to my place. All was quiet and peaceful; the night air; the apartment building, in complete, silent darkness.

'Good night,' said Posie. . . 'Thanks so much! I really—'

A sharp elbow in my rib interrupted me: I saw her lips purse into a tiny smile, her eyes, glittering their wordless intent. She pulled the door closed behind her. And I heard her exclaim as she rose out of sight, 'The kids're fast asleep. . . You two 'ave a good night!'

When Rey sat on the edge of my bed removing his clothes under the lamplight, I realized it was not only his Cadillac that was well-upholstered, but his ample butt, as well. My tentative arm reaching around his girth confirmed for me that it extended to a truly ponderous pot-belly: regrettably, a 'down-sizing' did occur—but not where you might want it. This was my first experience with a corpulent person, but not my last: (Since I'm still alive, I can't be positive!) However, he was a nice guy.

I barely had time to suppress a sigh, before he rolled over on top of me and the lights went out. He rolled, I rolled and gently, unbelievably fast—the deed was done!—although, for the life of me, I wouldn't swear to it.

The reason I know it happened (for *him*, anyway) was that in the split second that followed, Rey let out a tremendous roar. The night was rent with it!

'What's wrong?!' I gasped, as his howling body, hurled—catapulted over me!—in the pitch dark, onto the floor, bumping, crashing around, hollering like a butchered hog. 'Heart attack!?!' I thought, groping for the light switch, 'Stroke?!?'

'Stop! What's *wrong with you*? Stop! My neighbors!' What would poor little Mrs. Alpert directly above me think? Never mind her! What would Mrs. Miller on the *Fifth* floor think?!? Still, he wailed.

'Please!' I kicked at him under the lamplight until he stared up at me. . . 'Why did you *do* that?!'

'I *always* do that,' he replied, sighing contentedly. In the parlance of the day, Rey was a 'screamer.' (Most guys know what I mean— if they recall a certain waitress in Tupelo, or maybe Bethesda.)

But not in *my* backyard! No more, Tubby the Tuba!

A blonde bee-hive hairstyle, white knee-high boots, a short skirt, with a girl bazoomed in between, showed up at my door a week later: It was Rey's 'significant other,' Gracie. (I should have told her she needn't have bothered.)

'Are you Maura?' she said, sizing me up in my dowdy at-home clothing. I nodded. 'I'm Gracine, Rey's *fiancée*. I found the bill for the dress he bought you.'

'There was nothing at all between us. Nothing!' (And I had not had to *lie* to her, either!) I pitched her the 'act of kindness' story and after taking a good look at me, she bought it and left.

When I told Posie later that evening about Gracine's visiting me to stake a claim on her man, she said, 'Oooh, she must have heard it on the *'grapevine!'*

'Posie, the way that man hollered that night, I'm sure she heard it in *Acushnet!'*

I sometimes wondered what I was doing, playing with babies in the sunshine, eating Posie's suppers and soups, each day blending into the next, with no future plan or planning; alone, but for the silent subliminal remonstrance that lived within me, and occasionally stopped feeding on my innards long enough to erupt: maybe point a long-nailed finger at the face of the young girl in the mirror and accuse, *'What are you doing with your life?!'*

The remonstrance seemed to know as well as I, that New York was the center of the universe, and at least for me, not the sunny enclaves of New Bedford/Fair Haven, as enchanted as we each were with them. So I drank the water and swallowed the remonstrance back down to where it belonged, down deep in my gut.

'You have to apply for Public Assistance,' Posie said at one of her late-night French Salad dinners upstairs in her apartment. 'This— *Dick*; he is sending you no monai. An' believe me, now that he is out of the service, he'll take off.'

'Well, I—' I started to protest, still seeing some incandescent miracle happening in the future—'No help,' she shook her head firmly, 'will come from him. Other people do it. Food stamps are not enough. You must, too. For the children! At least until baby Jerry is old enough for you to get a job. N'est-ce pas?' A look of guilt passed over her face. She loved little Jay (Jerry) and his sister, Kay (or Kim) and felt she was stealing them away from my parents: 'Unless you think you want to go back home now—?'

I looked at her thoughtfully. 'No. Later, when Jay is just a little bit bigger. You have been so wonderful to us. Just like my own mother.' She looked matter-of-fact, swallowed, and turned on the heels of her white waitress shoes to go into her little kitchen, 'I must get the bread. . . '

As I sat and waited for her to serve me, she called out, 'I love them, too.' She came back carrying the warm French bread and set it down firmly. 'Then you must apply tomorrow.'

IN THE HOUSES OF MEN

So I applied for Assistance and while I waited to be accepted, survived on floating 'fives' in Mom's notes (always, *'written in haste!'*), Posie's cooking; the contents of almost any dented can; pressure-cooked beef and beans. I made many, many home-made soups and only quit much later, when I heard Jerry sigh wistfully to a small friend, 'You get <u>canned</u> soup? God, you're so lucky!'

At last, I was accepted for Public Assistance and though it wasn't much, I knew I could get by for a while.

Waiting Rooms to Perdition—filled with fanatically-bored children inventing games with one another; squirming bawling babies; chain-smoking zombie mothers and slack-jawed fathers who had been corralled to sit (blank-eyed) in attendance and keep them company on repeat visits—were about to pay off.

It was my final go-around (or so I innocently imagined) and my signature was all that was required to get that first check. A file of papers was pushed over to me by the Clerk, who made no eye-contact, undoubtedly in order to keep sane.

'Do you swear that you are finished with your husband and are getting no help from him whatsoever?'

'That isn't hard to do,' I said, signing my name to the document in several places.

I left, happy and confident. I would steel myself. I'd put my hormones 'on hold.' *But*—I hadn't discussed it with my libido first. Circumstances, a town full of fishermen and my Benedict Arnold hormones were soon to join forces against me.

One evening, a tap at the door. Exhaling sharply, my 'private parts' flexing involuntarily, I admitted—Dick. A little acned, a little seedy and a newly-formed baleful glint shone in his eye. But it was still Dick.

Although my heart fluttered, it was my 'private parts' that let him into the bedroom: there, they were soon relieved and therefore, was I.

A scant second later as I stretched out in bed, I suddenly recalled the words of the Aid to Dependent Children worker who had okayed my funds, her eyes shooting warning shots through her spectacles at me:

'If any *contact* is made by your *husband,* you must let us know at once, or you will be in *danger of losing your aid.*'

My corporeal needs having been temporarily adjusted, I immediately reassessed the financial jeopardy I was in: 'Are you going to *leave* now?,' my voice quavered, as I faced him on the pillow.

His shark-like eyes opened and rolled swiftly upward toward the ceiling as he spoke: 'I thought I'd spend the night. I thought you'd like that.'

'Well, I . . . I . . . I—'

'It's cold out,' he added hopefully.

'All right. But you have to go *first thing in the morning.*'

'Not *A* problem,' he said, barely contemplating my face, and immediately fell asleep. I, too, burrowed down deep into a sex-relieved dream— until there was that loud clang. And then another CLANG!

What—was—*that?!*

My eyes popped open in the frosty night, past Dick, who was awake now, too, and toward the window—as out on the lawn, there arose such a clatter—and an intermittently flashing red light—

'What is this—?! Times Square??'

People were yelling. That throb was fire engines! The horrifying sight of a fully-suited up Fireman dragging a hose, went by my window.

'Oh, NO!,' I cried, my body stiffening in the bed, 'My worst nightmare!'

'I don't smell any smoke,' Dick said mildly.

'Maybe if we just lie still, they'll go away!,' I prayed, relaxing slightly.

Massive fists beat upon my front door: 'Open Up! Fire Department! Everyone OUT! Outside!'

The steam from our nostrils curled up in the frozen New Bedford air, as Dick and I, and all the tenants from the building, stood amid coils of fire hoses, like giant snakes surrounding us in the Parking Area.

The old ladies, wrapped in their coats, looked at me, looked at Dick, looked at each other—snorted in the cold air like old carriage horses—stamped and looked away. Posie, who had probably just gotten comfortable for the night, was still in her waitress shoes. She nodded grimly at me and folded her arms. And, of course, looked away.

'*Look away, Dixieland*,' I thought, for no reason whatever, followed by a certain, '*I'm dead!*'

'*False alarm!* A cry went up. '*False alarm!*' 'Everybody can go back to bed. . . *Sorry, Folks!*'

Dick was the first one back inside. 'I might as well stay until the morning.'

'What *difference* does it make!?'

Once again, the banging on the door. . . Sunlight was streaming in my eyes.

This time, I sat upright much faster.

'Maybe a fireman forgot his hat,' said Dick.

'Ha-ha,' I replied over my shoulder; on my way to the living room to answer the door, I noticed the kitchen clock said nine a.m.

'Yes?!'

'It's Mrs. DuChamp—from Aid to Dependent Children!'

My legs froze stiff and my heart stopped. 'Just a minute,' I managed.

'Open the door *NOW*!'

'Let me put a robe on!,' I screamed, racing to the bedroom.

Dick was standing by the bed, filing his nails with an emery board and wearing white boxer shorts decorated with red hearts.

'It's the *ADC*! Get into the closet!' He looked up, lips parted, eyes steely.

'The *what*?! I don't want to. *OW!* You're stepping on my *toe!*' I pushed him. He didn't budge; smiled, conscious of the new power he wielded.

The banging at the front door continued.

'*Please*,' I begged tearfully, 'I need the money for the *children!*'

He stopped filing and as an afterthought, shrugged and stepped into the closet, staring straight ahead as I rolled the door closed past his nose.

I heard myself prattling hysterically to Mrs. DuChamp, who rubbed her sore knuckles, as she entered, at last. She was a short, stolid frizzy-haired woman. She peered around her, taking everything in.

'We had a *fire* last night—fire engines here—I don't—and didn't hear and we went back to *bed* and—' I shrieked, tying my robe in the living room, 'we overslept—the children and I!' She nodded curtly, taking a seat on the couch.

'So the last time you saw your husband. . . ' The notebook was out; the questions began. I lied and I lied and I lied, partially and completely. I lied like a rug.

She put her notebook away. 'It might work,' I thought.

She stood up to leave. My senses were still reeling. Suddenly, without a hint, she paraded into the bedroom area.

'Where are you going?!,' I clamored, running after her.

Mrs. DuChamp stood like a beagle on-point in the center of the bedroom; my heart pounded so loudly in my ears, I knew she had to hear it. It would be nothing for Dick to roll open the closet and stand before her in his BVD's, filing his nails: I saw it happening any second.

She walked over to the bed and 'fluffed' at the covers, pulling them back. She got down on her knees like a naughty gnome, peering under the bed; stood, and started for the closet, for the 'death blow.' (I knew he would still be filing his nails.)

She—stopped and turned: 'Where do the children sleep?' I opened my eyes.

'Children?' She nodded impatiently, 'Then you can help me find the front door.'

'This place,' I gasped, running like a fox, 'is shaped like the letter 'S'! 'Yes, it is,' she gasped, running after me on her short legs.

The children were asleep, their small, healthy bodies as warm as toast in their two cribs, as the sunlight filtered into their clean little room. Mrs. DuChamp looked transfixed for a moment by them. I prayed Dick would not come wandering along to look at them sleeping. She looked up.

'They have their own room,' she said quietly.

'Yes. I wanted to put the bigger girl in my room because I was lonely, but I thought it would be better for them to have their own room, to be more independent.'

'You were right,' she said, and looked into my eyes. I was glad that finally, I had told her the truth.

ONLY LORRA

Every good waitress knows that Salt and Pepper come in pairs. Soon after Posie, Salt of the Earth, became my friend and a major calming influence in my life, I met her Sascatchewan buddy, Lorra—definitely Pepper. I was enjoying 'un petit souper' upstairs at Posie's high-ceilinged apartment; clean, cluttered with many mementoes, when—came a grand entrance, involving snappy French-brown eyes and dark hair.

She wore a hat as only a French woman can, a small navy blue hat, worn at an angle, with a dart of a feather. Just so. The trim navy suit, nipped in at the waist. White gloves. White touch at throat; navy pumps. It was Jackie-Kennedy Time and Lorra was a fine proponent of her style.

'Maura? Mon amie, Lorra!' A deferential tilt of the head, a murmur of a smile and Lorra circumnavigated the room, treating it as her personal goldfish bowl, sashaying here and there, picking up trinkets, feigning an interest in them and putting them back as she floated by me, giving me dark, side-long glances. She was inspecting me! I smiled. I couldn't help it. Truthfully, I was flattered. No one, male or female, before or since, ever tried so obviously to impress me. Flattered.

Posie's eyebrows elevated, as she was well-acquainted with Lorra's shenanigans. She sighed aloud and went to make tea, while Lorra and I made small talk—very small on my part, as I was leery of The French Inspector. Still, I admired her stage presence. Only her big-boned hands and large feet gave away the farm labor and heavy maid work that she and Posie had endured as teenagers in the Provinces.

Suddenly, I saw acceptance come to her face: I was approved. We warmed up to each other as Posie and Lorrie chatted over tea and cakes, and from then on, we were a threesome: Salt, Pepper and Unseasoned. Not only did they add Gallic Spice to my life, but to the end of my days, they imbued in me a strange blend of Posie and knowing what is *right* to do and Lorra, savoring the pleasure of refusing to do it at all—but always correctly!

Lorrie spirited us around town in her spiffy blue Chevy while Posie was working at Mickey's. She had had a few husbands herself, so one might say she pulled rank on Posie for worldliness; Posie had been married and widowed once, and was waiting for someone named Manny to become a widower.

'It'll happen any day now, Posie!,' Manny insisted, *'She's a verra sick woman. . !'*

And who is to say she was not?

Manny had a raucous laugh. He also had emphysyma and big yellow hands with matching grosgraine yellow nails. The very first time I met him, he made a swipe with one ursine paw at my halter top and grabbed my breast, right in front of Posie, so she would think he was joking, I guess. I think it was the left one. We were in the parking lot of our building on South Sixth, and he reached out of the driver's window to do it.

After he drove off, she says primly (ignoring my shaking fist in the wake of his departure)—'Manny has to take care of his wife, so our time together is very scarce.' I stared at her.

'Well! He's not going to *leave* her just because she's *sick*, you know! He'll stay with her until she goes! That's the kind of man he is. But we have our little fun.' I nodded dumbly. A 'triple-threat.' And he was her guy.

But just to keep the books balanced, Lorrie's first love impregnated her with twins (Posie: 'She was so large, she had to turn sideways to go through doors!. . . In Lorra's eighth month, he got a member of the church choir pregnant; in her *ninth*, he had the nerve to go swimming and drown! Probably it was lightning! . . But whatever it was, she raised the girls by herself, waitressing.')

And coquetting—and reeling in another husband or two.

When I met Lorra, she was on her fourth husband, a fisherman whom she had come to dislike so intensely, it was well he was away a lot. Her twin daughters were now twenty-six, married and living in upper Mass., although, Posie confided, 'One of them is very sick!' A strange son, a male nurse, was in the military; I met him once.

Now, about Lorra's husbands number two and three; an aura of mystery surrounded two, and a gray mist of suspicion fell upon the death of number three. (Posie: '—though I'm sure if she poisoned him, he deserved it. I'm not saying she *did*, mind you, but—?' A shrug.)

All this, to explain a woman who played a palm-reading gypsy at Halloween, freely painting palms red . . .'—You want your palm *read*, eh?' And who took us to the New Bedford Zoo.

Lions, tigers and . . .The bear pit was free and open, four or five dark brown or black bears milling below, down there, over the fence and in the pit, minding their own bear business.

'Nize bears. Nize bears!'
God help me, I know what she's thinking!
'No, Lorrie, don't go in there!' Her black eyes twinkled.
Even as I spoke, she had one leg over the fence into the bear pit.
'God! You're—!' . . . 'Oh, pshaw!,' her eyes flashed at me, 'give me dat!' She pointed.
'*What?* Give you what?!' . . . 'Dat <u>stick</u>; dat long stick.' She waved impatiently and fearfully hoping she wanted it to climb back over, I handed it to her.
'There! Bad bear: Waaa!' She laughed and reached over, pushing the stick at the bears below.
Kay tilted her head curiously, smiling wanly at her Lorra. The red-cheeked Jay let out a happy hoot, which further enlivened Lorra. 'Ba-a-a-d Bear! Oooo, silly bear!,' she said, making her lips and eyes round, playing to the House.
'Naughty bears! Ho-<u>ho</u>!' (poke-<u>poke</u>!)
The bears began sidling over and pawing up at her ankles. It's no accident that the French are tightrope walkers and race-car drivers; no accident at all!—*Sont fou'*! My knees were weak: 'Get out of there

now, Lorrie,' this isn't funny. Here come the cops,' I added. As if that would matter to her.

Bump! She made contact with the stick and the irate bear, all eight feet of him, rose up furiously on his hind legs, swiping at her, roaring, so close that I could see the drool flying off of his teeth.
'See?!? He *likes* it!'

Lorra's house was magnificently tidy. I shouldn't say 'her house,' because she changed houses as often as husbands, but whether she owned or rented, she moved in with buckets of cleaning fluids and supplies, and in short order, the windows were sunlit and sparkling; the curtains, pristinely perfect; the living area, done in casual beiges and greens and eminently livable. She out-bungalowed those in H&G magazine and had the houseplants to prove it.

So it was that on the occasional visit to her domicile, I was filled with not only the urge to clean, but peace and happiness.

This day, however, I found her seated on her couch, in slacks and sweater; still, staring off like someone witnessing a plane crash.

'What's wrong?,' I asked and though her brown eyes looked right through me, I knew instantly what it was. I sat next to her in the unspeakable silence; near the staunchest of women. Yet I couldn't bring myself to take her hand. I cleared my throat, trying, dying to think of the right words to say to a bereaved mother.

She lifted her arm heavily, barely pointing to one of the pictures on her piano: the single, smiling framed photograph of Mariet, her head swathed in a gigantic white bandage to cover the brain tumor surgery—a red ribbon, Lorra's touch—stuck on the top; her mother joking as she pinned it there, saying that Mariet was *'everyone's* Christmas present!' that year. Her arm dropped as she turned her head away from me.

When she looked back, her expression shocked me for a second. She wished it were me instead. She dropped her eyelids down, either in grief or shame—too late, for I had seen. Before she could look up again, I kissed her cheek—it was dry—and said, 'I'm so sorry, my Lorra. Can I do anything for you, anything? Can I make you tea?'

She looked at me and nodded 'No,' smiling that twist of a smile.

'Tell me what I can do.'

'It's all right. She's resting at last.'

I was standing in front of her. 'Shall I go now?' She bit her lip and nodded. I walked to the door and when I looked back, I thought I saw that look again. It cut deep into my heart, but for her, not for me.

I turned the knob and called back, 'I love you, Lorra. I'll call you up later.' I think I heard a whispered, 'Thank you,' as I closed the door. I was walking down the path when I heard that one terrible sob and I looked back: the sun still sparkled on her windows.

Mariet's funeral was Upstate. A week after her return, she drove me to pick up my allotment of surplus cheese and dry goods: 'Lisette was asking for you,' she said and even though I had never met Mariet's twin—when I looked over into Lorrie's eyes, I knew that I now had a 'twin sister' and an impossibly insane French-Canadian adoptive mother.

'Oh, that's nice,' I replied as calmly as possible.

'Shhh!' she replied, 'I'm parking our *car*!

'Sure, the day is bitter and cold,' I thought, pushing the baby carriage down and around County Street in New Bedford, doing errands with the two kids in tow, 'but what is it? What's bothering me?' I stopped suddenly. 'Oh, God! I know what it is! It's exactly five years ago today, that I met Dick!'

I hurried home, depressed, buffeted mindless by the wind, as I pushed up the street to South Sixth: wondering if time passes more quickly in a coastal town, than it does in the Midwest. *('If it is true that a proportionally higher number of Nebraskans are over ninety, does the nation's breadbasket have a hidden advantage, and time actually move slower?')*

I wheeled the carriage into the parking lot—my apartment was at the back entrance—not really wanting to live that long, but sighing, anyway.

As the day wore on, my mood worsened and by the time evening rolled around, I was so despondent, I was dressed, combed, made-up and raring to go anyplace. My ears strained for the sound of Posie's car; for her tread on the stairs.

'*Please*, Posie! I never ask you to babysit; you know that.'

'I do. But today I worked a double shift and I'm tired. Ordinarily, I <u>want</u> you to—'

'But this is the anniversary of the day I met Dick: I just *can't* stay in the house tonight.' She looked at me and finally exhaled a long, 'All right; but only for an hour or two.' . . .

'Oh, great. Good. Thank you!

My lone 'sophisticated friend' Mister Scotch and Soda, joined me at the Center Street, the only half-way decent bar in town, where I sat focusing on the labels of distant bottles and in between sips, silently complimenting myself on my improving vision.

'May I buy you a drink, Miss?'

The 'may' startled me and I looked to my left at a Michael Caine-type '60's guy. Button-down collar, suit, eye-glasses.

'I already have one, but thank you.'

'. . . The one after that?' . . . 'That seems logical: All right,' I said.

I spat out at him right away that I was the divorced mother of two. He shot back that he was up here on business and was leaving in the morning for New York.

He served a 'Jason Clarke' and I volleyed a 'Maura Earhart. And I'm from New York, too.' He was shaking his head and laughing.

'What's funny?' I asked, thinking, *'We're even-up, aren't we?'*

'I wanted to say—what's a girl like you doing in a place like this?—because it seemed so—appropriate!'

'Well,' I shrugged, indicating the suit, 'You're not exactly a fisherman, either.'

He lowered his voice a notch: 'I seem to be doing all right in that capacity tonight!' (I wasn't about to tell him that by now, I was 'half-way into the boat.')

We enjoyed a nice evening together. 'It was a great kick talking to a New Yorker again,' I told him as he drove me home. 'I'll be back up the following weekend,' he said pulling into our parking lot and turning to look at me, added 'that is, if you'd like to get together again.' He walked me to the door.

'He seems very nice,' Posie yawned, heading for the door after Jason left. 'Yes, he does. And thanks to you, I had a wonderful time.'

It wasn't until I was in bed later that a chill ran over my scalp like a rat, and I realized that I'd met Jason on the same day as—'Oh, NO! The *Seventh!*'

I shrugged off the bad omen and snuggled up in a ball to dream the 'Nice Man/Good Father' dream of the single mother.

The Prisoner of the Diaper Pail began to look very much forward to those weekend visits that began to happen on a regular basis.

We went dancing and dining; Jason paid for the sitters, brought gifts for the children, had an effusive laugh and a very good operatic tenor voice, closer to Italian than Irish: this alone was too good to be true.

'Bright man! Carries an attache case! Has a job! Father for my children!' The old welfare rally-cry surged through me.

Kim and Jerry could have all the good things they deserved. Why *shouldn't* they?! He seemed to adore them and said he adored me. The thing that clinched it for me was that sex, though good, was not earth-shaking for me but often moved him to tears of rapture: '*He must be even more deprived than I!*' I figured. He might have been a Catholic, but in bed, he was strictly 'Presbyterian.'

Whenever I called his apartment in the Bronx, day or night, he was there. I was certain that he was not married or living with anyone. It all seemed too good to be true.

For a very glamorous while, I rode the crest of being coddled— with just the slightest fear of being 'codded.'

Yes, there were one or two gut-twinges; warnings. . . I wore the dress from Reynaud one evening, serenely confident and happy as Jason and I dined at the Manor in Fairhaven, just over the bridge.

'Waiter!' Jason suddenly called loudly across the posh room. 'Waiter! Come here!—which the waiter did.

'Just what do you mean by serving me this—<u>raw</u> meat!? I specifically told you I wanted it *well done*. I was perfectly *clear* about that!' Jason's face flamed crimson; the young waiter's turned to ash: 'I—I'm sorry, Sir,' he stammered.

'Christ! Don't be *sorry*,' Jason said, shoving the plate at him, 'Get it out of my sight and bring me,' he boomed in his singer's voice, '*Precisely* what I ordered!' The steak was hurried away.

'Jason. How could you *embarrass* him like that?! He's just a kid!'

'<u>He</u> knew what I was talking about! I don't countenance rudeness like that.'

'*You* were rude! You embarrassed me, and the waiter!'

The anger ebbed from his face: ' . . Did you think I came down a bit hard on him? Perhaps I did. I only wanted everything tonight to be perfect. I didn't mean to upset you.'

'You should apologize to the waiter.'

'He expects that!' he scoffed. 'You're being foolish.'

Jason worked for attorneys, investigating and preparing cases for trial. One big hapless guy who was assisting Jason came up with him one weekend and we double-dated.

The guy turned to his date and said, 'I was in the service. I was a *Pyro-trooper.*' Of course, we all laughed. All except Jason.

'What kind of idiot would think we'd believe a story like <u>*that?*</u> It's pronounced, '*Para*-trooper!' And I'm not driving any moron back to New York. I've had it with you!'

The girl and I were getting pretty embarrassed: 'How'll I get back? I need the ride!' the schlep begged. 'You'll have to find another way then, won't you?!? Try jumping out of a *plane*, you ass!'

Clues, decided clues, but I left them to lie there unattended to be readdressed in a different format, at a later date.

'Why don't you move back to New York? New Bedford is nice, but there really isn't a lot here for a person of *your* caliber.'

'I—plan to! But I want to wait until Jay is maybe two, three; then I can get a job and a sitter. At least, that's—'

'—Quite a long way off, isn't it?, ' Jason laughed, eyes twinkling: 'That's a lot of six-hour car rides up to New Bedford.'

'But you have to come up here on business anyway, don't you? . . . Didn't you?' His eyelids fluttered as he looked down. 'That's what I've been telling you,' he hesitated. Actually. . . Actually, that job was over a long time ago.'

'You mean—Do you mean to tell me you've been coming up here all this time, just to see _me_?'

'Well, that's not entirely—yes,' he admitted. 'It's true.'

It was impossible to know the real Jason. Never sitting, always standing, leaping or running off to go somewhere; leaving behind him a perfect smile and gifts; always gifts. Yet to me he was a 'will o' the wisp.' Something was hidden, something was covert or concealed; I couldn't say what. Something.

'Promise me you'll give it some thought,' he said, 'about returning to New York a little sooner.'

'I will,' I said. 'I'll give it a lot of thought.' And I did.

I talked it over with Posie.

Posie pronounced, 'He'll never get married.'

'Why do you _say_ that?'

'If he hasn't married by now, he never will: how old is he?'

'Thirty, he says.'

'He looks older than that.'

'Well, maybe he is. . . 'and he never was married?. . . He says, no.'

There was that significant Posie-pause: then that disgusting little smirk she reserved for 'naughty business.'

'Maybe he wants it both ways.'

'What—?'

'You know! He acts a little—fluttery. Maybe he's—?' '_No way_, is he queer! Believe me! He's just—nervous.'

Her eyebrows raised up. Another Posie-pause. 'Sometimes, they—'

'No, he's _not_!'

In the silence, I could see her setting up her French tightrope line, picking up her balance pole; getting ready for her final run: 'Well! Don't get your hopes up: he won't marry you.'

'Oh? How do you know?'

'I _know_. I don't know _why_ he won't, but I know that he won't.'

Inwardly, I agreed with her. Besides, I was searching for a special guy, not necessarily handsome, but with a true love that could bring me the happiness that a really good husband could bring. Maybe that was Jason.

But she had thrown the gauntlet down. Before I had a chance, really to pick it up and accept the challenge, a far greater challenge confronted Posie.

Manny's wife—did not die: Manny did. All the green oxygen tanks in the world could not restart that huge, ragged heart. Thus, all Posie's years of patience resulted in no net gain and the wearing of her black funereal 'ribbon-dress'—for an evening of night-clubbing with my parents (they came up for a first-visit) because, 'Bien sur, that's the way Manny would've wanted it.'

So the resilient Posie, my parents, and I went to a local burlesque club for dinner. These places were quite common in Massachusetts and were usually pretty tame, remarkable only for an adept 'tassel-twirler' here and there. But once the curtain raised on an unmade bed containing a woman, this show turned out to be steamy. I was extremely uncomfortable sitting with my parents and the bereaved near-widow at the little table, especially with my father there.

From under the stage-bed, a man's arms appeared, and he was soon stroking, petting and poking at this writhing, orgasmic woman. It was more than I could bear. I was about to stand up and bolt when my Dad said, 'This place is going to get raided.' He pointed to a man wearing a Stetson hat and a suit, and leaning casually, arms folded, against a nearby wall.

'That's a cop. And that's his partner leaning on the bar over there.'

'Oh, John, I don't know,' smiled the jovial Posie, sipping her C&C; 'That has never happened here in New Bedford.'

'Well, it's about to happen now.'

'Oh, don't be silly, Jack,' said Mom. . . 'Maybe it *is* silly, Mom, but I want to leave. Now.'

We sprang up as one, relieved to be leaving the couple on stage, now practically copulating. Dad lagged behind to pay the check and we three women waited for him outside on the gravel parking lot.

Just as my father was walking across the lot toward us, two police cruisers pulled up, sirens blaring, and detectives from other cars in the lot went running inside.

'That was close!' Dad laughed, as he opened the car doors. Jokes flew all the way home about it.

'Damn! I always wanted to be in a raid; it would've been so exciting!' . . . 'Oh, Maurie!' Mom remonstrated, 'How do you feel about being hand-cuffed?' . . . And Posie: '—that girl on the <u>stage</u> wouldn't have minded!....If it don't beat all! . . Never happened before. . . Good thing we left when we did. . . Mr. Connelly, <u>how</u> did you know that was going to happen?' 'Hmmmm,' said my mother, fixing him with a suspicious stare.

'With a show like that, it was only a matter of time,' Dad said, 'Now let's find a place to eat. Lobster sounds good!' And it was.

The trees stood around whispering about Spring. It was still a rumor; their buds had barely arrived. In that precipitous air, I prepared for the voyage home. I had Manny to thank for it: had he not died—precipitously—Posie would not've upped and gone to San Jose, California, and there married the Octogenarian John Rizzo and I would probably have stayed put and married unwisely in New Bedford, rather than in New York. Where are the pundits and seers when you need them? Busy answering '900' numbers, that's where. I might've called one myself, had one been available to me.

Local wisdom came for me in the dubious form of Lorra, clucking her lips, helping to pack my belongings into Jason's car; while exhorting the children to sit still and once en route to New York— Jason looked all about him, like a chicken about to be beheaded; making all concerned utterly exhausted. We were on the road: I was going back home.

'I will stay wid' you until you are settled in New York!' Lorra pronounced: it soon burned in my mind like a threat.

The curious thing about her admonishment to the children to 'sit still!' became obvious an hour outside of New Bedford: Lorra couldn't. She: cracked her gum straightened her skirt found books lost books fed snacks to either child on either side of her or simultaneously, until they turned a gray-green color and chattered along with Lorra incessantly.

Alongside me, the driver had turned Apoplectic Red, his jaw working furiously.

There was an odd pinging noise.

'Oh, no!,' wailed the nervous driver, 'I have to pull the car <u>over!</u> Under no circumstances,' he said, turning around and addressing Lorra, whom he now clearly detested, 'under <u>NO</u> circumstances—is anyone to <u>leave the car</u>: Is that clear is that perfectly clear is that—' Well, that was repeated a few times more.

Jerry, the two-year old sat, dull and glassy-eyed, his beautiful marble-eyes now listless, filled as he was with many hideous snacks and sweets; he, obviously going nowhere, it was not he to whom these entreaties were made. Kay, blonde, sweet and ever-docile, nodded: '—and he <u>certainly</u> doesn't mean *me!*'

Jason parked on a grassy shoulder off the highway; as the cars zoomed by, as he lifted the hood; thumping and listening. Then he walked to the rear of the car and opened up the trunk. With enormous alacrity, Lorrie sprang from the car, dragging a child by each hand.

'Lorra!'

'They have to make POTTY!' she called back, scuttling along the grass like some insane French crab towards a clump of distant trees, as the cars whizzed by her.

The trunk slammed shut. A roar issued forth from Jason, the first of many, that began with, 'I <u>told</u> you not to—!'

After the roar, the wee-wees and very pointed threats from Jason to Lorra (during which she consulted her compact mirror) we barreled on, car still pinging, in an unhealthy, intense, seething silence.

There was a tiny tug at the back of my hair.

'I didn't get to *go!*,' Kim whimpered, crossing her legs and pinching at herself, 'I have to *make!*'

5.

Most moves finish in the dead of night, dark and unfinished. I've never met anyone who enjoyed moving. That move, that Lorra, those children; that trip and the first glint of a hardness that went beyond being harried to horrid in Jason, all took their toll. That night I fell into a confused slumber, mercifully numbing the enormity of what I had done. I had cut my life-line.

I had cut *our* life-lines, and awoke to that knowledge with the sound of a coughing bus passing by.

Two children slept dreaming nearby, oblivious to the danger they were in: I was solely responsible for their welfare.

Another bus. I had rented the small apartment—right on busy Hillside Avenue, two blocks from my parents' house—for its closeness to them and to the very bus-line that was keeping me awake now.

A big-rig rolled by: nobody could bail me out now. Another bus. Another bus. Another truck and eventually, the Dawn rolled along, too.

While I job-hunted, lined up the baby-sitter, cooked, washed and tried to settle in, The Dream began, making regularly scheduled appearances, the one in which I wore a man's hat, way too big, the brim slipping down over my eyes, and men's trousers—again, too big, so that in between holding up the hat, I was hoisting up the pants; and shoes, the ponderous men's shoes, so heavy that when I tried to walk, I tripped.

The Dream increased in frequency when I started working at a Western Electric Supply facility out on the Island; my real-life smile, too bright, too tight; trying too hard; afraid to lose my job and afraid, always afraid, the baby-sitter was inadequate.

'Where do you bring the children when you work?' a neighbor down the street asked me one day at the laundromat. I put my wet clothes into the dryer: 'I don't. The sitter comes to me.' I slammed shut the dryer door, plunked in the coins, and, as the clothes began their slow tumble, I started to wonder. I turned round thoughtfully.

'Mrs. Reichert?' . . . 'Yeah—? Call me Ginnie.' . . 'Why do you ask, Ginnie?'

'S'just funny. I never see 'em. S'like, I didn't know anybody was *home* in there, s'all.'

Luckily, two days later, I got sick at work and went home at noon. As I fitted my key in the lock and walked in, I saw—nothing. But I heard the sounds of scuffling around, like the scuttle of rats.

I walked into the kids' bedroom and saw Jane, the sitter, standing at the foot of Kim's bed wearing just a bra and underpants. There was the flash of a man's rump, as he dove under the sheets. I turned and ran to my bedroom, the door of which was locked from the outside. I opened it.

Two of the prettiest kids in the world sat tousle-haired and sleepy, scratching the letters of the alphabet into my headboard with a pin. They jumped in guilt when they saw me.

'Mommy,' Kay said softly, 'I'm sorry!' Jerry just smiled; after all, he was only two.

'It's okay.' I kissed and hugged them and although the tight pain in my chest was unbearable, I did not cry. 'Don't worry. It's all right. 'Stay here! I'll be right back.'

'Don't leave!' Kim wailed. 'I won't. Just one minute, I promise.' I shut the door behind me and locked it.

When I walked back into the living room, the front door was just closing, so I caught no glimpse of the 'invisible man.' With all the aplomb of a Times Square waitress, Jane (dressed now) was dumping an enormous pile of cigarette butts into the garbage. She looked up, and one claw still holding the giant ashtray, placed the other one on a hip: 'I'll expect t'be paid through today.' For some reason, I had been struck dumb.

She tossed back her long dark hair and snatching up her purse, glared at me. Her thin face hardened: 'You owe me—'

I cleared my throat: I still didn't recognize my own voice. 'You better leave—'

'—fer Monday an' Tuesday; that's two days! An' today, I was here—'

'Now,' I said, moving menacingly towards her, 'Leave! Now!' She ran out, slamming the door.

After I gave them some soup, I examined the headboard, the entire flat, brown surface of it covered with thin spidery little pin-digs, here and there a visible B or a dominant A; a squiggle that could have been a tree and—what was this? A clearly visible 'happy-face!'

A sob caught in my throat: 'What could they possibly have had to smile about?' I whispered. 'How could I have been so blind?!?' I sobbed inwardly racked with a guilt that only deepened as I heard the happy prattle of my children at play, glad to have their mommy at home: 'Oh, God! Please don't let me have 'The Dream!' tonight. 'I don't think I can take it!'

I stayed home the rest of that week to line up a new sitter.

Ever since my return to New York, the difference in Jason was slight, yet unmistakable. There was a drawing-back I could feel, a definite cooling off. We still had our good times. I still saw him almost exclusively. But the exclusivity had its price. I thought, 'He doesn't want me, but he's tying me up by just 'showing up,' or making me cancel if I tried dating anyone else.'

When we went out, we would hit a piano-bar not too far away or on occasion, the Italian restaurant in the Village where the waiters serenaded you as you dined. Of course, Jason could always be 'persuaded' to sing by those who knew him—perhaps an aria from 'Aida,' or, eyes burning into mine, 'Maria,' from 'West Side Story'. . . 'On The Street Where You Live' . . .

'Aida?' Yes. Marriage—!? Always singing, always laughing, never able to be pinned down. Posie, damn her, had him pegged: I resolved to search with renewed vigor for somebody else.

'What's the matter?' Jason asked, as he drove me home late one night.

'Nothing.' I stared down at my shoe tops in the darkness of the car.

'You seem so serious.'. . .'I'm tired. Big day tomorrow.'

'Can I come up?' 'No. Not tonight.'

'Well,' he said, pulling up by my door, reaching into his pocket, 'Here's something for the kid—the sitter.'

'Jason, you don't have to do that.' He pushed the money at me. 'Please! You know I love the children!'

'You do, do you?' He looked at me strangely for a minute. 'Course I do. Say, how's the new one working out—the day-sitter?'

'Fine. She couldn't be worse than Jane, could she?'

Physically, the new sitter was as far from the rat-like Jane as she could be. She was a large rosy-cheeked woman named Carol, who lived (miraculously!) right next door to us. She had four little ones of her own and a husband, Big Jim, equally ample, who was 'in construction' and around the house a lot. The set-up seemed too good to be true: I went downstairs in the morning, dropped them off and hopped on a bus right outside for work.

One day, a few weeks later, I got a call at work.

'Maurie, it's Mom. On my way to work today, I saw the children out in the pouring rain in the sitter's backyard. Is she taking care of them properly?'

I was silent for a moment. 'Oh, they probably wanted to play outside in the rain. The *other* sitter never let them see daylight, and they'd be awake all night because she kept them in bed!'

'Oh, that Jane! I know. Tim used to go out with her, among others.'

I lowered my voice a little to below-office-level: 'She's a real sl—! Piece of work! But thanks, Mom. I'll keep an eye on things.' There was a pause at her end. 'I just wanted to make sure—they were all right.'

Carol dispelled the notion that a fat person smiles a lot. That much, I did notice; but she presented a calm, even lethargic, outward appearance and an easy composure that slipped only occasionally. Big Jim, her husband, was always jovial and relaxed. And my children were sun-tanned and slept like rocks at night: I was beginning to un-tense.

On a torrid July day, there was an employee walkout at our plant and the office help left at noon, in sympathy. I smiled on the bus, happy to be going home to try out the small air conditioner Jason had picked up somewhere, 'for a song,' exhilarated at the thought of going home and spending the day with my kids.

The bus pulled up to my stop farther back than usual, and I was treated to a view of Carol's backyard—and appalled to see Kim, lying listlessly under a hot sun in the dirt, like an unwatered dog. No grass. No shade. Just dirt.

As I got off the bus and stood there transfixed, fat-bellied little Jer trotted around the side of the house and tapped gingerly at the back screen door. 'Drink?' he called, 'Drink, please?'

'Shut *up!*' roared Carol from somewhere behind the screen. 'Quiet!' laughed children's voices from within, 'Quiet, Jay-Jay!'

Woodenly, I walked around the corner and up to the front door, still shaken, still unseen. Jimmy, Jr., freckle-nosed, shirtless and sucking on an orange ice-pop, answered my knock.

'Is Mommy home?' He darted away.

Carol came to the door, bare-footed, wearing a loose blue muu-muu, puzzled looks criss-crossing her forehead: 'What're *you* doing here?'

'I got off early, and—'

'Charlie! Go get the kids!' And Charlie, red ice-popped lips, ran through the cool confines of the air-conditioned living room, past the living room sofa—where everyone sat, sucking different color ice-pops—and on, out to the barren, blazing yard—to 'fetch' my kids.

I pushed past her: 'What are they doing *outside?*' I demanded, resisting the urge to add, 'like dogs!'

'They're *always* outside.' She stared directly into my eyes, her chin stuck out at me defiantly.

I grabbed my two confused children, leaving so fast that we almost knocked over Big Jim, as he came out of the bedroom carrying a big bowl of popcorn. He took one look at my face as I whirled past and wisely said nothing.

At home, Kim chirped happily, sipping her Kool-aid. 'I'm glad we're not going back to Carol's!'

'Why's that?' She gently pulled my ear down to her lip-level. 'No pants,' she whispered.

'What?!'. . . 'She don't wear any underpants!'

'*Doesn't* wear any underpants,' I corrected automatically. 'How do you know?' I dreaded the response.

'Cause when I lie on the floor, an' she crosses her *legs!*' she insisted. I exhaled a quiet sigh, strangely relieved, but trying hard not to see in my mind's eye what Kim must have.

'And also,' she said exasperatedly, draining her glass, 'We have to be so quiet when Big Jim and Carol take their *naps!*'

There was a local bar-owner known as 'Kruschev' for his strong resemblance to the Russian strongman.

Ginnie Reichert lived over 'Kruschev's saloon' down on the corner. She was what my mother would call, 'a common woman,' a dark-haired plain-faced New Yorker. Our city is full of them. Smoking cigarettes, popping gum loudly when chewing—which was what she was doing when she approached me that first week back home in the laundromat, when I had hired 'slut-Jane.' I recalled her misgivings and her words to me then: *Say, if yer lookin' for a baby-sitter, I'm more'n willing. I have my own two daughters, Sandy and Rosanne, and I'm right down the block from ya. It'd be easy for ya. I'd be reasonable, too.*

I had said I'd keep her in mind. '*Surely I can do better than this! Could I? Could I—do better?*' Desperately, I turned to Ginnie Over the Bar as a short-term solution, *'Just,'* I thought, *'till I can get someone really good.'*

Well, she was all wrong. She washed their little faces and fed them well, often taking money out of her own pocket, and took them to play in the park, and was cheerful and kind and—and—treated them like her own children and—! How wrong could I have been! The worst in my estimation, turned out to be the best break I had gotten in a long time. The children loved and deserved her. If she was all wrong, I was all wet. A phrase like undying gratitude would not be amiss. Nightmares lessened. Days developed an evenness, a sense of peace and even, at times, a tranquility such as I had not known in a very long time.

It seemed no time at all after Lorra went back to New Bedford, that she had returned. It was the 1964 New York World's Fair, a sight I will never forget. No, not the Fair: Lorra, cutting to the head of the long lines, beckoning me, one Gallic palm upturned as I followed, trying to keep up with her, ignoring the angry stares of those we bypassed on line.

'Lorra!' I hissed, 'No!' But she sailed onward and upward, hat fixed at a jaunty angle, using her bag as a battering ram, gaze, focused afar. Had General DeGaulle been as forceful in World War II, we would not have had to liberate Paris; Napolean would have taken his own arsenic to avoid confrontation with her.

This day, her sites were set on a dinner table—secured over the backs of many. 'See?' she smiled like Madame DeFarge, knitting needles poised after storming the Bastille, 'Just act like you belong. Easy!'

It was not until after dinner in The French Quarter that I found out what her large over-size bag was for: Swoop! One deft movement of her big arm and (eyes twinkling at me, confidingly) into the bag went salt cellars, napkin holders and ashtrays.

'You can't do that!' I gasped, leaning forward anxiously. 'That's stealing!' A delicate wave of the fingers: 'Oh, Poo! They expect that. These are souv'nirs, c'est tout. Ah! Forgot the pepper shaker!' Swoop, clatter, into the bag. Too late, I recalled Posie's comment: 'Lorra thinks everything belongs to her anyway, so it's not stealing.'

Rattle, clump, onto a new conquest! Chopsticks from the Chinese Pavilion. Beer steins from Germany. Sometimes, she would have the temerity to ask for an item, say, a wall-hanging in a BrauHaus (for which she was given a disbelieving stare) or a pineapple-shaped serving dish from The Islands because, a smiling Jamaican youth said, handing it over to her, 'You remind me of my muthah!'

All, all disappeared into the dark netherworld, the folds of Lorra's comport, it's maw perpetually open, ever ready to receive. We saw the whole Flushing Fair: It was pure luck we didn't get to see the Flushing Jail.

We stopped back at the French Quarter late that evening and waited for service.

'So? How is your Sweetheart, eh? Any marriage plans?' The waiter returned with our coffee and cakes, and I waited for him to depart before I answered, 'No. First he does, then he doesn't. I'm really sick of his stalling. I'm looking around for someone else.'

'But now you need someone to 'elp you; I know how that is!'

'He's not helping me by keeping potential suitors away, Lorra! No; I've made up my mind.'

We finished eating and Lorra had a good grip on the table candelabra, when our waiter—who obviously knew a thing or two—sallied up, wagged a warning finger at Lorra—and lit the candles, right under her nose!

'Spoil-sport!' she said looking up at him, and giving him her Very Famous Lorra-Grin: those chimpanzees at the New Bedford zoo, practicing their grins, still speak of Lorra.

But perhaps they should have been laughing at me. Because by the time Lorra went back home to New Bedford, I discovered I was pregnant again.

6.

'He was supposed to be here at six,' I murmured to the empty house. It was Saturday night and the kids had stayed at Ginnie's. For what I had to tell Jason, I didn't want any interruptions from them. Surely, he wouldn't let me down.

Obviously, he had a problem with commitment; wasn't a settled person. Yet I knew he loved children, and I believed he loved me. Since now was the time for scathing honesty, I had to admit that though I buried my feelings about it, there seemed always to be something bothering him, a thing that wasn't right. What was it? Surely, he would let me know what it was; surely.

The minutes crept by. Then an hour. The clock ticked clearly and efficiently, quietly doing its little job of driving me to distraction. *'Seven o'clock! Where is he?'*

Breathing, shallow; heart, pounding. 'Calm down! He'll be here. He'll be here. He'll be here. . . Perhaps he forgot!'

Horrified, I dialed his number. The phone rang hollowly.

It was past eight o'clock when he rang my doorbell. Talking, as he walked in past me, 'I'm sorry: I know I said six, but there was an—engagement—about which I had forgotten. May I?' He gestured to a chair before he sat in it, even more formally than usual.

'Of course.' Irked though I was, I still felt that very real 'something' that said something is very wrong.

'What is it, Hon? Jason loosened his tie in a weary and preoccupied way. 'What is it you wanted to talk to me about?'

All of a sudden, I flew around the apartment like a hummingbird, straightening the chairs, closing blinds and switching on the hanging light over the dinette table: It all seemed much too bright!

'Too bright!' I chirped noisily and turned it off again.

'We do need some light,' he said, drawing back and looking strangely at my antics. On, went the light, and off and then I turned to him and said, 'I'm two weeks late.' He seemed not to have heard me.

'I said, I'm—I'm pregnant.'

Jason got up and walked into the darkened living room. Finally, from the shadows: 'Are you sure?' I nodded. He turned away and cracked open the blinds, gazing out at the passing traffic. 'Maybe you're mistaken.'

'No.' There was an odd sound.

'Are you crying? You're not <u>crying</u>, are you?' My hopes plummeted as, when I drew nearer, I saw tears coursing down his face and heard his panicky whimpering.

'Jason, what's wrong? I thought you'd be *glad*. You always said you would love to have a child with me. Were you lying?'

'No! I mean, I am glad—it's just that—!' More sobs, blubbery noises, and his hand covering his face now made his words unintelligible.

'Jason, please! I can't understand what you're saying!' I drew back in an 'all at once' realization: 'You're married. That's it: you're married.'

'No! No, that's not it! I have to go—have to leave!' He rushed to the door.

'Wait! Do you intend—Do you want me to have an abortion?!'

'No, no, no! Please wait. I'll call you later! It's just the *shock!* Honest, Hon! Honest!'

He left, his face awash in tears.

That long, hard Saturday night came and went. Jason never called back. By Sunday morning, the kids were back home and I plodded through the day with great difficulty, a zombie with a gaping pit for a stomach, a robot in a diving suit, walking lugubriously on enormous, booted unfeeling feet, the dark icy sea of life, fathoms above me.

The children chirped buoyantly, playing with their Fisher-Price play-house, with the little wooden peg-people they called 'The Dumbos.' I couldn't bear to look at them, knowing how recklessly I had jeopardized their futures. Only Jerry, his round, blue-marble eyes staring solemnly at me, seemed to be aware of my distance; seemed to be thinking, *'Something's different with her today. I wonder what it is?'* How bad could I have made it; how much worse?

At last, after dinner and a little Star-Trek, they went off to bed. Methodically, I laid out their play-clothes for the next day and planned what I'd wear to work, which translates into 'grab something tomorrow.' I was now deeply into my own personal Hell, dreading the thought of tossing in bed till morning, so deep that Jason's words just behind my ear shocked me. I gasped and turned to face him. 'You left the door open,' he said unbuttoning his jacket.

'You look terrible,' I said, noticing his eyes, red and rimmed with tears. 'I didn't sleep well,' he said, hanging his suit jacket on the back of a chair. 'I'm going to splash some cold water on my face. Do you mind?'

As soon as he walked off into the bathroom, I did something I am not known for, only did once before and should have done a lot sooner: I looked in his wallet. There he was, in a photo with his arm linked around a beautiful, smiling blonde. I felt a knife-twist of agony from my heart down to my shoes. Then I saw the driver's license: it said, 'Jason *Kirkpatrick*.' Confused, reeling, I stuck the wallet back in the inside pocket where I'd found it. The room seemed to be moving and I couldn't catch my breath. I needed air, but had no strength to open a window. I teetered on the brink of madness.

'That's better,' sighed Jason, coming back. I watched him go to the window and peek through a slat of the blinds.

'Is your name Jason Clarke?'

He whirled around. 'You know it is.'

'Then *who* is Jason Kirkpatrick?'

'How did you—?! Wait. I'll tell you. That is my real name. And you were right. That's what I came over here to tell you.'

'I was right about what?' He forced the words out: 'I am married.'

Even though I had surmised the answer, the world receded farther from me. 'Why didn't you *tell* me?'

'I couldn't, I just couldn't! I didn't want to hurt you.'

'—And this is *better*, me finding out about it *now*? Who is she? Does she know about us?'

'I told her everything. Her name is Emma, but everyone calls her Skip. Actually, you'd *like* her.'

'I doubt that. The odds of me liking someone who suddenly pops up in a four-year relationship are not very good. What I want to know is, where has she been? I've been calling up at the Bronx for a long time, and she's never been there.'

'Once you talked to her, and I told you it was the cleaning woman; actually— he paused—'she really *does* clean there once in a while. But we've had separate apartments for years. She has one near her job in the city, and I stay in the one in the Bronx.'

'Why are you separated?'

'It was my fault,' he cried, bursting into tears, 'I was—mean to her!—and she got a boyfriend and I found out about it and followed her, and—!' he blew his nose noisily into his handkerchief.

'And, *what*?!'

'And,' he said, his voice hushed, 'I hid in a closet where they had their little love-nest, and she came home' (his voice broke again) and—she started—she was ironing his *shirts*! And I burst out at her and I—knocked her down. I didn't *mean* to, honest, but I did.' His voice dropped so low, I could scarcely hear him.

'You, *what*?'

'I fractured her skull.'

'You fractured her *skull*?' He nodded. 'I hit her and fractured her skull and right after that, she got her own apartment. Near the UN. She can well afford it; she has a big job.

'I don't blame her for moving out,' I said, as crushed as if I had been clobbered over the head myself. 'What happened to her boyfriend?'

'Oh, *that* was over immediately. She was just doing that to get even with me—and he didn't really love her, anyway!,' he added indignantly, 'I *told* her that!'

'Not the way you love *me*, Jason.' I went into the living room and sank down on the couch.

Jason came after me and when I turned away, he pulled my hand up to his hot, tear-stained lips.

'And now, you're the one having to suffer for it, you poor little thing. If I could change anything at all, it would be my telling you about this sooner. I'm so sorry, you poor little—'

'—I'm not a 'poor, little *anything*!' I said, pulling my hand down and away, 'You are! All this time, I've been hoping and praying that you would come to grips with whatever was bothering you and stand by me, and marry me, and—now! Now, I know! Begging you, *how* many times, to tell me if you were married, or what was wrong? Now, I know. After all your tears and your—protestations of love—! Now, it's too late to even consider having an abortion; so you can get out, Jason. Take your coat and get out.'

He started to leave, but he turned back.

'Maura, I want you to know I talked to Skip earlier, and she'll do whatever you want.'

He kept standing there.

'*She* said?. . .Are you waiting for some kind of an *answer from me*?'

He nodded; I pointed to the door; he left—just in time. I barely made it to the bathroom: I had to throw up. At least he had made *that* easy for me.

Of course, soon it was a little too late to do 'anything crazy,' or anything at all. *'I love you, I love her, I'll marry you soon—I can't marry you!—I can't hurt her! I can't hurt you!'* His words flowed past my ears like water over rocks, babbling, whimpering, droning on, assaulting my soul.

Incredibly, I fastened all my hatred on the photo of the slim blonde that I had tacked onto the screen of my imagination, and not on Jason, whose words fell like detritus—crumpled leaves without pity—and even though he had betrayed both of us, I felt overwhelming contempt for myself. I had let trust override sensibility and befriended a corruption that resulted in betraying my children— and one of them, an innocent baby.

'You should be *happy*,' said Jason, with his trademark-tears, 'Emma can't *have* a baby!'

I sat up in bed one night with an awful thought: *Emma was sterile. Had I been set up?! Had I been duped into having a baby—for them?*

Still, like a forlorn dog, I begged Jason to divorce Skip and marry me. I viewed Jason now as a gigolo or alternatively, a weak viper, but I still needed him. Welfare was not for me, but how long could I continue working? Tim, Cassie, my parents knew nothing about this pregnancy. I had fashioned this dilemma myself, so my dread was a private one.

Emma, Skip, was accustomed to 'discretion.' She managed a large private trust fund and was kept busy, according to Jason, ministering to the requirements of the heads of corporations and their minions. She had friends named Binky and Stu and John Witherspoon. I thought her need for privacy and a pristine lifestyle might serve my own interests.

Obtaining her telephone number from the Carnegie Group, I telephoned the incurious Skip, and was not surprised when she graciously and quickly decided to meet with me.

In the vast marbled holding-pen that was the lobby of 'any-office, midtown,' I watched tired droves of people exit the elevators, holding back their sighs until they'd spun through the revolving doors. Many people passed in that half-hour; no blonde approached me. My self-confidence all but eroded, I was preparing to leave when finally, a tall angular woman, her dark hair worn in a modified cap-cut, strode purposefully towards me.

'Hall-oo,' she said in a crooning business voice, 'Is it Maura? I'm Emma.' She extended a thin hand to me, which I shook. My strong first impression was that I was paying for an overdue library book; my mouth agape must've told her that. She raised two equally curious eyebrows at me—probably at the hideous home-permanent which I had just inflicted on my hair the night before, now rising up behind me like a bale of hay.

'I'm sorry—' I stammered, 'I saw a picture of someone else I _thought_ was you—in Jason's wallet!'

'Oh?,' she inquired, smiling tightly. 'Ah, noooh, that is, that picture, I believe, Jason with *Miss Denmark* on our trip there last year— although I, too, am Danish.' ('All along, I have been mentally sticking push-pins into the wrong voodoo doll!' I thought.)

'Shall we?' Emma asked (as I hastily ripped up the *Miss Denmark* mind-shot), and we headed off for drinks and a 'chat.'

'It's an unfortunate thing,' Emma said, sipping her whiskey sour, as we sat in a darkened cocktail lounge nearby, 'unfortunate. . . Jason is most upset about this. . . as _you_ must be,' she added, but not quickly enough. 'Just an unfortunate incident,' she clucked, apparently conferring with herself; shaking her head.

'It's hardly an _incident_! I've known him nearly four years and didn't know of your existence. He used a different name, and iden—'

'—Nor, I did I know of _you_!'

There was a long and mutually ugly pause.

'Well,' she added reluctantly, looking afar, 'obviously Jason is at some fault, too.'

'Too? Too!?' I echoed— to no reaction whatever. She nibbled on an h'ors doerve and took a swallow of her sour before looking up. When she did, her pale blue eyes were unflinching. She spoke in her 'business voice.'

'What do you expect me to do about it? We've been married for fifteen years. That's a long time—isn't it.'

'Jason tells me you've been separated for ten of those.'

'Ah, that is true that we've had separate residences for—several years. But we do love each other and care deeply for each other. You certainly don't expect that to change.'

'He tells me that he loves and wants to marry me.'
'I believe he thinks he does.'

By the time our drinky-chat was over, I knew that she suffered from perfect diction and complete denial where Jason was concerned; that if she saw him kick The Pope in the pants, she would carefully explain that *'The Pope must've had it coming to him.'* Further, I knew that she would stand pat, and there would be no further 'silly talk of divorce.'

Were I to guess at her state of mind, it would be that she had determined to protect Jason at all costs from the scheming little ball of bad hair that sat across from her, swilling whiskey sours. Apparently, I was just another one of Jason's dates 'gone bad.' It was simply a case of 'Katrinka-fix!,' in the phrase from an old cartoon. A baby? Oh, never mind: Katrinka fix!

Well, if Emma was the Queen of Short-Sightedness, was I the Empress of Family-Planning? Regrettably—not.

'Skip has agreed to a divorce.'

I started to close my front door on his face.

'Wait! Hear me out!'

'I'm tired, Jason; I'm tired. I have to get up early tomorrow. I can't hear anymore of this.

'You've been saying that for weeks,' I sighed. 'I have two other children to consider. I've got to have an abortion.' He bit his lower lip, a bit like Bill Clinton, and looked away. Finally, he asked, 'When?'

'Before the week is out. Before it's too late. I've got to.'

'No! I've told you; she's agreed to divorce me!'

'When?!,' I fired back.

'When—did she agree??'

'When are you getting it: the divorce!'

'As soon as—we can.'

'When is that?'

'It—This isn't easy for me. . . ! As soon as I can arrange it, to get away—I'd, I'd go to Juarez.'

'Mexico? Is that a promise? Do you promise?'

'Sure,' he nodded, 'Soon.'

'Soon,' came not at all that cold February.

'Call her Skip. Everyone calls her that nick-name.' I simply stared at him.

'Well?' . . . 'Well, what?' . . . 'What does *Skip* say—? About the—?'

'I've talked with Skip and she'd be willing, you know, to take the child—! And *pay*, you, of course. Or pay for the . . . if you wanted one. . .' Jason turned away, his voice trailing off, waiting for a response.

Rage filled me so that, like an animal, my throat closed.

So I had been right! Though I was far from a Vestal Virgin, I had been a sacrifice to Emma's frigidity. Waves of rage and terror alternated within me before I could speak.

'*My* baby? The two of you—want to keep *my* baby? *Our* baby?! Either that, or she'll *pay* me to have an abortion?!

'No! Tell her I say 'No' to everything!'

'I told her you'd say that! I feel the same way you do about the baby. She didn't mean it like you think she did; she's a very kind person.'

'I know the kind of person she is,' I said as cold as death, 'and it's too late for an abortion, anyway. The two of you can find another guinea pig! Get out.'

'I'll go to Juarez, I will! Don't do anything rash. Remember that I love you.'

'Get out,' I said dully, and pushed the door closed on his departing back.

All that cold Sunday and the many days that followed, I was battered by demons. I felt as if sand was pouring down my throat and I couldn't breathe. I ran around my apartment, turning light switches off and then on, gasping for air, afraid for my life; wanting to call 911 because I couldn't breathe but afraid they would throw me in a Psych Ward if I did. Couldn't catch my breath. A giant dump truck was pouring sand down my throat and I was trying to claw my way up to the surface to breathe—but— I could not!

'Air!' I whispered, afraid to scare my children if I were actually dying. 'Air! I need air!' I gasped, and for the first time in my life,

I realized that nervous breakdowns were something real, not exaggerated, as I had supposed them to be.

The dump truck and the sand pouring down, down in me, are always there to remind me of that truth. That panic attack and one that followed it, was the closest so far I've ever come to a complete breakdown, and it was close enough.

7.

'What are those bright pink flowers on the tree, Mom?' asked Kim, giving a happy little skip up the flat steps leading to our four-family garden apartment house.

'Those are crab-apple blossoms, honey.' The tree stood on some pounded-down dirt right outside our window. There was grass and some landscaping, but the hard-packed dirt marked the places where the children played. It was hard for all of us not to bubble with joy and hope: it was *Spring*, after all, and we had just moved as a family, into our very own first-floor, freshly-painted garden apartment! Never mind that we'd moved in under the name of Jason 'Clarke,' instead of Kirkpatrick, that we still hadn't married; that I was beginning to 'show,' and that he had yet to make the trip to Juarez—or that he still maintained his apartment in the Bronx. It was April, we were beginning a new life and Kay and Jay would be enrolled in a good school. Watching her wispy little braids bouncing up and down, I felt like skipping, too.

There was an aura of excitement around garden apartments in the 'sixties and early 'seventies, right up to the time that Alice Crimmins, the red-haired cocktail waitress, was accused of murdering her two darling children in one. Some said I looked like her, except for the hair.

Not quite the projects, and definitely not your own home in the suburbs, but with a vestige of greenery and minus the chaos of city-living, it was Blue Collar Paradise, especially if there was an easy commute to work. Some, however, some did not work.

By the time the bloom was off the crab-apple tree, some of us got up early of a Monday and after several cups of tea to 'get going,' sat around in a bathrobe and circled want-ads dutifully from the Sunday Times—that someone, being Jason—and then went back to bed to sleep for the rest of the week. Soon, this was a pattern as firmly engrained in my mind as Jason's bathrobe was—navy, red and thin-gold striped—while the gold in our garden apartment got even 'thinner.' This became especially true when I got too big to go to work any longer. I dreaded his 'cuppa tea,' I quickly loathed the bathrobe and I became a very prudent shopper.

A neighbor gave me a big old second-hand carriage for the coming baby and Kim, Jerry and I pushed it to Pantry Pride to load up with food that was either wilted or dented.

The Supermarket was the great equalizer: while I shopped, I not only occupied myself finding bargains, but even though I sweated-out the pennies and the coupons, I was respected at the store. I was a mother doing her shopping, like anybody else.

One day as Kim and I trotted to the store, a perky-eared brown mutt gazed longingly after us, cocking its head, its large brown eyes hopeful.

'It's a girl!' Kim cried, as the dog waved its upward swoop of a tail. 'Can we keep 'er?!' I hesitated, more than slightly charmed by the pooch.

'It's a *stray*, Mom!'

'We have to go shopping,' I said, plodding on to the mournful tune of Kim's whimpers. Looking back, I saw the dog's tail sag and my own heart did a little nosedive: 'If she's there when we come back, maybe.' 'Really?!' . . . 'Maybe. I said, *maybe.*'

Of course, it was hard to tell Kim to get Kix or pick up a head of lettuce, when all she had going on behind those big saucer-eyes was a brown dog and which block she might be lurking on now. Of course also, when we went back, the stray was nowhere in sight: 'Why didn't you let me keep it!? I never ask you to get me anything! I just wanted that dog so bad.'

My throat constricted. 'Sorry, Kimmy.'

We were putting away the groceries at home when Jerry walked in.

'Where's Jason?' he asked, looking around surreptitiously.

'I don't know. In the city somewhere. Why?' He disappeared and returned in an instant, staggering under the weight of—the very dog! Kim let out a scream. The dog flinched.

'Put it down, Jerry!'

'—Put *her* down!,' Kim corrected me. 'That's the *same dog* we saw earlier, Jay.' 'Can we? 'Can we?!' Imploring eyes met mine, one set of them, brown.

'No, I think—I think things are tough enough around here, without a dog: C'mon, girl!,' I said holding the door open, 'Out!'

Did she run for the door? Do pigs fly upside down on a Wednesday?

'It's raining out!' Kim cried. 'Pouring,' Jer pointed out, indicating the window.

Then I uttered that fateful line: 'Just for tonight.'

Thus, dog food was added to our next shopping list—for 'Scotch,' the name chosen and slurred over by my mother, who now had a serious drinking problem—and like the liquor, Scotch made you happy, too, only it lasted much longer. A combination of brown and white, street-dog and saint, with a fluffy coil of a tail that such a dog often holds high like a banner, she was the best 'Shopper's Special' I ever got. If she had any faults, they were only stealing an occasional steak or two and raiding the day-old donut bin at 'Dunkin.'

She became one of the few blessings of a truly awful union that was a long and terrible bus ride; an odyssey where as you went, the way became darker, seedier, scarier; where you are not sure at all if you are heading in the right direction; where, when finally you are sure, you are completely lost. Yet, you are never irretrievably lost until life itself is lost: that is the lesson you learn if your mother is a good teacher.

There I stood, a bloated farmer's daughter—a 'Quaker,' gone to seed in a pilgrim-gray dress with a white alter-boy's collar—all the religions, gone to pot, as the Clerk at the New York Marriage Bureau coughed and said, 'Join hands.' Jason held my hand with his two fingers, like it was something he found by the side of the road.

'I will' said I, and 'I will' said he. 'Kiss the bride,' said the Clerk, trying hard not to look at my stomach. I looked up from my (definitely!) yoke-collar at Jason.

Big surprise. Tears streamed down his face. Stoically, he managed to kiss my cheek. It was not only one of the most unromantic weddings I ever participated in, possibly, in all of history, but certainly the most unwise. And I owed it all to myself.

The baby was born two weeks later.

'For God's sake, don't name an innocent little baby 'Sarah!'

'Not Sarah, Dad—*Sally*.'

'Sarah, Sally; same thing,' he grunted. I knew who he meant. Dad's cousin, Sally, the family bitch from Columbus Avenue, who used deprecation and put-downs to put her husband Nick down into his suicide's grave: *'Don't curse her with that. Please.'*

'It's either *that*, or Sadie, after Jason's sister.' He thought for a minute. 'What's the *other* sister's name?'

'Anna Monica Veronica.'. . . 'As in, plays the harmonica?' He let out a huge sigh.

I don't know whether it was me, running around and thinking I was suffocating in sand while I was carrying her, or the 48-hour labor I endured without medication at New York Hospital at the hands of, to quote Jason, 'the finest doctor!' (paid for by Emma, of course, the good ol' 'Skipper') or an actual self-fulfilling prophecy, but she was Sarah, reborn. I'm trying not to call my baby a bitch, but Sally was as close to Goering in a diaper as I'd ever want to see.

In no time at all, she was following Jason around and at his behest, making and keeping lists of 'offences' allegedly committed by the bigger kids against her. 'Allegations,' as in, 'These Allegations,' one of Jason's favorite words and everyone's least favorite. It was no wonder that before Kim or Jer came in the front door, they would take turns and scout down the block to see if his car was parked there: they had to prepare themselves to come into the house. (I learned of this much later.) I, too, had a sick, sinking feeling whenever I saw his car pull up in front.

But for now, a doting, though unemployed, Jason emerged—and hung over Sally's crib constantly, babbling at her when she was awake, crooning to her when she slept. When she was three months old, and he left his post briefly, there was a palpable pause—and a short electric-personality charge emanated from the crib: 'Hey, *Dad!*' The eerie call came from her as yet untried set of vocal cords. Just once.

'Did you *hear* that?!'

Jason, rarely speechless, nodded.

'We must never speak of this.'

'It doesn't matter; no one would *believe* it, anyway,' he answered.

She must've blown out her batteries because it was not until she was five months old that she spoke again—in sentences. Indubitably, she got a double-helping of the speech gene. Who knew she was sitting on eleven or twelve languages, all waiting to erupt; that one day, she would write speeches for Ambassadors, and live in luxury in Switzerland? (She talked a lot in Family Court, but that was the tip of the iceberg, and not the Alps.)

It had begun as most marriages do, an experimentation in converging personalities, with contingencies. The contingencies for me, were Emma, the 'post-it wife,' stuck to his side, no matter what, and probably for Jason, Kay and Jay, my little liabilities. We were in a garden apartment on Spencer Hill, with no garden, *but* without passing busses belching gasses into the windows. It was quieter, except for us. The fights started soon, escalating from arguments, bursting forth like thunder claps.

'I don't want the children hanging their things near my—*our* clothes,' Jason said, disdainfully pulling Kim's sweater from the packed closet, letting it fall to the floor. 'I don't want them sitting on our bed, either: they're so—*dirty!*'

'What do you mean, 'dirty?!''

'Dirty,' he shuddered, 'from playing in dirt!'

'We have only <u>one</u> real closet: I can see <u>sweaters</u>, but some of the things—!!'

'You'll have to make some other arrangements, My Dear.'

'<u>What</u> 'other arrangements?' It's wall-to-wall bureaus in their bedroom, and the living room has those three huge desks from Skip's office.'

'They are <u>formica</u>! They were being discarded and she put them aside for my use!' 'Well, then, put them in the Bronx! You call that place your office, don't you?'. . . 'There's no room there, either!' . . . 'Jason, for God's sakes, the other day, a kid was visiting Jerry, and he asked me if this was a *store!*'

'Speaking of the Bronx, I had better go check my mail.' He grabbed his empty attache case and beat a retreat, before the mailman could deliver the bills.

We were just scraping by on food and utilities. His sporadic paychecks covered windfall shopping expeditions; my meager report-typing at night helped stave off the bill collectors and then, of course, there was always good old Skip. I took on Beginning English students for tutoring, and typing and editing term papers to make some cash.

'Jason, if you just *circle* the ads and go back to bed, you'll never get a job.'

'Don't be ridiculous! I have a few good prospects already lined up for next week.' He laughed, showing teeth, but without making eye contact. I soon found out 'Don't be ridiculous' meant, 'I'm lying.' He pooh-poohed my fears, told me my worries were groundless, drank his twelve cups of tea in his robe and my anxieties deepened. Were it not for Ben and Mary, who lived upstairs and gave us egg-salad, bagels and the occasional and delicious vegetable-cheese from their Jewish Deli, we'd have been a lot hungrier than we were.

When the way became impossible and the cash disappeared, a 'charitable donation' came in from Skip: 'Someone paid me some money he owed me,' Jason said importantly. 'Is it from Skip, Jason?' . . . *'Don't be ridiculous!'*

When at his Queens domicile, he ate his meals apart from us— London broil, or whatever it was I made, on a TV tray in the living room in from of the television: 'I can't digest at the table. The children make me nervous.'

The horrible Jason emerged in the months after the wedding, slowly unfurling one leg at a time like a dreadful spider; swinging, spinning; putting a strangle-hold on us all.

'Don't you ever comb the back of your hair?!,' he might hiss as we entered a crowded place, or *'Your dress is wrinkled.* You never learned how to iron properly, did you? You're always disheveled!'

Bedlam had begun and Jerry was a favorite target. Now in grade school, full of who knows what kind of identity crises or what dark thoughts or good ones; he of the dark-fringed eyes and the gentle-voice and the good looks of 'Air Wolf,' suffered in the profound silence of the wronged child.

What matter, the perplexities and doubts that assailed him? An error in judgment, large or small, resulted in Jer being placed on a chair and Jason talking 'at him' for up to two hours or more, until the great shining orbs of hope that were his eyes glazed over; till the small fingers clutched the sides of the kitchen chair, to keep from falling to the floor. Still, despite my entreaties, Jason's voice droned on: *'Clearly, you have no respect for your mother or me, or else you would not have cut school, would you? Whatever made you think you could fool me surely you have some idea that I would . . . didn't you?'* Rhetorical, all, the questions droned on, no answers expected or even tolerated, less questions, than a sounding-board for pomposity; less pomposity, than cruel verbal flagellation.

'What can he be thinking?' I worried, looking at the little boy.

'Jason! Please come to the kitchen!'

'In a moment—! And what, Jerry, <u>what</u>, do you think your teachers believe of you because were <u>I</u> your teacher, I would certainly—!'

'Jason!!'

'What is it? I'm *speaking* to the boy!' As he stood before me, I looked at the suit, the carefully-knotted tie. 'It's too long,' I said finally, 'You're lecturing him for too long.'

'You fail to understand that one of us in this house has to make some rules. I'm merely elucidating to the boy what is expected of him.'

'You're grilling him like a piece of cheese. You've made your point.'

'Oh? Well, at least he won't be a <u>slacker</u>! I'm here to make sure of that!'

'Don't you understand?! He can't <u>*hear*</u> you anymore. You're turning him into a serial killer!'

'He'll learn respect. He'll sit there until he—!'

'You're <u>killing</u> him! And you're killing me!'

'I'm not running away from him—like his father did!' he snarled.

Every day, I disliked him more. He slept late, contriving a meager business as a runner, a lackey for lawyers, a summons-server, calling himself a 'litigations expert'. One of the members of a law firm he did some work for called him an 'agitations expert.' 'I laughed,' Jason bristled, 'but I didn't think it was the least bit funny!' I thought there was more truth than humor in it; anyway, it helped me stay up that night till three in the morning typing his grossly Redundant Report and Affidavit, and preparing the grossly-inflated bill.

Two words he <u>did</u> like were 'piano bar.' In the beginning, we would frequent them a lot. Very popular then among marrieds and those seeking to be, people would go to lounges and sit around horseshoe or circle-shaped bars, listening and sipping while the performer canoodled the keys, offering his own rendition of the songs of the day—often singing along with him, occasionally stuffing tips into a strategically-placed brandy-snifter. If you were a favorite of the artist, you could be 'persuaded' to solo.

Joe Darise was an accomplished saloon-singer who combined the smooth style of Sinatra, with the casual manner of Hoagy Carmichael

(*'Stardust'; 'Ol' Buttermilk Sky'*). Joe became a great friend of Jason's, whose talent was not lost on Joe. Not only did he encourage him, he spent his time and energy in preparing a highly-stylized arrangement for an upcoming audition Jason had on the boards. Jason had an unusual (for the Irish) Italian timbre to his tenor. Unfortunately, he lacked the intestinal fortitude to actually *go* to the audition, so Joe's handsomely bound and hand-printed song notes gathered dust on one of our desks. We became less welcome at the club.

Before that unhappy incident, however, I loved listening to Joe D's mellow performances and even sang a solo or two in my 'pleasant, but weak and unsubstantiated voice,' as Jason correctly characterized it.

Long before Joe did, I had grown tired of Jason's elaborate pretensions to grandeur, and since baby-sitters cost money, I began electing to stay home, putting my 'piano bar career' in serious jeopardy. There was always enough money for Jason to go, and go, he did, stumbling home later and later, drunker and drunker. We all began cowering in our beds; now, as he raged incoherently almost on a nightly basis.

That he didn't work; that he slept days, following me around with a yellow note pad listing his grievances among the letters I had to type for him; that he began secretly to record my phone calls; all contributed, all paled, in comparison to my escalating dread of the madness provoked in him by nights of drinking and the bellicose days that followed them. Tantrum was his new middle name.

Neighbors flew from us; the police came to us. And always, it was Jason who called them. I learned why women complained about cops: if you had a Peeping-Tom and you lived alone, as when I did in New Bedford, they 'hit on you,' arriving uninvited, nervously chewing gum, doused with Old Spice Cologne.

Now, I found that in situations of domestic violence, they often took the man's part; this seemed especially true if the cop was Irish.

'Listen, Pal,' said Jason, drawing one cop aside and off into the bedroom, 'You know how these woman-things get started.' His voice lowered conspiratorially as they spoke, phrases like, '—*worked for Phil Murphy...on the job...*' drifted back out to me.

'He's *not* working!,' I called out.

'We'll *get* to you, *okay, Ma'am? Pipe down out there!*' 'What job?,' I snorted defiantly, '*He's* not a cop. And he's pushing me around,' I said to the other cop who was watching me, taking a sullen stance, arms folded.

'I don't see no bruises!'

'Hey, Frank,' the burly Irish cop called out from the other room, ''C'mere an' take a look at this. All 'ese kids, crowded into this little room!' He gestured expansively and dropped his arm. I could see him, his back to me, shaking his head negatively. Frank, trotting in to survey the damage, threw me back a dirty look. 'S'like a pig sty,' Frank agreed pleasantly.

'See that you keep it down now,' said the Senior Officer, thumping his notebook as they left, and looking right at me. I did not reply.

'Thanks, *boys!*' said Jason at the door.

'My name is Officer *Sorrentino,*' *Frank* corrected him. 'Sorry, Officer!' The 'Boys Club' had sided with him. Jason's manhood was vindicated: he would bother me no more.

But I was devastated. Why was I not believed? No blood, I guess. Why was I treated so poorly? No dick, I guess.

Time and again, if we had any significantly differing opinion, Jason dialed the police. Sometimes, he would frighten me just by lifting the phone off the cradle: 'You see that I can't reason with you. You're not behaving rationally. Perhaps I should have you locked up. Creedmoor is right up the road.' Up, went his eyebrows, up, the corners of his mouth: 'Yes, that's what I think I have to do, *for the children.*'

'No, Jason! *No.* Please do *not* call the police again. They were here *yesterday.* Don't you care what the neighbors think?'

'It's you who doesn't care. . . Hello, Operator? Give me Sergeant O'Malley. Yes. I'll wait.

'Sergeant? This is Jason Kirkpatrick. Yes, that's right. . . No. Now, *you* listen! I have a problem here! I need—What?! Give me your badge number. I want to speak to the Captain! You can't—hello?! *Hello?*'

So finally, miraculously, the police refused to come and stopped giving credence to his calls. They knew, after a while, that he was a Nut-Job. Once, when two newbies did come, they looked at Jason, over six feet tall, and exhaling tiredly asked, 'Okay, what did she threaten you with?' 'Why, she just—*threatened* me. Shook her fist— like this!'

'How big're you, Miss?'

'What?'

'What *height* are you?'. . . 'Five foot two.' The two cops looked at each other: 'GetOUTahere!' They gave Jason the one-armed chorus of disgust as they walked out.

But once they stopped coming, *oh, once they stopped coming*, it was so much worse. Jason called them repeatedly and as the police became nearly as defiant as I was, he raged. I awakened to find him staring down at me. My heart leapt, but I did not move a muscle: Kim lay sleeping near me. He leaned over and spat down into my face, like a snake. I groaned and turned away. From that moment on, I planned my escape.

I was thinking of just that a couple of mornings later, as Kim and I walked past the dumpster in the driveway.

'Look!' she gasped. We both stopped dead: A seven foot tall yellow stuffed giraffe with big orange spots. It peered down at us much as a real giraffe might.

'Let's get it outta there,' Kim said, gazing upward at it. 'It is in mint condition,' I acknowledged. . . 'Like new! Let's!' . . . 'But where would we *keep* it? I'm sure that's why they got rid of it in the first place—whoever owned it.'

'If we don't like it, we can put it back, can't we?' 'True. And we don't have to feed this one!' She bounded up the side of the dumpster and after a little tussle, we dragged it home.

'We'll stash it in here for now,' I said, shoving the geeky giraffe into Jason's closet, really stuffing it in there. . . . 'I wonder if it's all right in there?' Kim frowned. . . 'Take a look,' I shrugged. As she opened the door, the long neck came swinging out at an alarming angle.

'Wait till Jason comes home at three in the morning—!' I started to say. As our eyes met, we both burst out laughing.

Well, we shut the door again, went to the dentist for a toothache she'd been having and on to many other errands of the day, some of them involving the other two children. It wasn't until we were all tucked in our beds later that night and my eyelids, heavy with sleep, were closing that I remembered the giraffe. I smiled a little and dozed off.

Deep and away in some more blissful state, I started at the sound of a tenor's scream and a loud *Jesus Christ!* A suddenly sober Jason appeared in the bedroom doorway. 'You nearly gave me a heart attack!' 'Sorry. Forgot it was there'. . .

I was on the phone with my mother. 'You know, if you like that dog, you should have her 'fixed.' You've had her for a while now. Two years?'

'Scotch? Longer than that. Yes, I know; you're right. I've been thinking about it,' I answered, lifting up the kitchen curtain as we spoke, peering out under the crabapple tree. There stood Scotch wearing a guilty look, whilst Champ, the Super's Boxer, plugged jauntily away at her. I let the curtain fall: 'Never mind, Mom.'

'What do you mean? *I'll* give you the money to—!'

'Gotta go. Call you back.'

Scotch had six lovely, fluffy pups in the old crib, all born in those little black baggies puppies come in. The seventh pup—a scrawny pale runt that Jer immediately named 'Willard', (after a movie that was out about a white rat)— I had to pull out of Scotch at three in the morning. Her head was a pealed skull, the inside, probably, an empty stone dungeon with a few old bones in it, and maybe a moth flitting around in there. Willard liked to pee in Jason's shoes. Other than that, she had no special talent. Naturally, this was the one we kept. (Nobody wanted Cinderella.) Scotch lived to be twenty and Willard, about the same. Maybe it was the donuts?

He, who I had once thought of as the quintessential light-hearted bachelor, had morphed into the picture of Dorian Gray, with no visible line of demarcation. Mood swings began soon after Jason 'moved into' the house on Spencer Hill—sans luggage, but certainly not sans 'baggage.' I knew that the reason Skip had her separate luxury apartment downtown, not far from the UN, and he kept the uptown 'bachelor pad,' was that he had thrown her down and fractured her skull in a jealous rage. She forgave him, but never again to the extent of residing with him.

This forerunner of the Clinton-esque woman paid the price for her love or folly, footing the bills from a discreet distance, keeping him on as 'arm-candy' to escort her to various Carnegie functions—to smile, and telling him, I was sure, not to speak too 'authoritatively' on any significant matter. Hadn't he told me about his explosion over Skip's boyfriend himself, explaining how he leaped from a closet in their love-nest, confronting her as she was ironing the boyfriend's shirts? I don't know whether I was more surprised at his impulsive act, or the idea that anyone found Frigid Bridget attractive.

So had I interrupted all this happiness. He told me this amid copious tears at the beginning of our pseudo-union (in reality, a triumvirate) probably so I would not expect a grand future with him as a husband or father. Though this was patently obvious, I preferred not to see it that way. Instead, at the inception, I fought a losing battle to keep him 'home'—'home,' being a dubious distinction, to one who was truly never at rest.

Whether Jason suffered from an extreme insecurity or truly felt as superior as he acted was at last an uninteresting mystery to those who took the brunt of his madness.

I know he viewed me as lower-class than he, chuckling on a good day at my 'inadequacies' and pillorying me for, say, his perceived mispronunciation of a word like 'stu-dent,' demanding its repetition: thusly and thusly and thusly. Never could I draw him into any intimate or relaxed conversation, high, I think, on the priority list of any good relationship. When I tried, he literally drew back, like a large cardboard cutout of John Barrymore, with about as much depth. A profile would be proffered, a stage-smile. I wondered why he never let his guard down.

'You never mention your parents, Jason. What were they like?'
He stared at me, his face claiming an impassivity before he spoke:
'Saints.'

'What?'

'My mother and father were *Saints.*'

That was the extent of the revelation of his past, except once to
reveal, 'Mother closed the blinds every afternoon precisely at four-
oh-five.' He also confessed to me that he was 'profoundly grateful'
that his parents hid him in the basement for two months to avoid
his being drafted: whether this was for the Korean or Vietnamese
conflict, I wasn't sure and wasn't apprised; like Dorian Gray, Jason
never divulged his true age. Later, he admitted that the army did
catch up with him, that he served briefly; that he was discharged
'without honor.'

I broached the subject with Skip on a brief visit, the purpose,
now forgotten.

'Jason's parents?' she echoed. 'His father was a bootlegger during
Prohibition and the mother—Veronica, was—a good woman.'

'The sisters?' She stared at me, her opaque eyes unreadable: 'Anna
Monica and Sadie both died before they were fifty,' she replied and
perhaps anticipating my next question, tagged on the explanation:
'They were alcoholics.'

Mother Veronica—was she a Saint? If the proof is in her output,
she's shoveling coal way below sea level. Then again, maybe she was
a Saint.

My parents were continuing the tradition begun when we children
were teenagers of making long excursions to Jones Beach where
they were known as '*The Beach Nuts.*' Laden down like mules with
provisions for every conceivable emergency—especially my mother,
her backpack containing tuna sandwiches and vodka—we would
all trek miles to a mid-beach secluded spot on either Beach 3 or 4,
somewhere near the dunes and nowhere near the water, yet always
near the Point of Exhaustion.

There we would lie listlessly, we children, for the long day that
stretched before us, getting up the strength to make the ocean,

swimming against vicious waves, and dangerous riptides. My parents presided like The Lunts over a coterie of friends, upon whom they lavished snacks and sandwiches and vodka and as the day progressed, so did the jokes and the raucous laughter.

As the shadows lengthened, so did the burbled stories, the slurred and babbled punch-lines much appreciated by all, except for Cass, Tim and I, who didn't drink. As the sun sank over the distant sea, the dialogue was more staccato, coarser, so that even we 'got it,' along with advanced cases of sunburn.

Jason was added to this august group after we married, along with the children, for a foray or two. I was so busy, I was pulling my hair out. Frantically, I diapered the baby, found the swimsuits and slapped together the tuna fish sandwiches for our first outing with The Group.

'Can't you give me a hand? Why are you staring at me like that?'

'Are you trying to poison me? Were those mushrooms or toadstools on my steak last night?' Jason demanded. I stopped wrapping the sandwiches in waxed paper and brushed my hair back out of my eyes. 'Are you kidding, Jason? We all ate that steak. Didn't you say something about having chili for lunch yesterday? Maybe *that* was it.'

'No,' he said finally, 'I've never felt that way before. Ever!'

'Well, believe me, if I *were* trying to poison you, you wouldn't be standing there, *telling* me about it!'

By the time we got to the beach, the mushroom matter had all but been forgotten. Jason placed his blanket on the sand, away from everyone—no surprise, there!—and Lonnie, Terry and all my parents' other friends sat around having their coffee and sandwiches in subdued tones, in deference to the New Arrival.

I passed out sandwiches to the kids and, of course, offered Jason the first one. Terry poured him a coffee from her thermos. We all settled in and were enjoying sandwiches as Jason took a huge bite of his—and suddenly, he stood up, the food still a bulge in his cheek.

'What's the matter?' Terry said. 'What's wrong, Jason?' said I. He turned to me, ashen-faced, and as everyone watched, pulled—a bobby pin!—from his mouth. 'Did you put this in my sandwich?' he demanded, as if in a scene from *'J'Accuse!'* Everyone's eyes were on me.

'I don't know what you're complaining about, Jason' said my Dad after the long, uncomfortable pause that followed, 'She's just making sure you get your *daily Iron!*'

'Jason,' I said to him, once the laughter stopped, 'I'm sorry. I guess it was just that I was in a rush, flying around making the sandwiches and—and.' He said not a word, slowly lying down, face-up on his blanket.

My entire family saw through Jason like a sheet of glass and unanimously hated him.

One Sunday, Jason had made a delivery of some legal papers nearby, and we had dinner at Cassie's in Connecticut. She and her husband and children were low-key and pleasant and distressingly normal for me; I watched, yearning for a relationship like that.

Meanwhile, Jason postured and exaggerated his importance more than usual, which turned out to be a great deal: *'I had to get these papers to this lawyer—a <u>very</u> important man—at once! Of course, I overbill him enormously—Ha-Ha!'*—he laughed, inserting his hand, Napolean-like, inside his vest—'Course,' he added to the politely-elevated eyebrows around him, 'he's unaware that I'm *overcharging* him!'

'Must be a dick like you,' muttered little Rickie, their youngest, but we all heard him. To everyone's credit, there were no laughs, but there were a few suppressed smiles; his father quickly chastised Rickie, but not very sternly.

'That was very impertinent, young man!' Jason snapped, turning to me. 'I think it's time that we take our leave. I don't countenance rudeness like that from anyone!'

Hastily, we said our good-byes and were hustled into the car and as we were backing out of the driveway, were startled to see a small figure appear in the dusk by the garage. Suddenly, little Rickie pulled down his pajama-bottoms and 'mooned' Jason! We all sighed, knowing we would have a most unpleasant trip home as, indeed, we did, with Jason ranting, 'Never in my life! The parents are to blame—Such disrespect! Shocking!'

The phone rang soon after we got home and it was Cassie, apologizing, but tittering slightly. 'None of us was laughing, Cassie, and you know why, I think.' After a moment of quiet, she said, 'Well, he is a dick, you know.' I looked over at Jason, who was examining a glass of milk before drinking it. 'I'll tell him you said so. Thank you.'

The world was a dark and lonely place. From the horrified looks on the older kids' faces, living in a mad household, where the norm was always the opposite of what you expected, to a toddler who had turned into a paid-informer, I knew I had made a very bad mistake with Jason. *Father* material? I would have been delighted for any evidence that he was *human* material!

But wasn't it 'too soon' to do anything about it? Wasn't the baby too young? I'd been divorced once already; didn't divorce cost money? But you can't put a price on guts, can you. Apparently, I was severely deficient in these: Rather than realizing I was following in my downtrodden mother's footsteps, I busied myself in writing The Short Story, the genre then so popular.

One short-short was about Lou, a guy who owned a pizza parlor and who the mob made an example of—by baking him in his own oven. All I can remember of it is that he wore black and white checkered pants, and that it made an interesting pizza topping. I'd done a lot of short stories and considered 'Lou's Pizza' to be the dopiest of them all. However, the kids got hold of it and—remarkably—read it and loved it: Jason, too.

'I enjoyed the pizza-man story. You have quite a flair for this. Why not consider going to college for it—? Matriculating?'

'Oh, no I might take a course or two in Creative Writing, but—!'

'That's nonsense. You should matriculate'. ..'Oh, no, I....'

The 'one or two' gradually devolved into a surprising *best time of my life*, even, nestled as it was, down deep inside what was one of the worst. It took a long time to get there, but the trip to Degree-Land was wonderful and worth it. Jason, once boyfriend, then husband, ever the biggest bully of them all, had made a winning suggestion and a vital contribution to my happiness. It might have had at its root his desire to increase my earning power for him, or his perceived status in the eyes of others, or simply to keep me busy while he squired Skip to her many functions, but I acquired a BA magna in English Lit, and a lot of fine friendships because of Jason.

Matriculation just 'happened.' City College cost me eight dollars tuition tax per year plus books, which I usually bought 'Used' and sold back at term's end.

First night of class, community college; first class, History. I looked left, at an attractive, plumpish sepia-skinned girl sitting down next to me. We conversed for a moment.

'Say, I saw the funniest black guy on TV last night. His name is Flip Wilson. Did you catch him?'

Her eyes narrowed. 'Did you have to say '*black* comedian?' Couldn't you just have said, '*comedian?*'

I clammed up. The teacher, puffily 'from Harvard,' began his discourse and once class was over, I lammed outa there, making a mental note not to mess with—whoever the heck she was.

Next time, same girl, same seat, turned to me: 'Sorry I snapped at you the other evening. My mother passed away that day.'

I nodded, and as the Harvard guy droned on 'raising our sites,' I wondered at the kind of girl who could come to class on the same day her mother died and gazed covertly over at her. Did she have enormous feelings—? Or none, whatever. Knowing my penchant for picking crackpots, was this someone I even wanted to know?

A risk was taken on both our parts, the chasm breached and Marilyn and I became the firmest of friends. The incident about her mother was the first inkling of her self-containment, or 'repression,' as it might today be called. Indeed, extremely restrained, even formal, she never used profanity or reviled anyone: the rejoinder about Flip Wilson's color was the only time she ever criticized me, and was certainly a 'sixties gut reaction, when equality was still a smoldering issue, a long dream away.

She of the keen mind, missed nothing, excelled in math and advice-giving and her 'restraint' camouflaged a great and forgiving heart. Other than a 'Marilyn' (Monroe) complex for keeping people waiting and once drawing my fury by not showing up at all, Lyn was nearly perfect. We shared confidences.

After classes, we might hit Jann's ice cream parlor, wolfing down blueberry blintzes and yakking away. One night, someone in back played the song '*Honey*' on the juke-box. Lyn's eyes misted over and she gazed down. 'What's the matter?'

'Honey was my mother's name.' When she looked up, the mist had cleared: that was the closest I ever saw her to tears during our long friendship. Maybe if she hadn't swallowed all those tears. . . ? But we can't know everything.

By the time Lyn first visited my house, all our diversities had helped make us good pals. Jason was very cordial to her. By her next visit, he was laughing and saying things like, 'That spick owes me a favor!' and 'I didn't know he was a kike, did you?' I was horribly embarrassed, and stammered an apology to her as she left.

'I know what he's trying to do,' Marilyn smiled at me outside of my front door, 'don't worry about it. The funny thing about it is he thinks that's the first time I've ever seen that tried! Hey, I'll see you tomorrow in class. Give you a lift part-way home, if you want. I'm going your way tomorrow.'

After class, as she drove her big old black and white merc along Kissena, we laughed at Jason's flagrant efforts to make her feel uncomfortable, though I knew it had to bother her somewhat. 'Oh,' I said, 'when he's *driving* and someone cuts him off, he screams *Jew-nigger bastard*!' at them.' She howled over this: 'From now on, that's what *I'm* going to say!'

'But you're not like that! You don't curse!'

'I know! Only when somebody cuts me *off*, okay?!'

While she maintained a silence about it, I knew Lyn surmised that I was desperate to get out of the marriage, but hadn't quite figured out how to do it.

It was end-of-term and she was driving me, on our way to take Final Exams. I was telling her about a Hitchcock episode on TV a few nights before: 'The lady bangs her husband over the head with a frozen leg of lamb, cooks it and serves 'the evidence' for *dinner*—to the detective investigating her husband's death!'

'What? What're you talking about?' She slowed for a light. 'Too bad you missed it. It was really great!'

Marilyn put her foot on the gas pedal. 'She picks up the leg of lamb—like this—' I demonstrated, lifting my arms up in the air, holding an imaginary leg of lamb aloft. She turned to look. Smash! We rear-ended the car in front of us.

We were late to class and ached all over for the tests, but we both got good marks. 'US Grade A Prime!' Lyn quipped, when we got our papers back, 'and I never even studied.'

'Blame it on the lamb,' became our private catch-all phrase. It covered everything…Well, nearly.

'You're *what?*'
'Pregnant.'
'How did that happen?'
'Blame it on the—!'
'—Not *this* time. How long?'
'Not long; maybe two weeks. But I know I am.'
'Talk about bad timing. What're you going to do?'
(Lyn was in the process of, with Roger, adopting their first baby: *'I'm the only black woman in America who can't have babies.'* So I took a big breath before answering her.)

'I don't know.' Although I had a pretty good idea what I was going to do. I was half way through school and there was no way in hell I wanted another baby.

I made the appointment with a doctor in Kew Gardens who performed such a 'procedure,' as an abortion was delicately called, or murder, as the protesters called it. Lyn accompanied me.

We leafed through the magazines in the perfectly lovely outer office. When they called me in, I hopped up onto the white table in the sparkling-clean lab, as I was instructed. I was no stranger to this situation.

But then something I can't explain took over; some unrelenting sorrow in my gut. I jumped down from the table. The nurse turned to me in surprise.

'I'm sorry. I just can't do this—today, Nurse.'

'That's perfectly all right,' she replied and went out to get the next patient.

Startled, Lyn looked up at me from her magazine, raising both eyebrows: 'Back so soon?'

'I changed my mind.' I felt curiously light-hearted and depressed at the same time.

'Then,' said she, closing the magazine and standing up, 'How about some Chinese?' I nodded, and as we left, added in a burst of levity, 'No, I think there are enough Chinese already!'

She held the door for me: 'We blacks are gaining on them.'

We went to Sun Luck's on Queens Boulevard and chowed down.

'*Dim sum?*' Oh, yeah.

8.

'What a beautiful baby!' I heard, every time I ventured out with her. A doll-maker seemed to have taken up an extra-fine sable line-brush and carefully drawn the cupid mouth, the artful brow. Her blue eyes needed no further enhancement, fringed as they were with dark lashes. She was the Elizabeth Taylor in the Hall of Babes.

'Are you going to nurse that baby forever? How long have you been nursing her?' came Marilyn's voice over the phone. 'Oh, must be—nine months, now?'

'Nearer a year,' she sniffed back; 'bout time you *weaned* her, isn't it? Translation: When are you coming back to school?'

Lyn had it right. 'Nursing the Baby' was the great escape. I could lie down with this placid and perfect doll, performing an important function, while at the same time, exiling myself from the madness of Jason. It was The Year of The Cow.

Sally of course hated it, hated the baby, hated me and began scrawling her retaliatory lists with a vengeance:
1) Jerry ate my ice cream. Why does he always curse?
2) Kim has a boyfriend named Arthur Wendle. He bit her on the nek.
3) Yesterday K. and Jerry threw my list in the toilet.

A sad numbness overtook me and I viewed the whole show with glassy eyes, which made Sally even more furious for the attention she wasn't getting. Yes, I was a bad mother to her: too often, I was unable even to like her. For me, the light at the end of that tunnel I traveled was dim, diffused, underwater and somewhere way out beyond the Great Barrier Reef. As proof, each new day a wave of great sadness washed over me, engulfing me.

What was to be done? How could I forgive myself the luxury of having another baby? How miserable I made things for everybody!

'How very gorgeous your baby is!'

'Baby remained 'Baby,' a blank on the birth certificate, nameless for nearly a year. When Jason came 'home,' he spelled out, *'Where is that bundle of J O Y?'*—In part, to appease Sally's fomenting rage and in truth, because she truly was. Thus, she became Joy Marie Kirkpatrick, and not Anna Monica, a name that at the time, perfectly suited her.

Psychologists caution against naming your man-child Angel or Jesus (the prisons are full of them) or your precious daughter Chastity (a nearly foolproof recipe for white boots, miniskirts and car-hopping) but no amount of warning could ever have convinced me that Joy would become a source of pain, confusion, utter bewilderment and at last, despair.

Kay and Jay sought constantly to protect her. Surely no one, Jason included, despite smothering her in six sweaters at a time, intended to harm her. The real damage came later. No one could protect her from herself.

How nice it would be if dandelions were always yellow and happiness sang like a lark within us. But the structure of life does not permit. Dandelions need rain to grow. Trying to insulate Joy from the world turned her inward, toward a sorrow that was not to be breached—although it was impossible to foresee, when searching the clear crystal of her eyes and the magic of her child-soul. Cares warp us. Despite the daily ritual of wrapping herself in Denial against the cold fray of discontent; the blazing battles that flared to the tune of police sirens, irreparable damage was done to that sensitive soul.

Jimmy McFadden was a soft-spoken fireman, so soft, you could barely understand him. He was also Jason's best and truest longtime friend. He had silver hair and blue eyes, and spoke Chinese that he had learned in the Navy, a sing-song Chinese and he crinkled his eyes when he spoke it in a way that you had to laugh at him. He was a very nice man. It was something of a miracle to me that Jason maintained one or two good long-time friendships.

Once Jimmy took a cab downtown, and the Chinese cab driver pulled up alongside another cab, and started conversing with the other driver, who happened to be Chinese, too, talking about Jimmy, his fare, in a derogatory way. When Jimmy got out to pay the fare, he tipped the man generously and told him (in Chinese) that he hoped he'd have a good day, and that his other fares wouldn't be such 'shits.'

'Jimmy and I are going to Florida next week to look over some property.'

'What kind of property?' '—For his retirement. We'll be back in a week.'

'Jason, I thought you had a job interview with a Mr. Humphrey?—Humphries? Next week: Don't you?'

'Yes, but that can wait. This is important.'

'Why do *you* have to go with him? Why not go himself?'

'Because I'm his best friend. And you know Jimmy! He has to have somebody there,' he laughed, 'to translate for him.'

Jason had been gone only two days when I developed a wicked abscess that required surgery. I called Jimmy's sister—Jimmy lived with her—to get his number in Florida. 'Hello?' said a weirdly-wispy voice that could only be—Jimmy's! I was too stunned to say anything at first, then I managed a muffled 'Jimmy?'—my mouth being as swollen as it was.

'Yes?'

Jimmy?!? What're you doing *home?*' . . .

'Who is—who is *this?*'

'Where is Jason? Why aren't you in Florida?'

'He—ah, he's not here right now.'

'You two were supposed to have left Sunday night. What happened?'

Suddenly, the light went on in the part of my brain that wasn't abscessed. 'This was a *set-up*, wasn't it!?'

'No! I, ah—!' 'Don't bother lying to me, Jimmy! I know where he is!'

'. . . Geez! He said you wouldn't be calling here,' Jimmy mumbled. I crashed the phone down, and immediately dialed another number:

'Mrs. Kirkpatrick's office; may I help you?. . . No, I'm sorry, Emma's not here. She's in the Bahamas for a week. May I take a message? Certainly, I'll tell her Maura called—oh, she *does* she know your number! Fine!'

Well, it wasn't 'fine' with me. The trip to 'Florida' was cut short a day or two.

'You never should have called Skip at her office! They don't know about you there! She had no idea you didn't know we were traveling together: ours was a business trip!'

'You're the one with a lot of nerve—thinking I'm that stupid! Business trip! *Monkey* business! That's the icing on it. That snaps it entirely.'

'You can check: we had separate rooms. The poor thing! I went along just for appearances. They all still think we're married. I had to make the trip.'

'You did. And you <u>had</u> to drag poor Jimmy into it. And you had to make up that lie about Florida.' 'She honestly knew nothing about it.' 'I can believe that. She's just stupid enough!'

'How *dare* you call Skip stupid, the woman who—!'

'—The woman who pays our bills and keeps wrecking any chance we might have to have a *family* together? *Her,* you mean!? You mean, poor *me!* . . but not anymore.

'You can have her! If you defrosted her for a week, she'd *still* be frigid!' I walked out of the apartment, still woozy from the mouth surgery but noticing Jason's eyes starting to bulge, and frightened that he might hit me.

Phoning her proved equally fruitless. I was thoroughly disgusted with the 'kept woman' arrangement and in an effort to see that faltering 'light at the end of the tunnel,' threw myself into taking care of the kids and typing up school assignments for my evening classes.

But after that trip, a subliminal light had gone on in my brain, and it was an enticing shade of red. It beckoned for me to follow to a place of new, furtive excitements.

'There! He *is* looking at me. Finally!' I had been flirting outrageously with my Sike teacher in Community College night classes; reading the text, but reading far too much between the lines. To his credit, he tried not to make eye contact with me, an attractive married woman a couple of years older than he; trying persistently to ignore me. But I was equally persistent, resorting finally to an eye-catching dark brown floppy-brimmed felt hat, mini skirt and knee-high leather boots, typical 'Seventies gear; gear best worn by someone ten years younger than I. But good looks and the straight blonde hair that the hippies wore then, 'made it happen' for me.

He had brown, wavy hair, blue eyes and the same last name as a famous composer. He was single.

I was married to a man with two apartments, an empty wallet, an empty attache case which he carried shield-like all the time, and a doting ex-'wuff' who footed all Jason's bills (except for me and the kids!)

I knew all about cheating, except that, so far, I never had. This would still have been a pleasant fantasy excursion, only my 'green card' came in the form of Jason and Skip's Undercover Charitable Convention Adventure in the Bahamas. I was of the opinion that charity, Carnegie grants included, begins at home. So I determined to slip the bonds of matrimony and eventually release myself—or was that, '*relieve* myself?'

No matter. We'll skip the semantics, the philosophizing, the phony excuses: I 'went there.'

To wit: I ultimately found myself in the teacher's bedroom, with the lights on, but without my hat and my boots on—or anything else.

I realized, starkers, perched upon his bed and looking back at him, that his head was *also* cocked, and further—that we were facing a full-length mirror. I gasped.

'What's wrong?,' he said, grinning back at me in the mirror. '. . . Nothing. It's just—a shock to see that we look— beautiful.'

'Would you like me to take a picture?,' he asked, pumping. 'I have a camera.'

A dim bulb from an old attorney went off in my head, and I recalled something about never putting it in writing and never taking a picture and though it was probably too late on both counts, I got momentarily smart. (Maybe it was the additional lighting equipment I saw standing around?)

'No, thank you.'

Well, it was a pretty decent interval. I ruined things, maybe intentionally, by writing him a letter which sounded dangerously proactive and job-losable for a teacher at a time when—in fact, on our very campus, a sit-in had occurred, large cavernous holes had been dug and a huge wooden crucifix erected at the Main Gate—job security was hardly at a high. He avoided any eye contact whatsoever after that, perhaps envisioning his own not-too generous balls affixed to that 'ad-hoc' crucifix.

One night during a fast and furious rainstorm, I chased his car after class, skipping over the puddles in my boots, he nearly ran me down, but reluctantly said, 'Hop in,' and gave me a ride to the nearest bus stop, commenting only. . .

'That was an *interesting* letter.'

I blushed, and felt a burst of steam sear my sordid soul— but at that same instant, a 'flash-bulb' went off in my mind's eye—of the long mirror in his bedroom; his camera by the bureau.

I smiled, and got out of the car: 'Thanks for the ride.'

So much for shrinks—though I probably could have used a good one.

School remained my solace, the stem-source of my self-esteem and balm for the third-degree burn that was my marriage. I hoped it would afford me a way out, though I never dreamed its real value to me would always be a warm, intangible and internal thing. I also met a wonderful friend, Lyn, the very best companion one could have. And all these gifts came down to me initially, through Jason, the worst companion I ever had.

Steve Doran was Guest Lecturer at one of Marilyn's Business elective courses on a Tuesday evening. He worked for Honeywell, as a liaison for the budding science of Computer Technology and Its Possible Applications in Business, the subject of his lecture.

The sad turnout that night was indicative of how few realized at that time, the potential of a giant industry that would soon out-stride the Honeywell thermostat business by several light years. But Steve had a clue, as did Marilyn, with her quiet analyst's mind. She asked pointed questions of the speaker, who seemed amiable enough. I thought I saw him shoot a few glances at me and was unsurprised when, after the few lackluster attendees drifted away, he said, 'Would you ladies care to join me for a cup of coffee?'

'I'd like to,' said Marilyn, packing up her things, 'but I have to be at work early tomorrow.' I just started working at the Medical Library.' 'Oh? Which one?' 'Sinai,' she replied. He smiled at me as he handed her his card, 'Maybe you'll give the Manager over there my card. TRW has a new computer that will really facilitate your operations. It's tailor-made for libraries.' She took the card and nodded.

'Then, you?' he said turning to me, 'perhaps you could go for a cup of coffee.'

Steve, I learned, had a gentle personality, a good head for business and a wife who hit him over it with a potato masher every chance she got. He resided now mostly in Columbia, Maryland, working out of TRW and then at home on Long Island, where the four daughters lived with Mickey, real name, Marsha; she of the martinis and the potato masher.

It didn't take me long, blowing over my coffee cup and laughing for what seemed like the first time in years, to divulge that I also knew an 'Emma,' who took the name Skip and who, though not outwardly violent, was every bit as controlling. I thanked him for the coffee and he offered to drop me home—which I suggested he do around the corner, by the dumpsters. He kissed me right on the lips, despite being a low-key kind of guy, and as I had one hand on the door, I jumped out, smiled and said 'I enjoyed your lecture.'

'It's the first of three. If you liked it,' he laughed, 'the *lecture*, I mean!—there's another one Tuesday.'

By the next lecture, we had graduated to martinis. By the third, we were very good friends, though not yet intimate ones. Marilyn said nothing but looked rather glumly at me. As she packed up her book bag that third lecture, however, she said, 'I hope you know what you're doing. You're still *married*, you know.'

'Marilyn, you know Jason's a rat, and it's wonderful to be with someone who doesn't scream and throw tantrums.'

'<u>That</u> is what I'm talking about. The tantrums. Be careful.'

Steve was almost distressingly normal compared with Jason. I looked forward to secretive dinners with Mr. Doran and 'Mr. Martini' and chose to think we commiserated and not that I was what no one ever thinks of themselves as: bad.

I was actually having a wonderful time. For the first time in my life, I enjoyed talking with a man who actually listened to my views, without an immediate 'given' that they would be discounted or ridiculed. What heaven!

Of course, the 'PI' at home was highly suspicious by now. Where once, through the day, he called home when away three or four times, now it was eleven, twelve—twenty times that these check-up calls came in: 'What're you doing?' 'Washing the dishes.' Ring, ring! 'Hi, what're you doing?' 'Same thing I was doing five minutes ago: washing dishes.'

It still wasn't 'time' for me to leave: no guts, no diploma, no money. I merrily went from being bad, to doing worse. The dinners with Steve of the big brown eyes and the bedside manner lengthened, as did the drink list.

One evening when Jason was away 'on business,' we had a late dinner-drinks date that evolved into a mad parking session in a local lover's lane. We were groping around in the back seat of his car when police floodlights struck my besotted eyes: fortunately, the driver was not quite as drunk as I was.

I remember the martinis (it *must've* been them, though that was no excuse) yelling, 'Why don't they <u>all</u> jump back in here?!' Steve winced then, as I do now. After placating the cops, he hastily drove out of there while I removed my blonde wig, opened it up, and threw up into it: that was the last of our three-martini dates, but not the last of our association.

The Bad Woman of the Western World was about to claim her official title.

We planned an illicit trip to the cold upstate region, a weekend getaway. It would be so much fun. Hell, it was only a weekend. Jason and Droopy-Drawers had gone off to the Bahamas a few months ago and that was for a whole week! It was only fair. Only it wasn't fair to four little children. This was one of the meanest things I ever did. I find it hard to forgive anybody for anything. It's impossible to forgive myself, especially when there is such a high degree of guilt. I was supposed to be the responsible one. I was supposed to take care of them. Jason was not competent to do so.

We went away—after I blithely dropped my telephone book at home behind a huge bureau, to protect the innocent and the guilty from Jason's merciless phone calls.

The minute we left, I began looking over my shoulder—as did Steve, and for the same reason. We both knew Jason was a nut and we were culpable. We approached the snowy hinterlands and what proved to be a lovely little inn.

Later, I learned Jason frantically called the police many times— and as many times, they told him gruffly, 'Listen, Mr. Kirkpatrick, if she told you she was going away for the weekend and she'd be back on *Monday*, call us *Monday*, if she don't return. Okay? You got it? Don't call uz back till *Monday!*'

'He kept asking us where you went,' Kim said, 'waking us up and asking us questions.' 'Where did you *go*, Mom?' asked Jerry. 'Tell us where you went!' demanded Sally. I regret, to the end of my days breaching their trust, more than what followed next.

All that weekend, Steve and I knew a grim fate awaited us back in New York.

Was it worth it? Steve was nice enough, but the kind of guy who turns so hard in his sleep that he cuts you with the sheets. And I couldn't sleep that well anyway.

Blackness descended in my life on my return, engulfing me in the purest form of torture I have ever endured. There was no sleep, no rest, only questions, murmured or screamed and from me, no answers. I refused to answer him, but the questioning continued, until—

'What business is it of yours <u>where</u> I went? You and Skip went on your little trip! Leave me alone. Stop screaming in my face! Let the children sleep, you idiot!'

It ended with me flat on my back on our bed with, somehow, a carpet sweeper under me: '*Talk* to me, I won't hurt you,' Jason said, gripping my throat, 'I promise.'

'You're hurting me right now. Let me up!'

Suddenly, he backhanded me across the face; there was a jolt and a pause: I felt a slight sting in my nose.

'Talk!' he snarled, 'Who <u>is</u> he? I'm going to find out anyhow!' Water or blood started from my nostrils, but he still held me down. Then I saw it, moving swiftly across my face, a small black gun; felt its cold pressure against my temple.

'Now you *tell* me,' Jason said, one knee trembling on top of my chest, 'You *tell* me.'

Fear washed like a cold wave over me. Everything stopped, except the fear. I felt my eyes closing. Then, what felt like ages later, somebody (certainly not me) said in a small voice, 'Go ahead. Kill me. I'd rather be dead than live with you.'

I heard a 'click' from the revolver and I don't know why, but I didn't wet my pants. Jason drew the gun away. He snarled and straightened up and said, 'I've got to get out of here! You make me sick!' Thankfully, he went to the Bronx. In a night fraught with nightmares, finally, I slept.

The next day, he called. 'That was only a starter pistol. I couldn't have hurt you with that.' I said nothing.

'The reason I called is to tell you that I know who the scumbag is, and I had a nice little talk with Mickey. She's a very nice woman. You'd like her, except, of course, that you're sleeping with her husband. Do you know what a piece of—?'

Quietly, I hung up the phone; desperately unhappy at all the trouble I had unleashed on an unsuspecting family, and my own small children, solely for my own gratification and for getting whatever I thought 'even' would be! At least, I knew that Steve and Mickey already lived separately; that it was one of Steve's daughters who had helped him to relocate to Maryland and that they, too, were victims of domestic unrest—not that that exonerated me.

A greater fear I had was that Jason, having all the time in the world, would exert his efforts to bring Steve to financial ruin. (Steve prudently advised his loyal coworkers to tell Jason that he was no longer with the company, and concentrated on working in Maryland. This actually worked in his favor; we all know that the computer end of it was not a dead-end for any good businessman; thus, he prospered. Whether he found anyone else to drink martinis with or not, I cannot say, but I hope he did.)

'You have a broken nose. What happened?' Dr. Honig said. Jason sat near me in the doctor's office, reading the paper. I looked meaningfully in his direction, and did not answer. As the doctor's eyes followed my gaze, Jason's copy of the New York Times rose slowly up, up in front of his face.
'Can you set it?'
'It's a straight break. But it's going to give you trouble later on: sinus problems!' And he was right 'on the nose.'
My father, though fearsome, was not without perspective in a bad situation, and using good judgment—where the outcome did not affect him. Maybe he could give me some advice.
'Dad, I don't think I can stand living with Jason any longer. First of all, he— . . .' He waved a hand of dismissal and put on his thinking-face: '—A list of his offences isn't necessary.
'How much school do you have left?'
'About a year and a half; maybe two years.'
'Then I would wait it out. Get that degree. Because if he knows you're leaving him, he'll never let you graduate. He'll spoil it for you; that's how he is.'
'But Dad, I—!'
'—Just think of it as the light at the end of the tunnel.'
'—That's what I've been *doing*, Dad!'
'You know that expression: a long, dark tunnel and there, at the end, is that little, faint light. As you draw nearer, it'll get brighter for

you. You'll see. Hang in there; it's not that long. And it'll be worth it for you.'

I nodded glumly. *('Light. Tunnel.'* I thought to myself, *'A goal. I can do it. I can. Just like that damn little train.')*

'And if he gives you any more problems—talk to Timmy. He's a cop; he can take care of him.'

I thought of Jason, following Skip; and knocking her down—and nodded again: *('Tunnel. Timmy.')*

Of course, my marriage was doomed. It wouldn't be the first time, or the last. Timmy and I had begun to play a game of 'marital tag,' not that it was a favorite game of ours. It's just that each time I got married, Tim was getting a divorce. When I had decided on a divorce, Tim had found the woman of his dreams. This went on about six times, if you count it as ping-pong ripostes, until we got sick of it and our partners ran off or were equally demented or sick of us.

So at the last count, he was married twice, with a long cohabitation-run of eleven years (which I maintain didn't count) and I had chalked up two legit unions and no illegits. Who won? You tell me. Cassie refused to play. She had coerced her importer, Raoul, into a long-term, superficially monogamous union. She always seemed to have all the eggs, dammit, and the basket they came in.

I wondered if she had any full-length mirrors in her past?

'If I did,' I'm sure she'd say, 'Do you suppose I'd be stupid enough to admit it?' Not on the life of Cassandra Winters!

Tim's first union in his early twenties, was with a beautiful Italian girl, Tammy, who walked out almost immediately: she served dinner promptly at six, and he showed up at six—the next day; she threatened to leave; he threatened to choke her while she slept. She left. He never really got over Tammy.

The second wife, Italian, too, looked like Ma Kettle but bore him a son. Begrudgingly.

One day, a neighbor and I were visiting Marie and The Boy, then two, for cake and tea. She had just sent Timmy, Jr. flying across the dining room with a murderous smack in the face for dropping a cookie, when Tim came in, filthy as could be, from doing some kind of construction work until he could get on The Force.

The neighbor and I exchanged glances and bit our tongues about the boy; we didn't want to cause any friction. Tim nodded at us and kept walking.

'Where're <u>you</u> goin'?' Tim stopped short and turned to Marie: 'To take a bath.'

'Not in <u>there</u>, you're not!,' Marie snorted. 'I just <u>cleaned</u> that bathroom!'

We all sat there sipping tea, the kid ruefully rubbing his cheek and looking an awful lot like his father at the same age. Tim turned around and headed for the door.

'Where th' hell're you going <u>now?!?</u>'

'To find some place to take a bath,' he said calmly and left. And I guess he did, 'cause that was that.

She and Timmy, Jr. moved to Florida, and he supported the boy. He only had the one.

I, on the other hand, was very open-ended about it—as poor a choice of words as you could want, having two children with each spouse—a lot more than the spouses' net worth. But in the game of marital ping-pong, I must be considered the big loser.

Some Marriage Counselor said it before me, I am sure, but the only difference between the words 'martial' and 'marital' is a misplaced 'I.'

Clearly, I recall misplacing my 'I' on *two* infamous December the Sevenths, five years apart; clearly, I went for double or nothing, and lost. That much was now very clear to me.

Unbeknownst to me, the Defective Detective had planted a telephone bug as big as a breadbox under our bed. The funny thing was, he called home or spoke on the phone so often, that all the incoming calls were his! So he had the dubious pleasure of listening to his own mellifluous caterwauling, lies or bent truths lisping back at him. That he feared he was losing control was no secret. He took to following me.

A girlfriend from school gave me a year's pass to Jack LaLanne's.

'I'm under a lot of stress. . . '

She handed the pass over: 'Here. This'll help you; I have an extra.' I am forever grateful to that woman, who I barely knew, and it really helped a lot. Of course, he followed me there, too, but he gave that up after a while.

It came time for Joy to go to Kindergarten. This was a milestone for me: I'd be able to get part-time work and crawl out from under some of the despotism, until I got my diploma.

Jerry had missed a lot of school last term and lately, his eyes were often suspiciously red and he had the 'munchies,' but as everyone back then knew, pot was nothing to worry about. . . Oh, right. I didn't want to take a full time job because of Jer and Kim, too, now tall, blonde and, in loathsome deference to a past expression, 'hot to trot.'

'I don't want Joy to go to Kindergarten,' Jason said flatly, his flat eyelids gazing opaquely downward in an uncompromising stare at the floor.

'What? What're you talking about?! I told you that the Catholic school doesn't *have* a Kindergarten.'

'I'm not going to put my child on a public school bus where she can be raped by the bus driver,' he calmly replied.

'But *all* the children go on that bus and it's to a good school.'

'I'm warning you,' he said menacingly, 'not to do it.'

No more was said about it. Of course, I enrolled her.

On the first Monday of school, Jason left to go on an 'investigation' early that morning and my heart leaped 'for joy.' I dressed her in her new dress and shoes, and we happily waited with the other children and mothers at the bus stop; I looked around furtively, but saw no one.

'There it is!,' Joy cried as the yellow bus approached. They lined up and filed on, and as she put her tiny foot on that first step up, a roar ensued: all looked in the direction of our building's basement, as Jason came charging up the stairs, confronting us:

'Take that child off the bus! My child is not going on any bus!' He marched onto the bus and dragged the stunned child off and across the street to our apartment.

I went over to a neighbor, Irene's house, and we sipped coffee in silence. In deference to my feelings, which were incalculable, she said very little: *her* child was *on* the bus, heading for school.

Finally, she asked me, 'Are you all right?' 'Yes. Thank you for the coffee.'

'What are you going to do?'

'I don't know. But that is the last straw. When that nut refuses to let me send my child to school—that's it.'

'I have the name of a good divorce lawyer,' Irene said softly, 'if you need one.'

'I have to wait a few months; I'm graduating in June. Hold onto it for me, will you please?'

Later in the week, I spoke to Jimmy McFadden, who prevailed upon Jason to let up on the bus issue, '*for 'the kid's sake—Geez, Jason, it's only for one term! Then you can enroll her in Lady O' Lourdes. Right? Right, Jason?*' And I guess after he chewed it over with 'mother,' Emma, he acquiesced. He agreed to send her, but *not* on the school bus: I had to walk her there. It was a little bit of a walk, but the bus driver wanted no trouble, so we did it: two miles a day. Cold days, when he was in the house on Spencer Hill, he would drive her there.

Spring had to come: everyone knows that. Nobody waited for it more than I did that year.

Before it came, Jason punched me in the eye. It is hard hanging onto the cooking stove the day after you've been punched. It is an indescribably violated, humiliating feeling; it is as though you are an animal. You glare bitterly at the master of the house, but you are confused and frightened of the tower of venom who has done this to you.

'*Tunnel. Timmy!*': These two words popped into my befuddled brain as my possible salvation.

'I'll be by at four. I'm off then,' Tim said.

When he dropped by in his uniform, I rolled up my sleeve to show him my arm, too, black and blue from the shoulder to my elbow. He made a funny grunt and turned away. I rolled down my sleeve. 'Want some coffee?' 'Nah. I'm going to go home and get out of my uniform. I'll be back later.' Fear gripped me. 'Timmy, I'm trying to wait to leave him till June. Can you—?'

His eyes were always like blue steel, but they got even harder then: '—That's why I'm changing out of my uniform. Can't do something like that in uniform. Don't worry. I'm going to take him for a walk and have a little talk. Nothing earthshaking, I promise you.'

Jason was very pleased to go for 'a little walk' with Tim, who he admired as a 'member of the force.' Maybe he thought Tim was going to confide in him about some mysterious aspects of a case he was working on, or something; I don't know. I do know that after that walk with Timmy, Jason never touched me again.

I worked, I lived, I waited for Spring. Love might come for others in June, but not for me. I longed for freedom, or what is now all too commonly called, 'having a life.'

The brand new suitcase stood, loosely wrapped, in the center of the floor as Jason came in. He was dressed in a black Security Guard's outfit, a job he had 'stooped to, temporarily' in his own terminology.

'What is this?'. . . 'It's for you, for your birthday.'

'My birthday isn't until *July*.'

'Well, it's a little early. Open it.' He pulled the paper off, stared at the suitcase and realizing the significance of the gift, looked slowly up at me. His eyes blazed, but in a rare show of reticence, he said nothing, and left for work.

Kim had turned into a Viking of a girl, tall and blonde, but with the straight back of a Native American Indian. Her dish-pan blue eyes still lit up with delight, but denied persistently what they saw in our house. She had the nervous skitter of a little horse about to bolt the stable.

I recall it so well.

Kim would go to Rod's prom at Molloy, wearing a form fitting strapless white gown with faux ermine trimming, loaned to her by a girlfriend, and with her golden 'Swedish' skin, she looked absolutely stunning. Rod presented her with a corsage and couldn't keep his eyes off her as he pinned it to her dress.

When finally she came home towards dawn, that flower was gone. Her dress askew, she was laughing so hard, she fell in a drunken heap into the puppy box in the kitchen, feet up, in a halo of white satin. Saved, from being a vision of debauchery, solely by her youth and beauty. The puppies had fortunately just been relocated.

Later, this 'fall' had a deeper significance. Rod not only couldn't keep his eyes off her, he couldn't keep his hands off her, either. All too soon, they had married and gone to Texas, where Rod was an engineering student, where his parents now lived and where they would await the birth of their first baby. She was barely eighteen.

It was a trying and horrific time for Rod's parents, and for me. Though they recognized that she was a pretty and kind girl, they knew Rod's future was compromised and that the couple's youth was against them. I suffered a strange mix of relief that she was marrying well, and leaving an unhappy setting for, I hoped, a better one, and a great guilt for pushing my baby out of the nest—*'before,'* as my friend Marilyn commented, *'her eyes are even opened!'* But when she was gone away from us, scared and far away, I would be relieved that she was gone.

Jerry was still a problem, but I naively felt that once Jason was out of the picture, he would spend more time at home and all would be well.

The time had come.

The picture is still in my album, two beaming girl-graduates in caps and gowns; Joy, from Kindergarten, and her mother, from college, with a degree in English Literature that it had only taken me nine years to acquire.

It is too bad I don't have a photo to remember Jason's face two weeks later, when the summons server arrived—too early!

The children and I were supposed to be out of the house by ten; he arrived at nine o'clock, while I was still at home. 'Make sure you send a guy who can take care of himself,' I told the attorney, 'Jason has a terrible temper. Although I've told him repeatedly that I'm leaving him, I'm sure he doesn't believe me.'

'Don't worry, I'll send a man who can handle him,' Lawyer Dan Daniels assured me.

'I wonder who that can be?' Jason said, going to answer the door. I could not believe my eyes. A ninety-year old man, hatless and weightless, peered at me from underneath Jason's arm. I gasped, as I saw the summons tucked under one of his pinny little white-shirted arm. Our eyes met—literally! He was no taller than I.

'Good morning,' he said in a quavery voice, extending the envelope to Jason, 'Sir, this is for you.'

'What's this?' Jason fell back as he read the contents—and so did the little man, with Jason pursuing him out the front door.

'Who sent you?'

'Don't touch me!,' cried the elfin, ancient man. 'I'm just doing my job!'

'Don't touch him!' I echoed from the kitchen window, as they stood out there by the pink-blossomed crab-apple tree in the bright sunshine.

'What, is he a *black-belt*?!,' Jason yelled back at me.

He turned, at the sound of venetian blinds being pulled up by neighbors all along the block—and the little man took his chance and scurried off around the corner, presumably, to a breakfast of crumbs and cheese.

Why is it that the psychopaths never know the answer to: *'Why? Why?! Are you doing this to me!?'* Towering over me, raging and screaming, I was so glad that the children were not home.

Vengeance is mine, saieth the Jason. Immediately after I filed for divorce, he charged me with Child Abuse.

9.

Long ago and far away, the sound of a train whistle blew, its mournful whistle soft in the distant past, but not forgotten. Tim heard it long before anyone else did, hurtling through the house like a sun-suited juggernaut, baby curls bobbing madly.

'Not even dogs can hear that,' mother muttered, 'Get out of his way!'

He stood tip-toe on the toilet seat, baby thighs stretching, growing an inch, straining to see—

There! There it was: that snake of a Hammermill train, loaded up, puffing round the distant bend, its smoke curling back against the dark green of the lindens, desperate to leave Erie behind. What a row! Oh, the wonder of it! I stared too, over his stampede of curls, until the very last little bit of it quit the bathroom view, till the noise faded away. . . Cunning toddler.

I sighed, and scanned the dim photo; yellow curls and sun-suit sitting on a long-gone back porch step; beyond the screen door, a glimpse of mother's apron.

It was confusing to me now, nearly inconceivable, that the sun-suit had graduated into a policeman's uniform—oh, how the years roll by!—and the wearer, retired into fat ex-cop-dum and the prevailing cynicism of the empty beer can.

Then, all was magic and toy cars and dolls with wooden heads and eyes that moved, winking luscious, even-length lashes. And a little sister, to poke them out with a pencil or a popsicle stick; a little sister who consulted a looking glass, the first presentiment of great beauty peering back at her past the baby fat and her mother's rouge, nodding sagely, at the U-shaped face of the future movie queen, forming chrysalis-like before her gaze.

Quiet ever, Cassie and Tim, of the trains; preserved in silence in my reverie. And I? Only in the sun-drenched solitude of the fields, the sweet stench of milk-pods, the hum of the bee, the heavenly swing-by of the butterfly, did I find peace and was free of my usual prattle. These were my gentle Gods.

Where are they now? The children; the dreams?
Have the stars lost their footing?

In our family, the closest people to you are the farthest away. It's not geometry, but it's true. I can wish it were not so, yet it is. Yearning for a call from Tim or Cassie is utterly pointless.

If they call me, it is to report a death or at least, a significant illness. Part of the problem is probably that I wonder why. I should know by now they don't care. But after a while, I burst at the seams and ring Cassie, Tim being so noncommittal as to be not worth a phone blip.

'So, how are you?!'

'Well.'

'What's new?'

'Let's see. Daryl and Caryl are starting the first grade and I have to go to school about them.'

'What're you—? What're you *talking* about—?'

'World! In *'World!'* I told the head writer I didn't like it, because how much trouble can a first-grader be? But she said, 'They're *twins!* Then she rolled her eyes up at me!'

'You do that, Cassie; you roll your eyes up.'

'On *me*, it looks good.'

125

'. . . Well, I guess you have to play it as it lays.'

'Yep. . .How're <u>you</u> doing? How's Jason? . . .

'Crazy.'

'I know that, but is he working?'

'Why *would* he, when *I'm* working? Especially, not since I filed for divorce. In fact, I have today off, and I just wanted to see how you and the kids...'

It was good to hear her voice, all the way from Connecticut, yet it was never enough.

I'd wonder, then, if Cassie or Tim ever missed me. . .

. . . Hell, he *lived* twenty minutes away from me, so there's your answer. He had never—well, maybe once—been inside my house. 'Course, if I *needed* him, he'd be there.

Tim pulled up in his gray van with the door stove-in—from being broad-sided five years ago. I think that he considered it a status-symbol.

'Get in! Get in! It <u>opens</u>!'

I climbed in and clanged the door shut after a few tries. Tim looked over at me charily: 'It's not on the driver's side,' he explained, 'or I would've had it fixed.' I said nothing. He was driving me to the DMV in Jamaica to get my license renewed and no way, did I want to ruffle his feathers.

We lurched up to a light. 'How's your knee?' *(An inaudible grunt from Tim.)*

A steering post had ripped open an old wound below Tim's kneecap during a high-speed chase. It was constantly re-infecting and oozing pus. It was to be the main reason he would go out on a Disability. I'd seen him pour iodine directly into that hole, that ugly maw, staring stoically right up at me, like a slightly bemused Charlie Bronson. Tim had a sense of humor—and lost it—and I'm sure the people he locked up never found it, either.

Today was not a Happy Day for Tim. If you drink all night, you can appear sober, but you can't appear cheerful in the morning. Tim was scowling.

He had mastered the art of police driving so well that he could not stop at a single light; so well that I could not stop flinching and saying 'Woo!' as he tailgated, changed lanes in front of others—no signals, of course—or stopped cold, ignoring the frantic horn-blasts around us.

'What's the matter with <u>you</u>?!'

'Nothing.'

'Then <u>stop</u> it!' he snarled.

True, he was not driving in reverse, so I clenched my teeth and tried to look away, but it was like watching carnage-footage from 'Amazingly Stupid Police Chases For No Goddamn Good Reason At All' . . . You had to look.

'Thank God!,' I thought, as the recalcitrant van released its cargo and I stepped down just off Sutphin.

'I *said,* I'll be right over *here!'* Tim shouted.. . . 'Gotcha. I won't be long,' I called back.

The DMV was amazingly fast. I was eating a banana when they snapped my picture. I gasped aloud, not sure just how 'unappealing' that would be, but I took my papers and hastened outside, gratified to have been processed so soon.

Tim's chin, angled firmly against his chest, promised me a ride to Hell, not home—and I got it.

It wasn't the stream of curses, blue, green and otherwise from his lips; it wasn't his driving horizontally across three lanes; it wasn't even the bullets rolling around on the floor of the van and scudding into my ankles when he slammed on the brakes. It was his verbal abuse as we drove along Archer Avenue. When he wasn't nearly running down old ladies, he was completely 'running <u>*me*</u> down.'

'. . . I can't *believe* you don't know your own exit number . . . what planet are you from? . . . How long have you been driving, anyway. . .what kind of a <u>moron</u> doesn't use the highway?!. . . You don't know your ass from your elbow. . !' He hated Dad, and he had turned *into* Dad.

There it was! A subway entrance! Hurling my shoulder against the bent door at the next red light, I landed on the sidewalk. I ran toward the entrance, as the commanding cop voice ordered, 'Maura! Get back here: Where the hell do you think you're going?!'

'Home!' I headed down the stairs, tripping over a friendly wino, and back home. It took me the long trip back to calm down.

'Never, never,' I vowed, 'will I ever be the victim trapped in his car again!'

Both Dad and Cassie had warned me about it, but I really didn't know the extent, the pure hell it was, the true extent that Tim made you hurt.

'His poor prisoners!,' I muttered to myself, 'I'll bet they *leap* out of the police car to do time, when he's driving!'

10.

A cloud covered the sun. I looked up with a shock and the sick feeling that always accompanied it, to the sight of Jason's car pulling up smoothly to the curb— firmly disproving any notion that psychotics cannot be good drivers. I inched the lawn chair back up along the small stretch of grass, toward our kitchen window. As he strode up, his pants legs flapping heartily in the September breezes, fear engulfed me. *('No one is at home!' There's no one in the building, in all four apartments!)*

'Hello! Sitting out here all by yourself?'

'I have an ear infection. I was just treating it.'

'Let me!,' he cried, grabbing a Q-tip from out of my lap and learning over me. 'Which ear?!'

'Please! Don't! That won't be necessary,' I said, leaning forward protectively over the bottle of rubbing alcohol. Too late: I felt the tentative tickle of the swab in my ear and leapt up.

'Did that hurt?'

'No, it's fine. Don't! I just *did* that!' He smirked, Q-tip in hand, and cast a hasty look around: 'Anyone home?' Anxiously, I turned to go inside.

'Don't call the police. I merely want to talk to you,' he said, in a forced, level voice. 'I want you to reconsider,' he harrumphed, adjusting his shirt collar, 'about leaving. The children need a loving home to grow up in.' His eyes were saddened, his pale cheeks, gaunt. I stopped, one hand on the back of the lawn chair and, for a moment, I hesitated. 'Sweetie, you know I love you!' Jason took hold of my elbow: 'C'mon, Sweetie, we'll go *inside*!'

Then I remembered: just two days ago, he stood staunchly in court, lying about how I 'abused and neglected the children,' swearing out a petition against me. I looked at him: he had even worn the same suit!

'No, I can't. There've been too many things—I can't.'

'Think about the good things!' . . . 'What good things?' 'The *good* things: remember the good things?' He stood there expectantly.

I honestly tried, tried hard: 'There *weren't* any. I'm sorry, Jason.' He made a noise of disgust and shook his head. 'You're being *ridiculous*!' (Could he have said *anything* to alienate me more? I couldn't imagine what *that* might be!)

He began to smolder; I began inching toward my door.

'What about the time I bought you the five dresses? And all the shoes I bought for the children that day?'

'That was after you <u>hit</u> me!'

'I never <u>touched</u> you!'

'Oh, what's the use! It's too much—'

Keenly, He looked around to see if anyone was observing him, and in that split second, I raced in the front door and slammed it shut. I leaned against it, breathing hard. From the other side, I could feel the fury.

'You are making a serious mistake,' came the icy tones.

'Jason, there's no reason we can't part as friends, for the children. We should—'

I heard a rattle and realized he was trying to unfasten the kitchen window.

Racing there, I snapped the lock shut; he slapped his hand flat against the pane, his eyes blazing through the glass at me with animal anger: 'I tried to be reasonable with you, and now you're going to regret it. You will lose them all—cunt!' . . inarguably, to any woman, the worst word in the English language.

'I have an Order of Protection,' I reminded him without looking into his eyes, 'and I'm calling the Police!' He nailed me with my least-favorite word once again, and once more with his eyes. Then he sped off.

I brewed some tea, shuddering and reflecting on the rapid transition from 'Sweetie' to 'Cunt,' and also wondering how an Order of Protection could stop a fist? A bullet?

It was a dark and stormy night, as the story goes, about a week before Halloween. Most of the leaves were gone now, but the few that were left were being driven by the cold winds, scudding up against the huge living room picture-window, the window that was our one enduring source of apartment-pride.

Kim shuddered, turned away from the window, to go and play Candyland or Hoops & Ladders with her friend, Barbi Steiffel, who was sleeping over (who would later reciprocate by showing Kim the finer points of another game, shop-lifting.)

But for now, they were innocently engaged over a game-board set up on the pull-out couch where they would sleep. I pulled the venetian blind half way down, smiling to myself at their little chucklings, and went to make them cocoa. It was good to be indoors while the wind whistled and howled outside. With promises to 'perhaps' go shopping with them on Saturday morning, we all turned in early: besides, Sally's father was to pick her up early for the weekend.

Still smiling, I rolled up into my covers. It was good to have the bed to myself and not have to worry about someone coming in drunk and waking me up. I drifted off to the scratchy tune of branches tapping against the windows.

'Those are mighty big trees!' I thought, jolted awake. My eyes were wide open, but it was my ears that were paying attention. There it was again!

'I believe—someone is trying to break in!,' I whispered, creeping out of bed, worried more about the children than what miserable swag an interloper might take. Were it not for the children, especially the girls in the living room, I might have stayed right where I was, in bed. Then I would have missed that unmistakable light-bulb shaped head at the kitchen window, trying to undo the latch. I glared out at him.

Jason was drunk of course, but there was a new and supercharged insanity in his eyes.

'Let me in! I'm here to pick up my daughter!'. . . 'You're, what? What time is it?—Jason! It's—three in the morning! Come back tomorrow: she's sleeping!'

'Let me inside! I'll sleep on the couch!'

'You can't: the girls are having a sleep-over!' Jason swayed drunkenly in the wind outside the window, glaring stupidly up at me. At last, he blurted out, 'You fucking liar! Let me in! I won't touch you. You have my word of honor!'

I took a deep breath. 'Jason. Listen. All the children are asleep. Go away now, or I'll call the police.' He started to shake and rattle the window. I sighed, unwilling to have the police over, scaring the kids and making yet another scene.

Apparently, he was giving me no choice. I went to call the police and got my Order of Protection from a bureau drawer in the bedroom.

As I did, a sudden ominous chill engulfed me. I turned back, my scalp tingling: I knew now what he was going to do! Racing back into the living room, past the sleeping girls, I saw him standing outside the picture window. His features were distorted by the darkness, not clear, but there was no mistaking the wave of pure evil that emanated from him. He snarled and slowly raised a big boulder with both hands; it was so heavy, he could barely lift it.

'No, Jason! *Don't!*' But I stood back, frozen in futility, as the gigantic boulder hovered over his head. It came crashing against the window. The sound of breaking glass rent the night.

The girls sat up in bed screaming and crying, as the wind entered, howling like a mental patient on a pass! All of us, Barbi and Sally, too, picking glass *off* the floor *off* the bedding *off* the couch. Slivers and shards everywhere! Nowhere to be seen, was Jason.

When the police came, they took a report. 'Do you have an Order of Protection, lady?' I showed it to them. 'Well, you shoulda called sooner. It's no good now: you can't prove nothing.'

'Hey, Mac,' called a cop from outside the window. 'He musta done it with this.' He shouldered the boulder that had been lying on the ground in front of the shattered frame.

'Looks like it.'

'Oof. I can hardly lift it.'

'Yep. Looks like it. Well.' He said turning to me, 'anybody hurt?'

'No.'

'Thanks Gods. So, we're outta here. You better find something to stick in that window until tomorrow an' you can get it fixed. It'll cost you, *that* one!. . .

'Give us a call if he comes back. An' like I say, it's his word against yours. Anybody else see him?' I shook my head. 'I'll tell you one thing,' he said. 'You're gonna be sweepin' up glass for a long time. G'night.'

He prophesied correctly. Winklets of glass were still surfacing a year later.

We found a large, empty box and stuck it in the giant hole, but it was still mighty cold in there. Kim kept dry-sobbing, largely in embarrassment that her friend was there, and they all doubled up in the little bedroom to try to get some sleep. I refused to take another look at the hole and slapped extra blankets on everybody.

Scotch would be my 'extra blanket'— her job title was 'canine comforter'— and as I put my Order of Protection back in the drawer, I knew it wasn't faster than a speeding bullet—Or a flying boulder. The only thing it ever protected was the inside of the drawer it was kept in.

Jason had established my vulnerability. Now, for once true to his word, he set out to ruin me.

It was five minutes, door to door. A three-minute bus ride. Home at five-oh-five, to cook dinner. The pay?—A fantastic one hundred weekly. It was a small construction company. I answered the phone and took dictation for Joe Mazzeratti and 'Tonio, the President, who never used a desk or a last-name. There was an on-site Job Boss, but it was Joe who did all the hiring and firing, bills and in-house management. He was the guy who took all the shit.

The men on the work crews hated him for trying to short-change and overwork them; the Job Boss berated him for mismanagement and strangely missing monies or equipment and Tonio wailed on him if one of his horses lost. Joe's newly-divorced wife (who also despised him) spent too much money.

Joe knew a life in Hell would be a step up, but he took it all in silence with an implacable face, like a fighter who took one punch too many. He was always very well-dressed and wore a tasteful diamond ring.

One day as I glanced over just inside his office door, I saw an attractive business lady sitting and chatting with Joe in his office. She looked back at me in a telling way, and the thought struck me that she was there for my job! I giggled nervously but began typing rapidly. Next thing I knew, she'd pulled a chair up alongside my desk.

'Yes?'

'I'm Madeline Hubert from BCW.' I gasped as, without missing a beat, she tossed a pile of photos onto my desk, of clothing, of ironing to be done—and of my own dirty laundry!

'Mr. Kirkpatrick has brought these to our attention and claims that you—'

'—Just a second. You come to my place of business, and you show me pictures of—pictures that idiot took?!' I stopped, realizing I was making no sense, choking on my words; that my face was aflame. I unclenched my hands, exhaled and spoke softly, my voice still shaking.

'I'm very angry! I know that I shouldn't get mad at you, Miss—?!'

'Mrs. Hubert.' . . . 'Mrs. Hubert: But I'm furious that this creep who has no job himself, is sneaking around and taking pictures of _my_ laundry piles, while I'm here, working to support my family!

And this jerk! And you—! Please leave. Don't come back to my job anymore; I can't lose this job! I'm—sorry; I'm angry.'

She extended her hand and stood. 'I'm sorry. I won't be back.' Tentatively, I shook her hand.

'May I call you at home,' she said, as a statement; not a question. I nodded, miserable, unable to speak and when she and her neat navy blue suit had departed, I looked in on Joe's open door.

'I'm sorry, Joe.'

He looked up from his papers. 'It's nuttin',' he said, 'Just do your work, 'kay?'

One week later, same scenario, different actor—a bad one: *Jason* sat at Joe's desk!

He began raising his voice from a challenging tone to the familiar loud rant. It took all of two minutes for Joe to scoot Jason out the front door. This time, Joe stood in his office doorway, one massive bear-arm holding up each side of the door jamb, silently regarding me as I trembled. 'Listen,' he said finally. . . 'Please don't fire me!,' I blurted.

'Yeh, but we're tryna run a business here.' He turned his big head slowly, 'Good thing Tonio ain't here. . . It better never happen again.'

'It won't. I promise!'

He kind of shook his head at the ridiculous notion of me promising anything, muttering to himself as he lumbered back to his desk.

It was almost Christmas, and no more visits from Jason or the BCW. Joe gave me a very nice compact-locket that crisp Christmas-Eve morning, but by closing time that day, Tonio came in and announced that the company was closing down immediately. He gave the part-time bookkeeper and myself a bottle of wine and one-week's termination pay.

I cried like a baby the whole three-minute bus ride home.

But you know what they say, about bad breaks turning into good ones: it was fiercely cold that winter and I got to stay home with my 'babies' and keep them warm and happy and feed them—carefully, because Unemployment Checks don't go very far. But I had had a whole lot of practice skimping, so it was 'duck soup' for me—and homemade chicken soup for everyone else: piece of cake.

Here's a *Jeopardy* question I learned the answer to the hard way: What is a combination of madness and boredom? What is sitting, sitting, sitting; a fear that something will happen or nothing ever will? If you can imagine being locked up in a bad school in a worse neighborhood, breathing the combined stale air of the strangest bunch of people you will ever encounter, you are close to realizing the dread those faded-lettered words on a dirty, chicken-wired glass door evoke: Family Court.

There, there is no escape. There, amid the listless, the lackluster, the pot-bellied and pony-tailed; there, amid the No-Shows and the Never-Should've-Showns; there, were my visits plus adjournments laid out end-to-end, I would have spent six solid months of my life, straight time.

I, too, have sighed and survived on those hard, hard chairs among the desperately pregnant and unmarried—a situation, to be sure, not foreign to me—among beautiful children, facing the huge obstacle of a full day or more inventing the most ingenious mental and physical games, darting in and around the solemn rows of chairs like road-runners, to while away the dreary hours.

There, among the hard-used women, among hard-users and non-users; the few stray fathers corralled to 'face up to it,' sullenly filing their fingernails or grimly gazing up at the dirty, hopeless ceilings, as if there might be a trap door up there, somewhere. Luckily, most had been scanned at the door for guns, because had I known one of them was 'packing,' I might have grabbed the weapon and shot myself.

And if it was like that for me, what about the poor stymied staff, sailors in a sudden, raging storm or becalmed otherwise, on a Dead Sea of Humanity?

My case dragged on for years and years, till *'your files!'* had swelled to an overflowing three suitcases and could not easily be dragged out and accessed. Why? Paper engendered from hundreds of rambling *MoneyGrams* Jason sent, *'Attention! The Court!'* Or when I appeared, he did not: More paper. When I had a lawyer, Jason's quit or was fired: More Paper!

Of course, I missed work and took temporary assignments. Family Court was my part-time Penal Colony.

There was now no pretense of Jason getting a job. Photos of dirty pots was only the beginning. With Skip helping him, he was about to launch a full-scale assault on what was fast becoming my crumbling castle on Spencer Hill.

I think, in retrospect, my worst crime was looking like Alice Crimmins, the cocktail waitress accused of complicity in the murder of her two darling children.

That day, I even glanced at her photo in the News, captured with giant foam rollers in her hair: 'Why, she looks—just like *me!*' I murmured, putting the paper back on the coffee table and absently touching the pink curlers on my own head. I had a date that night, although my divorce was not yet final, and I wanted to look my—but what was that?! A knock at the door. Crimmins-like, I scampered to answer it.

A plumpish woman with dark curls stood there, her eyes glittering like tiny black beads behind her cat-frame glasses.

'I'm Amanda Neiderman from the BCW.' Her voice throbbed in a full contralto, her glance, moving upward to my curlers—and freezing there. 'May I come in?'….'Well,' I—really wasn't expecting you,' I stammered, as if I had a chance of stopping her.

'Mr. Kirkpatrick asked me to stop by,' she said, moving an ample hip inside: 'I won't be long. Sally—?' Strangely, as if on cue, Sally came into the room. 'Sally, I want to talk with you.' Amanda Neiderman smiled at me with her lips: 'Do you mind waiting outside for a moment, Mrs. Kirkpatrick? I have a few questions for Sally.'

Sally stared me with her terminally baleful glance; obviously, she wanted a Private Audience; probably, no obviously, it had been prearranged.

'Not at all,' I murmured.

I took the sick feeling in my stomach outside to look at the crabapple tree. At its base, lay a jump rope and some GI Joes, waiting for some kids to play with them. The early winter sun gleamed smartly through the few leaves remaining on its branches. I felt no comfort gazing upwards, none at all, just overly 'made-up,' and despite the nippy breeze, my cheeks flamed.

Eventually, I went back inside.

'We aren't quite ready for you yet!'

Amanda and Sally looked up at me like two dining lions being disturbed by a vulture: '—just another moment. Or two,' Amanda added, a harder edge to her voice. No newsflash necessary: she was in *charming* Jason's' camp—never having seen or met the other one. Inwardly, I bridled indignantly; wondered, 'Is it still my home?!' The way she spoke to me, I felt like a person I wouldn't like.

I adopted a similar tone: 'All right. Another moment, but I do have a lot of things I have to do.'

'I see your hair and makeup are set for it!,' she retorted.

'I'll be on the stoop outside!,' I glared back.

'Really!!' I fumed, hopping from foot to foot, fretting for too long a time out there. I was just about to go back in—when I was empirically summoned to come back into my own house.

'Are you through?'

Sally had gone back into the bedroom. Neiderman snapped her handbag shut and swooped up her ledgers: 'You are being charged with Child Abuse by Mr. Kirkpatrick.'

'Oh,' I scoffed airily, 'that's his response to my filing for divorce!'

'Some of these charges—' she looked in the direction of the bedroom and Sally, 'bear looking into, and,' she raised her voice presumptively—'just might hold water! There will be some more questions.

'Someone will contact you next week. Oh: you are not to discuss these charges with Sally.'

'What—charges? I just started a new job!' . . . 'Doing what?' . . . 'Secretary in a construction company.'

I saw Amanda Neiderman gazing over at the News photo of Alice Crimmins on the table, but even *I* was shocked that we, Alice and I, shared not only the same pink rollers in our hair, but also the same *job* title!

'Mrs. Neiderman, I gave all that information in already. Mrs. Hubert interviewed me. Now, what *sort* of charges are you bringing?'

'I'm late for another appointment,' Neiderman replied, moving toward the door. 'I really can't address that now.'

I dashed over and opened open my own doorknob, before Neiderman could.

'Oh, and I think you should know,' she said, smirking and delivering her final riposte, 'Jason—Mr. Kirkpatrick—is seeking custody. Of both children. Sally and Joe.'

'Joy,' I corrected her, even as my heart stop beating. 'Skip!' I spoke aloud.

'What?' she asked, but the little cat-smile on her lips betrayed her. She had heard that name before.

'Mrs. Neiderman: 'I have no money for a lawyer.'

She shrugged. 'That will be your decision.' She pulled the door closed behind her, while I thought, *'You dog from Hell! If I were Alice Crimmins, I'd have money for a lawyer!'*

I started for the bedroom door, going to talk to Sally, when I remembered the harpy's admonition not to 'discuss the matter' with her.

'I'll let things quiet down for a while: maybe Sally'll soften up a little before the next person, the next caseworker, gets involved. Maybe I can still win her over. Maybe.'

Someone shot a Family Court Judge the day before the day of the Final Custody Hearing, so there was a long queue at the Checkpoint before the elevators. I sighed as they dumped out my purse and patted me down, and I sighed again as I picked up my lipstick and all the rest of my junk, 'reloaded' my weapon-free, purse hoping that before I got on the next elevator, any of the large, burly characters in line behind me didn't grapple for a gun and shoot me in the back, so naturally, a shiver raced down my spine while I waited.

I was at an all-time low that morning, before I ever got patted down. Jer had been missing a lot of school; for most of the eighth grade, I discovered, he had been forging absent notes. He had a lot of suspicious, equally red-eyed friends. I didn't know who to turn to about him.

Not to be outdone, Kim The Innocent had been caught shoplifting. I went to the department store and when I confronted her about it, she screamed and railed at me in a most un-Kim-like manner in front of the Store Manager. I shook like a leaf, in shock, unable to cope with her uncharacteristic response. Luckily, it was a 'first offense' and she was released in my custody, somber, but chastened.

All these things were on my mind as the infernally-slow elevator coasted to the second floor. My heart thumped a sad dirge. I thought I'd been a good mother. I'd taken them for walks in the fresh air, fed them well and kept them warm and bought them shoes and tried so very hard—but perhaps I had not tried hard enough. I had never given them the one thing children need above all else, stability.

I had broken the other societal taboo, too: I had no formal religion. Whatever ethics I had imparted to them were, I thought, for the good of all whom they encountered in life and for their own happiness. A druggie and a shoplifter! How successful had I been?

Furthermore, as I walked down the dirty, pealing, greenish hallway on the second floor, I felt a stabbing lack of faith in the Justice System. How much more of this could I take? How could I ward off the savage arrows, hurled from the mouths of grey-suited, slick-haired, high-priced, powder-puffed Irish lawyers, who kept climbing out of Skip's pocket-book, coming at me with a vengeance, the word 'retainer' stenciled in the back of their brains and cash stuck in their inside-jacket pocket for any lame-brain judge who wouldn't see it their way?

I wouldn't have believed it possible, if I hadn't seen it for myself— the 'honorable' doctor lie under oath; the cash-payoff to the sitting judge. I trusted not my own glibness—all was for naught! I trudged alone to the battlefield.

'*Part II*,' read the lettering. This corresponded with my summons. I took a seat, and waited the long wait, until I would hear the exasperated Bailiff cry, '*Kirkpatrick-Kirkpatrick!*'

A woman of significant girth entered and found seating in a space that normally should not accommodate five inches of her. I listened with appreciation to the accompanying groans and a sharp epithet or two from the oppressed flesh; this, the only bench, was the last available seating. All the chairs had been taken: I grabbed the last one! A man toting a potato-factory for a gut, smiled and came up to her, but the groundswell of groans and angry looks from others kept him at bay. He retreated against a wall.

It was there in an alcove that I spotted Jason, staring above the heads of others, his eyes fixed on a mean and distant point. I was glad that since we were in contentious litigation, he could not speak to me; sorry that in his macabre way, he loved me still.

'*Very Jekyl. Very Hyde*,' I was thinking, when it dawned on me that I had better stop viewing other people as subcultures, and consult the roster of cases for my own name, to make sure I was in the right place.

Sure enough—'No name! No name!,' The Court Officer ran his finger down the clipboard: 'Moved to Four/Part Four!'

Out of the corner of my eye, I saw Jason following me, as, panic-stricken, I hurried to avoid Dismissal of the case.

On Four now, I hissed, 'No roster! No listing! *Where is it?!*'

I ran and ran in my tight black pumps: '*Part IV!*' I noticed the palms of my hands were clammy, the first time in my life I had experienced this condition. It was also the first time in my life I faced losing my children.

'This time,' I thought, 'he's here. In the building. I saw him with my own eyes.' This time, unlike all the other times, all the adjournments, all the put-asides, the postponements, the cancellations—this time!— the hearing will take place.

As I turned the corner into Part IV, I saw: Mary Siegel, the Deli Owner; Katie Baugh, Mary Carlyle, Jerry Wall and many other friends and neighbors. All, all had come to testify—for me. For me! I had asked for a few people, but this—this turnout was—! People

I had not even *approached* were here. There must have been twenty of them.

All looked me in the eye. All smiled supportively. My eyes scalded over with tears, but a wonderful glow enveloped me: they thought I was okay. They had come to help me.

There was a tap at my elbow. I turned and saw Madeline Hubert.

'Mrs. Hubert? Are you here to—?' She nodded, '—to testify for you, yes.' She took my hand. 'But I thought you *liked* Mr. Kirkpatrick—Jason,' I whispered hoarsely.

'I did,' she said. 'At first. Not after close scrutiny. But now?! —I'm probably the reason they called in 'Gun Control' downstairs!' My laughter came euphorically, lifted upon the sea of love I felt surging around me.

The euphoria lasted until Jason's bombastic stuffed pelican of a lawyer got a glimpse of my phalanx of witnesses, and made a hasty phone call, somehow petitioning, somehow asking for the 'Final Hearing' to be set aside, for yet another delay and somehow, someway—did it!—got it 'Set Aside,' got, in those magical, jellical Jasonly words, 'Another Continuance.'

I thanked all my witnesses profusely for coming. All these people, who had taken time from their own businesses or jobs, who would go home disconsolately, thinking they had come for nothing that day. Maybe *they* thought so, but after that day, never in my heart was I ever lonely again.

Her eleventh birthday was approaching. I realized with a sense of anxiety that I had been far from a good mother to Sally. I knew that Skip would give her some wondrous bribes—er, gifts. 'But I'm her mother! What can I give her?—A birthday party! A *big* one!'

Twenty of her classmates were invited. Anxiously, anxiously, I baked a big cake and bought ice cream and the soda. Painstakingly, anxiously, I hand-made paper decorations; a giant white swan drifted serenely by, a teddy-bear waved at the shy wall-flowers, also hanging from the ceiling on strings. Games were bought and the event was, in short, orchestrated. Truly, the place looked marvelous.

Her friends had assembled and a selected one escorted in the 'Birthday Girl.'

'*Surprise! Surprise!*' everyone yelled. Sally stopped. The same diabolical smirk she always wore was on her face as, without a glance at me, she strolled over to her stack of presents. I was humiliated, too embarrassed at being ignored to tell her that the present-opening was for later. She opened and examined them all, pleased with each; re-stacked them and politely thanked her friends. Still, she hadn't gazed my way, once, even after the song had been sung, the cake cut and distributed.

As they played their party games, one lost-looking girl stood aside: '*Sally*,' I heard her say, '*Sally, you didn't thank your mother!*' Her fingers reached up, touching the paper swan wistfully, 'She must've worked hard to do this. They're beautiful.' Then, to my complete shock, the little girl wheeled around, burst into tears and ran outside.

'What's wrong?' I gasped, 'What happened?'

'Annette's mom died a couple of months ago,' said a matter-of-fact voice from the group. 'Sometimes she gets upset.'

'Please go to her!,' I pointed out the window, crying inside myself, 'Try to comfort her.' I feared that if I went out to her, it might make things worse. 'All right,' sighed one girl reluctantly; and, 'She does this all the time,' whispered another. They brought her back in and I gave her a Kleenex and hugged her to me, feeling the sorrow welling from her in waves.

I lifted her small chin: 'Annette, would you be in charge of the Grab Bag? I need somebody to help Sally hand out the gifts to the girls.' A snuffle, a nod and smile and later on, I was relieved to see her running and playing happily with the others, almost as if nothing was wrong.

The friends left the party jubilantly. The had had a good time, even Annette. Of the day, the main file in my memory bank consists of Sally's smirk and Annette's tears, something like the harlequin mini-masks of comedy and tragedy. Was there any irony involved?

I'll say!

Right after the guests left, Jason's car came rolling up. Sally loaded all her presents into his car and left my house for good. To her, it had never been home. I wasn't surprised, only appalled at the terrible timing.

'Thanks for the party,' she said as she left, said in the very same tone as 'Kiss my ass.'

When I was able to, I called Mrs. Hubert and told her about Sally leaving.

'What could you do? She wanted to go: you had no choice. Now, what about Joy?'

'What—do you mean, what about Joy? *She* doesn't want to leave.'

In the silence that followed, I could almost see her brown eyes, sizing the situation up over the phone: her rejoinder hit me like a slap. 'It won't be long,' she said gently, 'before she does.'

'No; no, she doesn't want to leave. She's happy here with me! We get along well.'

'I know. I know that you do. But they'll work on her and eventually—I know you find it hard to conceive of now, but between his brainwashing and sibling pressure—'

'Stop. Please, I just can't stand anymore today.'

'Well—unless you want to consider running away. We'll discuss that option later.'

'I don't understand.'

'It would involve changing your names and leaving the state, but often, women—'

'—I couldn't live like that. Looking over my shoulder; afraid that someday, I'd come home and she'd be gone (I could hear my own voice getting husky now) 'or going to pick her up and school and he'd have—taken her away. No.'

'Well.' I could see her smiling sympathetically over the phone. 'It's an option and you can think of about it. With Mr. Kirkpatrick, Jason, it's not about the girls. It's about revenge: he'll never leave you alone, you know. He'll never let it rest.'

'But these are his children, too,' I moaned, 'Can't he see what he's *doing?*'

'No, he can't. He doesn't care. It's payback time for you. That's the only thing he knows. . .Hello—? Mrs.—Maura?'

'I'm here. I'm here. So even though I 'won,' I've lost. All those court appearances, the threats, that so-called 'Final Decision' and the Order of Protection: all that was for *nothing?*

There was dead silence. Finally, she said, her voice lowered, 'Look, you're a young woman. If you cut them loose, give him what he wants, maybe the 'sicko' will stop bothering you. You'll have a chance to find someone else and be able to start over. You deserve it, to have a life. If you keep trying to hold on—'

'But to give up Joy up, *too*? I can't. I love her. I have to fight for her.'

'I understand.' The tired social-worker tone took over. She had reached the end of a song she had heard so many times before, that she knew every note by heart. 'I understand.'

'Jay! Hurry up and set the table: it's almost on.' For once, he moved without being told twice or thrice, putting out the plates, positioning the small black & white TV to face the table, so the three of us could watch 'Star Trek,' our favorite show and our 'seventies equivalent of 'down-time.' He was humming. *'Much happier since Jason's gone,'* I thought. *'That trip with the Healeys must've done him some good.'*

'How was the Cape?' . . . 'Hmmm? Oh, that. Good. Except they're always babbling a lot of Jehova-stuff, especially Mr. Healey.' 'Really? I didn't know he was into that.'

'Yeah. He is. Especially when he has to scrape somebody off the subway tracks.'

'Oh, my God! I knew he worked for Transit. Is *that* what he does?'.

'Yeah. They call for him: he's 'The Scraper.' Not everybody can *do* that, y'know,' Jay said importantly.

'I should think not!'

'But Virginia—Dennie's sister— says he gets real nutty after a Jumper.' (I made a mental note not to push Jerry on the Healeys any more.)

'Well. . . What did you guys do for fun?'

'Ah, there were sailboats, like, bobbing around out on the water; windy; and leaves blowin' 'n stuff. An' it was cold: Man, it was cold! Yeah, I had a great time!' He shifted around on his chair.

'Only on the way back, Mr. Healey's car slipped on the bridge and nearly turned over and the *door* opened up—! An' it was just luck that Virginia grabbed hold of me, or I would've gone right off into the water. I figured I'd say something in case they told you about it. I'm okay, though. Now.'

I shuddered, setting the milk on the table, glad that Jerry, watching me, waiting for a reaction was okay; glad that Jason was not around to scream and rant at him.

'I'm glad you got home in one piece,' I said finally. 'Tell Joy that dinner is ready—and please don't tell her about what Mr. Healey does for a living. She eats little enough, as it is!' He nodded and went to get her. '—and definitely a lot less time for *you* with The Scraper,' young man!,' I muttered.

Joy sat her tiny butt on the chair and picked up her fork. 'My best dinner,' she smiled. Spam 'n onions, mashed potatoes and pork and beans, and a 'voyage to another world' on the Good Ship Enterprise.

'Did you finish your H.W.?' Jerry had gotten us in the habit of using the initials.

'Don't have any,' he replied, clearing his plate. I turned to Joy, eyebrows raised, 'Same question.' She smiled and nodded, her mouth full, swallowing: 'I pasted the leaves on, but you have to ask me the questions on the paper.' She ran to get it: 'Here.'

I smiled at the clumps of white-pasted yellow and red leaves. 'Red are the leaves that drift from the trees—mumble, mumble—Okay, here it is: the question. Now all the leaves have started to come down, Joy. *What season is it?*' Her eyes grew round and introspective. 'Is it—*duck* season?' Over our laughter, Jerry cried, 'You Little Crazy!' It's *Fall*! You've seen one too many cartoons!'

'Not as many as you, Fatso,' she huffed.

It was just another ducky-day for us in Star Trek Land, and we were smart enough to enjoy it while it lasted, sensing perhaps that as surely as summer turns to fall, an awful winter sat, huddled and bitter, waiting around the corner for us.

As soon as the custody change was made, they shipped Sally off to a convent school in Western Ireland. Whatever happened to L.A. and her singing career—? Had I been talking to Jason, I'd have asked him that very question. That was just another fable told to her by an Idiot and I'm sure she fumed away at this, not the first of many betrayals. Hell, I wish I could say betrayals never bothered me, that I'd had so many of them, they were like kin-folk, but betrayals are the sucker-punches of life. You just never see them coming and they leave you stunned for quite a while.

Soon she was across the ocean, buying into their idea, Skip and Jason's, that it was a 'good plan,' so Sally had to do her fuming without Joy or me as a scapegoat, quietly, during Evening Prayers. Yet out of it, she learned a grudging patience.

I knew Sally was staying at Jason's in the Bronx for her Spring Break, so I called for news of her there.

'Hello?'

'Sally! Sally—is that <u>you</u>?! It's Mom! How <u>are</u>—?!'

She cut me off. '*Mother*,' she said, as though she were saying 'Dracula,' I really can't talk to you now. Dad is in Intensive Care at NYU with heart palpitations.' She hung up.

I wish I could lie and say that in the following minute or two, holding the receiver, I was filled with curiosity or good will. And that this is why I called the hospital. But the truth is, all the anguish and isolation from my children begat in me an unbiblical, evil plan, festering within until I dialed the New York Hospital and asked for Jason in Intensive Care.

'Who's calling?' asked the hushed voice. 'It's his wife,' I whispered earnestly.

'Halloo, Bub,' came the tired, phoney 'Lord Fauntleroy' voice I knew so well at last, over the hospital IC hook-up.

'Jason? Is that *you*?' I preened, in my usual best-ever slightly 'prune danish' Skippy imitation: 'How are you feeeeling? Bet-ter?'

He heaved a long sigh: 'A little bit, Bub, a little,' following it up by an extensive list of aches and problems and how 'they are not just exactly *sure* what is wrong with me.'

'What do you *mean*, Jason? I don't understand.'

"Well, they've run all the tests I just *told* you about,' he replied (slightly testy now) and they won't be sure till tomorrow.' He sighed again. A long pause from me, followed by another long sigh.

'Well, is *that* what they call a hospital? Please explain that to me again!'

Normally, Jason's hair-trigger tantrum button would have gone off by this time, but Skip was paying the bills and he *did* love to talk

. .

So he exhaled and launched into a thorough explanation of the perilous process being undertaken by the medical profession to ensure that he, their valued patient, would live—though surely not ever productively. After he concluded, there was a troubled sigh, a considerable wait and finally, a tentative '..Skip?'

I covered my mouth, remaining silent for a long and tedious time, counting to twenty twice to myself. ' . . . Skip? . . . Are you— there?'

'*Yea*-ahs.'

'Do you *follow* me? Because I'm quite tired now and I wish to—!'

'Do you know *whooo* this is? Hmmmm? Hmmm?'

There was a dreadful pause: 'Is it *you*?!' he screamed, 'Why you— (least favorite word!).

'Do you know where I *am* how *dare* you *never* call me again (least favorite word again.) Do you know how *sick* I am?!

'Nooo,' I replied carefully, '*Explain* it to me!'

Laughing like a maniac, I slammed up the phone.

11.

Maura Connelly Earhart Clarke Kirkpatrick. . . . I had acquired so many last names, I felt like a section of the Telephone Directory. Still, in an era when self-validation and feminine expression had not yet gone from an 'art form' to the norm, I was bound and eager to add yet another name; to jump back into the fray, into the dark and dismal deep-end of the dating pool, flailing around, trying to find the elusive, ephemeral *Mr. Alright: Light my fire!*

Deirdre Devereaux, a Queens College acquaintance, tipped me off to PWP (Parents Without Partners) Dances, held around Queens and Nassau and other counties at about the same time as the Time Share Chicken Dinners, and affording just about as much entertainment value.

The PWP Dances. . . Hmmm. . . how best to depict these motley aggregations of bald-headed and bespectacled men; of plump and emotionally burnt-out women, all thrown together to 'make music' on a little ginger-ale plus chit-chat? If there is any way a 'live-wire' got in there at the few dismal affairs that I attended, he must've been underground, or he quickly short-circuited.

So there am I, in that dark corner, not yet plump, but definitely 'burnt'—fending off polite digs from a tall, sarcastic veteran of these hooplas; fencing as hard as I could now, my back to the wall. I glanced around under the dim lights for my traveling buddy, Deirdre.

Deirdre. A low-key delusional, prematurely white-haired, victim of her own addled, still-active marital union: Bronx Irish girl, manic Frenchman.

She smiled back benignly, waved limply and quickly turned away, ignoring our 'double-head pat' prearranged signal to leave. She had not yet become discouraged enough to leave.

'I gave her every chance,' my tall fencing opponent said defiantly, 'but, honestly, when she took our rent money and got on that bus to A.C.—!'

'—A.C.?,' I interrupted. 'Yes, Atlantic City!—then, By God, I knew it was over.' Tall and thin sighed poignantly, took a sip of orange soda, waited for the expectant murmurs: *'How sad. You're better off without her—!'* Dutifully submitted.

'Oh, without a doubt! Still, except for the gambling bug, she was a good woman!' My eyes glazed as he droned on, then wandered over the dance floor. There in the dim-distance, a familiar light-bulb shape head emerged apart from the other dim bulbs: I recognized—*Jason!*

'Oh, My God,' I whispered aloud, *'He's here!'*

'Who's here?' Before I could get out, 'My Ex,' Orange Soda was gone, fast as a rabbit, without spilling a drop. . . talk about your mixed blessings.

I had my Order of Protection with me, so after the sighting, he, too, vanished. It was just his way of ruining another evening for me—

'Not,' I said to Deirdre (who had enough PWP now) on our way home, 'as if he could make a PWP Dance much worse!' She nodded: 'They were a bunch of rejects, but you have to keep on trying. You just never know.'

Jason must've had the PWP Schedule of Events. The next Jason sighting, he came up and said, 'How are you, Slut?' Now, I had a good excuse to by-pass the dreadful PWP Parties.

'He'll never leave you alone,' were Mrs. Hubert's words and with each day, there was more proof that she was right.

One afternoon as I rounded the corner, I saw the patrol car in front of our house, and raced up the front stairs. 'We have a report you abandoned your children,' the cops said, 'it was phoned in.'

'You don't understand, Officer. I just went to the Dairy Barn, right there on the corner for milk and bread. My husband is harassing me.' So I showed them the court papers, they inspected the 'condition of the house,' and left.

Right after they did, there was a tap at the door. I stood rooted to the spot, making the 'shush' motion to the kids. Still, the tapping continued. I saw a shock of blonde hair out the peep-hole, and recognized a member of the construction crew that was working on our street. Slowly, I opened the door.

'Yes?'

'The guys an' I saw you running up the street, an' the cops here, an' we wondered if you were all right—especially me!' he grinned. I couldn't help smiling back a little at this cute guy, who was about ten years my junior. 'Yeah, I'm okay. I just have an ex-husband who never leaves me alone.'

'Can't say I blame him.' He lowered his voice and looked back over his shoulder. 'I have to get back on the job. I don't suppose you'd go out on a date with me, would you? Or maybe just coffee?'

Well, you can't keep a good woman down—though I must say, he tried.

I ignored the age difference: we had our couple of dates. What the heck. It was spring, and Phil Buchanan dispelled the jaundiced taste that the flotsam at the PWP had left in my craw.

I felt safe that evening, going to the movies, knowing that Jason, Skip and the girls were out at Montauk for the weekend. I wore my white eyelet blouse, though it was a little early in the season, and a slim, black skirt. I felt beautiful, a delusional full ten years' younger. Phil and I had just seen the 'Pink Panther,' and were laughing so much, we could barely navigate the pathway to my door. 'The way his manservant—' 'Cato!,' Phil supplied.

'Yes—the way he *jumps* Peter Sellers!,' I snorted. '*Attacks* him!,' Phil corrected.

As we reached the steps, Jason leaped out of the bushes by the stoop and in a motion like we had just seen at the movies, reached out with one hand and ripped my blouse straight down the front.

'Slut!,' he cried. Turning to Phil: 'I'll help you take it off, Pal!'

'You Son of a Bitch!' Phil started after him, but Jason raced down towards the Dairy Barn, and his cowardly butt rounded the corner.

I grabbed hold of Phil's arm, holding my blouse up with my free hand. 'Don't! He's leaving, and it's just what he wants you to do!'

'It's just what *I* want to do, too!,' he said, shaking free of my grip, 'Let go! I can catch him!'

'No, Phil! You'll ruin my chances in court!'

Phil hesitated—not knowing that what I really meant was, *'A kid like you doesn't need an assault charge.'*

'Well,' he said, half-heartedly, 'at least, let me make sure you get in the house all right. C'mon.' *('I know what that translates into,' I thought, 'but I'm in no mood for company.')*

'Don't worry; I'll be all right. He's not going to hang around here now.'

'Still—.' He waited, while I searched for my key. Then I noticed the door was slightly ajar—and pushed it the rest of the way open.

The place had been completely trashed, like a bomb had gone off. Everything was turned upside-down. Contents of drawers, linens, clothes, food stuffs, were strewn all over. You couldn't walk without stepping on clothes or silverware. 'I've been robbed!'

I saw Phil staring at me curiously. Of course, Jason had done this. I just couldn't conceive that he would.

'How could one person have done all this?' I picked up what was left of my jewelry box, one that Sally had wanted when she left. It had been stomped upon and broken to bits. With an eerie premonition, a chill ran along my scalp, and I knew that Sally had played a part in this destruction.

'This guy's a nut,' Phil murmured. I nodded, picking up a broach from the floor, feeling a tear slide down my cheek. 'Want me to call the cops?'

'It'd do no good, believe me. You need proof he did it. I'd really like you to—go, if you don't mind.'

'But where will you sleep?' 'I'll clear a spot off the bed. I'll be all right. I'll clean up in the morning.'

'This's gonna take a few mornings. . You sure, now?' 'Yes.' We kissed goodnight.

'I'll call you,' he said, but before I locked my useless door, I knew the blouse was history and so was Phil.

But I knew that even earlier that night—when he laughingly called me '*Mom*' in the restaurant.

The telephone rang lustily in that richly personal pre-cellular jangle that phones no longer have. I was practically '*padded*-cellular!' because it had taken me over two weeks to sort out and try to reconstruct my wrecked apartment.

'Hello?'

'Hello,' said the pleasantly dull-yet-familiar female voice, 'My, you sound down.' Who is this?,' I asked in the patient 'pre-Caller ID' parlance of the day.

'Why, it's Deirdre! Don't tell me you don't re-_cog_-onize me?'

'Course I do. How are you?'

'Well. As I haven't heard from you in so long, I thought I'd give you a call. Why so glum?'

'Oh, that would take too long to tell. For one thing, I had a date a couple of weeks ago and Jason got jealous and trashed my apartment. I found out later he had Sally with him.' 'Your *daughter*—?! That's terrible!'

I sighed, 'I know; I'm just now getting it back in shape. And Jay is always off somewhere and—!'

'—Sounds to me like you need a night out!' There was a long silence from my end, and a lot of internal wheel-clicking: '—Deirdre, not that I don't appreciate it, but I just can't take those—!'

'Just a minute,' she interrupted sternly, 'It's *not* a PWP dance! This'd be a blind date. For Sunday. A guy I know wants to take me out, *us out,* to dinner; a nice place in Richmond Hill. He's bringing along a friend. Naturally, I thought of you.'

'Nope. I just went through an episode with my nutty 'ex.' Sorry. I'll pass.'

'Maura, you think you're the only woman with a nutty 'ex?

Mine is *French!*' 'No, I don't think that, it's just, I'm—!' 'Oh, I'm *sure* you have something *wonderful* planned for Sunday evening. What is it?!'

So I 'folded my cards.'

'Okay. What time?'

As I climbed into her car, I said, 'Rockaway? Where's that?' Deirdre leaned on the steering wheel, giving me that far-off 'alien' stare, and I'm sure it was more than the long black gloves I was wearing.

'By the beach.'

'Why do we have to meet there?' 'Cause that's where *Ed*-die lives.'

She batted—slowly—her lashes over her oddly opaque eyes and drove—slowly—to the Irish Circle, the meeting place.

'I mean, most people living in Queens have heard of Rockaway. You haven't gotten around much, have you?'

'No, I don't drive and if I did I'd have to find my way back.' 'Oh, that's right. You're the girl that always has to leave by the same door every day. At *Col*-lege.' (She always called it, College.)

'Yup. I even went three times when it was closed for a holiday.'

'Well, that was just stupidity.' (I laughed.)

'And you probably wanted to get out of the house, anyway,' she added, still without smiling. (She never smiled.)

'Deirdre?' 'Yes?' She drove on. 'Did anyone ever tell you that you look like a plaster-cast of a Saint?" 'Do you mean Our Blessed Mother?' I nodded. 'I think it's my eyes,' she said sagely. 'I'm sorry there's no air conditioning; isn't it awfully hot for June?'

No, actually, it was sweltering for June. We both had worn long dresses (mine, a top and a long black skirt with a side- slit).

'The rest'rant will probably be air-conditioned,' she said without smiling, 'and Rockaway's right on the ocean, so it shouldn't be too bad.'

Right on the ocean. It might have been, but by the time we walked into the *Irish Circle*, we not only couldn't find *'the boys,'* as

Deirdre playfully tagged our dates, we couldn't find a cool breeze anywhere inside this hub of Hibernian/Heinecken activity.

Frenzied dancers whirled by on a sea of sawdust and though it was only six in the evening, many were 'well-oiled.' The music was lively and loud; the attire, decidedly casual, even T-shirts—the white kind without slogans. (Maybe I did see one or two 'Kiss Me I'm IRISH' imperatives.)

'I feel like a *Rockafella*, around here' said Deirdre, from the side of her mouth. 'I still don't see *the boys*.'

'Look,' I chuckled, 'Over there. See that big guy? You can see his stomach! His undershirt has a big hole in it. And he's drunk as a skunk!'

Deirdre's plaster-cast face grew even more impassive: 'I believe— why, that's Mike Connelly.'

As she turned to look at me, I realized—'You mean—he's my *date*? Oh, *No*! And did you know that '*Connelly*' is my maiden-name, Deirdre?'

Deirdre was doubly-stricken. As we looked over at his six and a *half* foot frame, his bleary red eyes closed and he sank down onto the floor next to a quickly-vacated barstool. 'Now, how would I know Connelly was your name?' Saint Deirdre snapped; then suddenly yelling, 'Eddie!' she disappeared, having spotted her '*boy*' in the throng.

Smiling ruefully and shaking my head all the way, I made my way to the ladies room.

Now, I'm one of those people who rarely perspires, but I felt an intense heat building up in my face. Off came my 'top' in the bathroom stall, up, went the long black skirt, and it got pinned to my black bra, effectively turning it into a 'Suzy Wong dress.'

Ah! The first cool breeze of the evening traveled up the side-slit, unimpeded by panty-hose (now tucked snugly, along with top and gloves, in my purse).

'There's no reason I can't be comfortable,' I told my feeling-naked self, going out and sitting at the bar in my black lace panties and skirt/dress: 'A Scotch and Soda, please!'

A fresh breeze came in through the Western-style saloon doors. I sighed and sipped contentedly. Life was not so bad.

Deirdre scooted up. 'This is *Ed*-die.' 'Nice,' I smiled, 'No T-shirt!'

'Oh, yeahr,' Eddie said, 'Sorry about my friend. Mike's an ass.'

'—A *drunken* ass,' Deirdre politely corrected him.

'Yeahr.'

'Don't you two even think about it; Deirdre. I'm happy over here.' I took a sip of scotch. 'You two have a good time. Nice meeting you, Johnny.'

'*Ed*-die!' Deirdre corrected me.

'Yeahr. You wanna dance?,' he asked Deirdre. As they walked off, he took a nonchalant hop back to me. 'Hey, you're real class. Mike's an ass.'

'Yeahr,' I said. 'One more, please, bartender.'

I sat there, like a dime-store snob, watching with a jaundiced eye assorted carpenters and plumber's assistants, happily taking wild turns on the dance floor with their chosen ones. I was enjoying myself; I was Jimmy Breslin, or maybe the entertainment critic, reviewing the joint.

A plucky lad came up to me and asked me for a dance. 'Sure,' I said, shrugging a shoulder.

Once out on the floor, some reel or other caught my passion (along with the scotch) and I jigged and jogged saucily about, hands on hips, smirking away, my side-slit flipping up in a most 'un-Wong' fashion. I really, in short, didn't care. What new plague could attack me? I didn't want to know, nor cared I. I was young enough, still, that this was possible: The Devil, be damned.

In the midst of all this hilarity, I scarcely noticed a tall, white-shirted man wearing black pants, giving me the well-known 'eye,' and working his way toward me.

After tossing back yet another scotch, I was just about to accept a short fellow's invitation to trot.

'I'm a *roofer*,' he said persuasively.

But suddenly, a pair of black slacks intervened, intruding themselves between the roofer and me.

'Is your dance card filled?'

'Is my—?! No,' I laughed. 'Then, c'mon.'

He had his shirt-sleeves rolled up and as we twirled, the heat rose up from his well-muscled shoulders through the yoke of his shirt. I moved my hand slightly: 'It's nice to see a man in a white shirt.'

'Blanche Dubois. Streetcar,' he murmured.

'What?' I said, looking up at this big, average looking-guy for really the first time.

Interesting amber glints played in his eyes, but a kind of a 'Dead-End Kid' sneer on his face gave him a look that almost said, *'I've done everything there is to do.'*

He smiled down at me. 'I've been in theater for a while. Out of it now for a year or two.'

'What kind of theater?'

'A road company. Traveling around, doing stage productions. Fiddler, Kismet; Childrens' Theater.'

'That sounds wonderful.'

'It was. I loved it. Made a living at it for about ten years, but just barely. Drove a cab for a while; now I work at the post office.'

'Do you like it?'

'It's all right. I don't love it: it's a job.'

Like a one-two punch to the gut, I gave him my history, in case he wanted to 'run.'

'Divorced recently, four kids, insane ex-husband—any phone calls you have to make?'

He smiled indulgently. *'My* divorce is final next month! No children; no insane ex. She was an alcoholic, if you were about to ask.' I had been. He held me tighter as we finished our dance.

We found a spot at the bar and I told him my name as he ordered the drinks. We clicked glasses and began the guarded fencing match, but in a more relaxed way than normally.

'Maura Connelly,' I said.

'Mack Jones.'

Disappointment flooded over me. 'Oh, *please!*' I couldn't help rolling my eyes.

'What?!' He looked confused.

'I've just ended a relationship with an 'alias.' I can't take any more phony names, I'm sorry!'

He laughed. 'I know it sounds phony.' He pulled out his driver's license and showed it to me: It said, '*McKenzie Jones.*'

'Family name. It's Mack. But you can call me whatever you want to.'

I felt my cheeks redden. 'I'm sorry—Mack! It suits you.'

The lion-eyes looked amused: 'Only one in the phone book! My agent likes it; otherwise, it's a nuisance.

'But I'm glad I stopped in tonight. I was on my way back from a wedding in Maryland, and as I drove by the open door, I saw you sitting there in that Suzy Wong dress. Did you come here by yourself? I know you're not from around here.'

'Blind date,' I said, pointing my glass in the direction of Big Mike, who, with a befuddled expression, was being helped to his feet.

'Who, him? I've seen him before. Oh, he's *blind*, all right.'

'My friend, Deirdre, fixed me up. That's her, over there with Eddie, her date.' Mack said, 'They look pretty cozy.'

'Yes, that's why I was wondering—do you live around here?' 'Not too far.'

'Do you think you'd be able to give me a ride home?' 'Sure. Let me know when you want to go.'

'Pretty soon. Right now!'

I waved good-bye to Deirdre, who flashed her no-smile.

'Nice car,' I said of the red T-bird. 'It's a rental,' he said—like it was a strange, honor-bound thing to divulge— before inserting the key in the ignition.

As we drove along in silence, visions of me appearing in parts-separate, black-bagged, compactor-housed conditions, accompanied the strange telephone poles and black wires leading to—nowhere I recognized!

Quickly, I turned my head to see a sign pointing to—*what* airport? Which way was Oz? My brain was a bit fuzzy, but the way got stranger and stranger, till finally—'None of this looks familiar to me,' I said coldly.

He turned to me and smiled—the cold smile of a serial-killer! As he pulled the car over to a grimy curbside, a lightning-fast chill shot over me: 'Where are we?!' I demanded, my heart thumping, 'You said you were bringing me home.' (I was suddenly remembering a fine, fat fellow who, one night, under the pretense of giving me a lift home, placed my hand on his crotch, wailing, 'I've got Blue *Balls!*,' and me, fighting off the chance to give them a color-check.)

Mack sat there for a moment, staring at me: 'All right, so it's *my* home.'

'Did my ex put you up to this? Because it wouldn't be the first time he hired—!'

'Hey, *wait* a second! Just let me use the bathroom and I'll bring you home—all right?'

'Is there a subway nearby?'

He got out of the car and looked back in the car.

'Calm down. Do you want to wait down here?' I nodded. Then as he was walking away, I grumbled, 'Oh, I might as well use the bathroom, too. But then I want to go straight home!' He nodded, locking the car.

He was sitting on a green leather footstool as I came out of the bathroom, elbows resting on his knees, perfectly relaxed; beyond him, lay the leopard throw-covered studio bed.

'How appropriate,' I thought, as he held his fingertips together, the hint of something or other playing on his lips. 'And why not smile? *He's in his lair,*' I thought. But then, all thought ceased, my last one being, 'Why not?'

Part stupidity, part boiler-maker, part who knew what part, I sat down on his knee and kissed him. 'That,' as many have said before and sadly, will continue to say by rote,'was all she wrote.'

The boiler-maker part had me stand up and mumble something about 'getting rid of these clothes!' He smiled wickedly as he watched me toss my garments one at a time ('damn pins!) ceiling-ward, to settle on the floor like leaves.

After the slo-mo strip, he smiled, I smiled and after the lights went out; he must've followed suit, because I felt the warmth of his chest come down upon me.

An absolute stillness penetrated to the core of my being deep in my chest. Hushed by its presence, I knew that everything would be all right. And it was.

Later, standing naked and drinking a raspberry Shasta in front of his refrigerator, I mused: *'That good feeling in itself is a worry. Have I spoiled everything by caving in too soon?!'* I hoped not, because he was the best lover I had ever had, size-wise, tender-wise and wiseacre wise. He was tops.

And what *about* that near-religious feeling I had before? 'Don't tell me he didn't feel it, too. Don't tell me he won't call me or want to see me again!' I took a big swig of Shasta: *'Please* don't tell me that,' I murmured aloud.

Sunday sunshine, walking in the park, observing each other in the hot glare, and others, as they milled around us and in between; my 'dress,' wrinkled and disheveled in day's light, was definitely now more wrong than 'Wong.' 'I hope he likes wrinkles,' I thought; actually feeling lucky that my skin, at least, was pretty free of them, considering the plights and fights I'd had. Luck of the draw, and medium-texture skin, I guess, were working for me. But Mack seemed to notice neither that, nor the dress.

Shortly after our Sunday saunter, he drove me home to await the girls' return from their weekend in Montauk; then, on to return his rented 'T-bird.' As I turned to go inside, ignoring the abandonment-fear that clutched my lower-abdomen, I heard those glorious magic words: 'Will I see you again?'

'Sure. Well, the problem is—I have no phone right now. Also, I have a court-ordered 'shrink' appointment in two weeks—both my ex and I have to go in order to determine fitness for custody.'

'So?'

'So,' I exhaled, suppose I call you up in exactly two weeks from today at 8:00 PM. Would that be okay?'

He nodded, we kissed goodbye.

Two weeks later, he answered his phone on the first ring—a trifle breathlessly. *('No games?,'* I thought, 'Now, I'm really in trouble!')

'So what did the Shrink say?'

'He said I'm crazy,' I laughed, 'What about you?'

'My mother says I *must* be,' he replied. And he wasn't laughing, either.

Each time I got on the 'R' train to visit him, my heart started pumping. The bell at each stop meant I was one stop closer, and by the time the train rolled into Steinway Street, when the bell clanged and the doors parted, my heart nearly burst with happiness. Racing up the street, I thought, 'I'm going to see him in three minutes!' (Or five, or however far away my breathless self was from Mack's house at the time.) I was not only happy in his arms, I was safe there. The apartment had become my sanctum on the weekends when the girls were with Jason. I jumped on the train, joyous, my destination unknown to Jason.

Sometimes Mack let me stay snuggled in the bed in the morning, when he had work on a Saturday, just asking that I 'lock up,' if I had to leave, which I never did. 'Nothing can happen to me here,' I sighed contentedly.

I'd get up a bit later and clean his already tidy place, and inhale the musky, masculine smell of the place, and dance around and listen to *'Beatles'* records, singing loudly, blissfully; bothering no one. He was in a big apartment building on the ground floor, right off the elevators. Colors of happiness permeated all of, and everything about that place for me.

When he got home, I'd fix him a steak and we'd watch TV together while we ate. It was the best time of my life.

Meeting in the city was fun, going to the movies or bowling, then coming home to Astoria or maybe eating at a Chinese or Greek or Italian restaurant. I smiled so much, my face ached. Oh, the richness, the decadence, the splendor of love! The fact that the dirty, littered streets of Astoria were Paradise and the 'R' train was the brilliant, speeding chariot of gold that conveyed me there, filled the aching void within me with a grand hope. The hope was that he loved me, too. If you had to ask me, if I had to 'put my hand in fire' (as Posie used to say), I would swear that he did by any and all of the knowledge of the infinite contained within me. How much this was, I don't know, but I do know it was enough to carry me along, to convince me that he did. Ever since the beginning, I felt that he did. Somehow I hoped, somehow I prayed with all my being, that the synchronization of feeling when we first made love did occur and further, that we would love each other forever.

He had no children and no crazy ex-spouse; I had 'all of the above.' Yet the 'feeling' would not be denied.

'What are you; about thirty-five?' he asked me one night over dessert at the Neptune Diner. The strange warmth in his eyes gave me a chill. I put my blatant honesty on 'hold' and took a sip of coffee before nodding.

'I *thought* so!,' he said, seeming relieved. I knew it was about having children. I felt a twinge for not having told him I was four years older than that, but was so happy in my mad delusions, I said to myself, '*Later. I'll tell him later.*'

I put the near-lie on a pile of mental gray stones in a corner of my mind, quite close to the other rocks in my head. 'He wants a baby,' I thought exultantly, '*with me!*' I didn't listen to the old hag saying in my ear; 'he's two years *younger* than you; he's able, you probably aren't.' I didn't even ask myself why I would *want* another child: I put a fresh coat of lipstick on the old hag's lying lips, and we left the diner.

He was gentle and good, he loved kids and animals. He was—destined to meet the fly in my ointment.

We took Joy to the zoo one day, and had a lovely time. She liked him, too.

Soon after on that day, we came face to face with Jason, walking down the path from my apartment. His usual irritated and stultified look turned to disbelief when he saw us. He stopped in front of us, and he looked *up* to confront Mack—just slightly taller—who stuck out his chin at a defiant angle and glared *down* at Jason. To think height had never been important to me before! It certainly has the 'bully advantage.'

I skirted the standoff and went to open my front door. When I looked back, a cowed Jason was mumbling and smiling a retreat, like the coward he was. A great warmth enveloped me. I knew Jason would find a way to take vengeance, but just then, I was protected and loved and life was grand.

Mack was the kind of man who *was* a man; who stepped back and looked things over before proceeding. He had a dependable job with the post office and an overriding calmness; each of these qualities, absent my whole life, would obviously appeal to me. Also, he was bigger and stronger than Jason. How lucky could I get?

He and Jerry hit it off at once, sharing calm attitudes and an intense dislike of Jason. Joy greeted him with a guarded equanimity, as she did the whole world: at her tender age, she was a Master of Self-Defense.

Sally, more a Mistress of Defiance, was a different story. On the day when first they met at the house on Spencer Hill, Mack sat relaxed, his arms akimbo on the back of my couch. When she entered, she appeared not to see him. 'Hello, *Mom*,' she said, emphasizing my name like a pejorative, 'How are you?'

'Fine,' I said, kissing her cheek and hugging her, 'it's great to see you.' In truth, we hadn't seen each other for quite a while, yet my stomach muscles knitted together reflexively, knowing I lied: it was seldom that great to see her.

'I can't stay long. Dad is waiting outside. I just dropped by to say hello.'

'I'm glad you did. I'd like you to meet Mack Jones. You've heard me mention him.'

'Hello, Sally,' Mack said in his rich, deep voice, standing up and smiling. She walked directly across the room, brushed right past him, leaned over— and patted the dog!

'How *are* you, Scotch? I've missed you!' As she straightened up, it was impossible not to read the gleam of triumph in her eyes. Even the dog looked embarrassed.

'Sally! That's very rude of you! Mack came all the way to—!'

'I have to leave now,' she said and flounced triumphantly out.

'I'm so sorry,' I said, 'I'm mortified.'

'Forget it—it's only natural,' he said, but it was impossible not to read the glint in *his* eye, either.

'Well, *that's* the beginning of a great friendship,' I thought later on that evening, 'and probably the end of Mack's and mine!'

But it wasn't. There were too many plusses for us, too many shared opinions and pleasant differences. He was well-organized and neater than I; I, more outgoing and impulsive than he: I made him laugh.

I met one or two of his cousins, some of his co-workers, his best friend. It seemed to me like my first taste of a normal world. We complemented; we filled each other's needs; we were a happy, delirious combination of loneliness-no-more.

Jerry and Mack got along very well and Mack had convinced him that instead of cutting school, it would be worth his while to join the Air Force. 'It beats the streets, Pal,' he said. Two of Jay's friends had died in drug-related incidents that year, so he was giving it careful consideration. And Joy; Joy laughed when she was with us.

Soon, however, she began to take on Sally's cool judiciousness where Mack was concerned. The new chill was apparent.

I told Mack of holding Sally on my lap by the window before she left to stay with her father: 'I asked her why she wanted to go.'

'What'd she say? That you two didn't get along?'

'No, not that, although we really don't; she said he was going to take her to L.A. for a singing career and that they'd have lots of money and *rugs* on the floor—not,' I choked out, 'dirty old wooden floors, like *I* have!'

'Don't be upset; it's not your fault,' Mack said.

'I know, I know. And I trundled her on my lap, and I searched for the right words. I think I said something like—those promises sound good, but they are never going to happen.'

'—Oh, I'm not pretty enough to have a career? Are you saying Dad is *lying* to me?—' That's what she asked me.'

'What did you tell her?,' Mack asked me.

'What could I do? I took a deep breath and I told her— *yes*, he's lying to you. And she moved out right after her eleventh birthday party.' He looked into my eyes, but his thoughts were unreadable.

'He's her Dad,' he offered finally. I nodded. 'But now, the other one is acting like I'm a criminal. Mrs. Hubert says Jason will never leave me alone, and I should let them *both* go,' I blurted out, 'but I just can't do that!' His mouth was a thin, grim line. 'She's right, you know.'

Then, suddenly, it was taken out of my hands. I had been brought to court yet again, by Jason, demanding custody, and charging me with abuse.

The Family Court Judge declared, 'Constant wrangling is not in the best interests of these children. Until these people can come to a reasonable compromise, the children will be put in Foster Care!'

The gavel slammed and with a shock, it was over for a period of at least two months. After a month, we were to be given separate supervised visitation.

Sally went to a facility for older girls and thanks to the intervention of Mrs. Hubert, Joy went to a 'comforting, nurturing older woman.' I trusted Mrs. Hubert and found out that this was indeed the case. However, guilt at the relief I felt at not having to make a decision and at having the chance to enjoy Mack's company flooded me. I often gave in to tears, alternating with bewilderment.

'We're going to the beach, so you can forget your troubles for a while,' he said. This involved taking a couple of busses.

I had my hair in bobby-pins and plopped a big sun-hat on my head. It was still early in the season, but I had on a blouse and a pair of blue-green shorts that were a little too short; my legs looked chunky and pale. I dragged along a tote-bag with sandwiches and sodas. A completely lackluster expression topped off my ensemble.

'Where are we going?' I asked dully, waiting for the bus, 'I mean what beach?'

'Rockaway.'

'Oh, that's where we met; that's right; it's near the beach.' He rolled his eyes up and smiled a little. 'Yeah.'

'I should have brought some sun-block. It's a good thing I wore lipstick, anyway. Will we get a seat on this bus?' He looked off into the distance. 'We'll get some sun-block when we get there; here it comes.'

Everyone got off the bus at the last stop, the flip-flop-wearing herd turning madly, dragging picnic stuff and beach umbrellas, off in the direction of what I was *sure* was the water. Mack cut off sharply in another direction. 'Isn't the water down that way?' He didn't answer, walking at a good clip. 'Mack, how come everybody's going that way and we're going—?'

'Short cut,' he said, striking me as oddly reminiscent of the night we met. He must've thought of that too, because he smiled and said, 'I have to take care of something. It'll just take a minute.'

Very suddenly, he turned and held open a cyclone-fence gate for me; so suddenly, that I kept on walking straight ahead.

'Hey, c'mere!' he called.

I turned back in surprise: 'Where're you going?' He beckoned and I followed, followed him up the few stairs, as he rang a doorbell. 'He *wouldn't*,' I thought! But he had!

There, at the open door, stood the sweetest little lady I had seen in a long time. Her eyes smiled before her pretty mouth did. She seemed to be expecting me. And so was his father.

Her eyes traveled down to my chunky thighs. I groaned and tried hiking my shorts down as Mack said, 'Maura, I'd like you to meet my mother—and my father'—the tall gent behind her, peering over her shoulder.

'Come in, come in,' they said, while I mumbled, mortified, something about pin curls in my hair. ('I'll *kill* him!' I thought, as Mrs. Jones, a chubbier version of me, fixed us lunch.)

Sitting at the kitchen table with my thighs safely hidden, I felt some relief. She had a much less cynical aspect than her son did and her questions, though occasionally probing, were always delicately put. I, too, spoke carefully. I didn't want to create an even worse impression than I already had.

'Take off your hat, Dear; oh, come on, do!,' she said and when I did, she laughed spontaneously and so did I. It was a pleasant lunch, and afterwards, he and I went down for a swim. The house was only a block and a half from the ocean.

As we walked along the shoreline before going back up to the house, he said, 'You know, you're the one I want to spend the rest of my life with. If we can work things out, do you feel the same way? I think you do. I'm pretty sure you do!'

I walked along as if I hadn't a care in the world.

As of that moment, I hadn't. I turned to him, my arms flapping, legs splashing, and said 'What?'

'Do you feel that way about me?' I nodded, but he kept looking at me, so I said, 'The rest of your life? Do you know what that sounds like?'

He smiled and we held hands as we walked and thump, thump, thump went my heart. I wondered, had he told his parents about what he was planning? I wondered, did his Mom still think he was crazy to be involved with me? I wondered, but I just couldn't wonder any more. I was too 'pinch-me' happy.

12.

The month was up in no time and the court-supervised visits began, and were a horror.

I was a stranger to Joy. A flick of her lashes dismissed me; she turned her blueness past me, to the sky outside the court-room window. The woman who cared for her was a grandmotherly figure, smiling, ample, neatly dressed, and she had done the same for Joy, whose sweet cheeks were rounded and polished with care, her face, the jeweled center of a flower; the hair, combed waving back in wings of sunshine. 'I bought her the coat,' the lady smiled, pointing with an open hand at the belted pearl-gray trench coat, 'and the dress (pink floral)!,' waving her hand with the accomplished pride of an artist. 'Thank you,' I said sincerely, 'thank you so much,' and my heart broke in two.

What was I to do?

'Daddy says you don't care about us, or we wouldn't be here,' she uttered softly while I sat with her.

'But that's not my doing, Joy! The Judge decided that!' Indifferently, she nibbled at the snacks I had brought her; indifferently, she watched me leave and despite the kisses and hugs I heaped upon her, she refused to be encouraged when I told her that I would return.

What was she to do?

Bitter tears scalded the back of my throat as I pressed the button for the elevator—and only worsened, as Jason exited the elevator before I could get on—his arms loaded with toys, his heart, with poison. 'Hel-ooo, Darling Joy, how's my Darling?' 'Daddy!,' she cried— and another door slid shut.

The lengthy train ride out to Little Flower to see Sally, was an even worse nightmare. She was waiting outside for me, and we sat under a tree so we could talk. As we settled down on the grass, she had not yet said a word, looking down with the merest glance at the wrapped gifts I had brought along.

'How are you, honey? How are they treating you here?'

'Do you know where you've sent me? Do you know what they *do* to me here?' My heart leaped with fear.

'Has—anyone touched you?'

'Are you talking about *sex?* Is that all your perverted mind can think of? They haven't done that *yet*, but give them time! They're very mean to me; they call me a lot of names, and it's all your fault for sending me here, Bitch!'

My hand flew up and I slapped her face. I shouldn't have. It was the long journey, filled with, as I now saw, an unrealistic expectation that she would be glad to see me. She slapped me back. Some people from the front of the building, obviously Supervisors, came down the stairs.

'Is everything all right here?' The Security Guard called out, walking toward us as he spoke. We both stood there, crying. Sally picked up her packages.

'The Bitch is just leaving,' Sally said. She turned and walked away.

'She's right,' I said in Mack's arms later that night, 'She's right.' The trip home could not alleviate the pain. 'I *am* a Bitch. But her personality is so rotten that maybe she's making it up, when she says the other girls are mean to her!'

'Shhh, shush, never mind. Give it up! Go to sleep,' he said. I knew then that I *would* 'give it up.' I would commit the un-motherly act of giving up my own children. And Mack would be the bonus to me, the solace I needed for the loss I would endure. How great would that be? Oh, how great would that be!

'Don't go making—conversation—la-da-dah; I never want to go that far—,' the radio sang out and while I held on for Mrs. Hubert—*'I love you just the way you are,'* it said. And I sure hoped he did. I needed a lot of loving, though personally speaking, I wasn't sure how much I deserved. 'Hell,' I rationalized, 'as much as anybody else, I guess.'

The morning of the day: the last day she lived in my house. Joy walked out to the corner of Spencer Hill under a brilliant sunshine, her hair in braids, the last day of school; wearing her uniform, the white blouse, the little blue plaid jumper. Poised mid-step, she turned, looking back at me. It is her look that is etched in my mind until the last breath I draw in my life. She knew. She knew somehow, as I did, that a mournful event had come to pass. We could not tear our eyes away. I put my hand to my lips and blew her a kiss and like some dainty bird, she was gone.

'You're doing the right thing,' Mrs. Hubert said, 'this way, if he has the children, maybe you'll have a chance to have some happiness for yourself. You deserve it.'

'I do?' 'Of *course,* you do.' ('Hmmm, I thought, 'Hmmm. Why don't I feel good about it? What is that 'grab' at the pit of my stomach; that *clenched fist?* What is that?')

I never thought of asking my friend, Marilyn from school, to go to court with me that day. She was always busy now with her own two adopted sons; her job; school. She had maybe a credit and a half to go, to get her degree. Marilyn knew and loved the girls and I couldn't have subjected her to that, or myself, to her dispassionate disapproval.

It was bad enough. . . that day in Court. Court: God, how I hated it. I would rather clean toilets than be a lawyer and spend my days in that vile setting.

Why am I angry? Anger should not be confused with despair. That day in Court, I knew as I was signing over custody of my children that I was doing the 'wrongest' thing I ever did. The fist in my stomach told me so. Always listen to 'The Fist.' It never lies, even when you lie to yourself. I wish I had. I would've run, flown, hidden in the woods; anything else. Maybe I should've shot him, or anything else, or something along that line. I don't know.

'Blah-blah-blah,' Jason swore, 'You'll see the children all you want and every other weekend and blah-blah.'
'You'll be fair?'
His signing, my signing, made the lie more palatable.

Later, Mack held my hand on the outskirts of court, by the elevators. The girls were paraded in front of me by Jason and he stopped them there, right in front of the elevators.

'Say good-bye to your mother,' he said in deadly, vaunted tones. He didn't have to add, 'forever.' For a fleeting instant, before they were marched into the elevator like little soldiers to their doom, I was shot by the nine-year old's gaze; felled, by guilt unabating. Joy's innocent blue eyes were saved from utter clairvoyance only by a frame of dark lashes, imparting a look of unusual judiciousness. There was much to judge, much wrong, but these were her parents, so the cloak was wrapped tighter, the judgment turned inward, like a dagger. How harsh! Harsh, are we all to each other, and to ourselves? Ruthless.
'*Open the door!,*' I yelled, crying, banging with the side of my fist. '*It's me!* You know I'm here! It's my day to visit!'
('*Daddy, it's Mommy! Let her in!*') I paused, straining to hear Joy's voice, pleading from somewhere beyond Jason's apartment door—stifling my streaming, ragged breath; gulping back the gasps. A murmur—then, no more. Silence. (*He must've taken them into the distant bedroom!*)
Instantly, I resumed pounding like a mad-woman on the door, finally leaning my forehead against its cold, unrelenting surface, and sobbing, '*I knew*—I knew you wouldn't be fair!'

All the way home on the A-train, my swollen eyes stared at nothing and no one, of course, looked back at me. My thoughts buzzed like flies, sitting, hopping, changing direction.

Had I gone to the police, it would have been a waste of time. They had no Warrant to search; I had no Visitation Papers with me and even if I had, the day would have been shot; the children traumatized even further, fearful and sick at having to visit with me under such tense conditions.

'What are *you* doing here—?!' Mack set down his bowling bag and wrapped me in his arms, while I sobbed.

'Cops!?' I replied to his suggestion. 'What good would *they* have done?' Of course, he held me: 'another few minutes, and I would have been gone,' he murmured as I gave way to fresh tears; of course he comforted me—and skipped the bowling.

'It's all right. It's only practice. But if I have a team-meet, I have to go.'

'I know, I know; I'm going to call Mrs. Hubert on Monday and register a complaint. But right now, I'm so tired, I just want to sleep. I'm going to try to call them up later. Maybe I'll get lucky and get them on the phone,' I whimpered, trying not to think of how the girls felt, or of the wounded knot at the pit of my stomach. . . 'Just need some rest.'

Drifting off, I heard him say quietly, 'Mom was right.' I opened my eyes for a brief second and saw him staring up at the ceiling. Then I fell asleep.

Now, there was just Jer, Scotch (the girls had taken the pup, Willard) and I, left living in the old house on Spencer Hill so even though we had 'plans,' there was still unfinished business, and I held onto it. I started a new job right after I gave the girls up to Jason, with a national retailers' supply company down on Fifteenth Street. It helped me combat the dull feeling of horror within.

Sure, Mack comforted me, but now when I was in his arms, even at our happiest moments, there remained that spot of pain between us, like an inoperable cancer. Though I held very still, I sensed he could feel it, too; he was intuitive, as most actors are.

My next weekend visit to the girls went off without a hitch, despite the pounding of my heart. (Mrs. Hubert, after unleashing a choice curse or two when I told her about Jason not answering the door, must've laid down the law to him, and she threatened to question the custody decision.)

It made no sense to use up the whole weekend traveling back and forth, or to give Jason a chance to infringe on my newfound privacy, so the next time, they spent a long Saturday with me, with me returning them to Jason late-evening. We saw a Disney film, ate at MacDonald's and did a little shopping. Both Joy and Sally seemed to enjoy it. When I brought them back that night, there it was again—that ache in my gut.

I began to empathize with all the single daddies I saw on those weekends, sitting forlornly in picture shows with their daughters and sons, or schlepping around after them in zoos and museums. They were easy to spot: I wondered if they spotted me, too. Like them, these trips—in my case, to the Bronx to see my children—became the Oasis in the Sahara of my life. If my plans were circumvented, my tongue hung out with thirst for the sight of them.

And then it happened again. I made the trip and no one was there and there were tears of frustration and Mack held me, as before.

'I know what he's doing. He's keeping you off-balance, that's what he's doing. It's a control-thing.'

'It's so cruel!'

'That's right. And there's not a thing you can do about it. He'll probably say he had made other plans, or he got the weekend mixed up.' Indeed, he said he got the day mixed up and the next time, was fine; the time after that, Jerry and I showed up with a picnic basket—a friend dropped us off—and we set the basket down in the silent hall: no one was home. . . The usual tears, the usual phone calls.

Sometimes late at night in Astoria or Spencer, the phone would ring and all hell would break loose, the girls yelling and screaming— Sally and Jason, fighting, arguing!—and little Joy would get on the phone at midnight and say, 'Don't worry, Mom. It's all right; they're calming down now. I can take care of it!'

173

No sleep could come as I lay awake, staring at the black ceiling. With all the MailGrams and phone calls and tortures Jason dreamed up and inflicted on me, the nighttime phone calls were the worst. I scarcely noticed the new silence that had come over Mack, a quiet contemplation, a drawing back.

One Saturday night, we had tickets to a concert, a group that Mack really loved. There was a knock at the door and when I opened it, I saw Jason's car roaring away up toward the corner of Spencer— and Sally calling out, 'Bye, Dad.' She came up to the door, smiling all the way.

'Sally, what're you doing here? I'm not supposed to have you till next week.' 'Dad had to go someplace. He said to tell you he'll pick me up tomorrow.'

'Oh, no,' I said. 'He can't do that: I have plans made. You can't stay tonight.'

'So, *change them*! I've got nowhere to go. If you leave me here, I'll call up Mrs. Neiderman!' Of course, it was out of the question that I take her to Mack's place and get a sitter.

If I was angry, Mack was furious. First he laughed.'Very funny! What time are you coming over?' When he knew I was not kidding, something happened between us: a line that had been there all the time had been crossed. He gave the tickets to a friend. Forgiveness was not forthcoming.

I was handling things all wrong. I needed to talk to Marilyn, to have lunch with her. She was always able to calm me down just by her presence, and perhaps I could think more clearly about Jason and Sally and Mack, and everything else. She could give me a few ideas; her suggestions often came in the form of questions, but valid ones. Yes, I'd better have lunch with the 'mental health expert.'

But when I called, and called back again, she wasn't there, nor was her secretary. I had to leave word with the girl at the Board, who came across as very odd, almost rude. Come to think of it, Lyn had either been 'at a meeting' or 'away from her desk' or 'at a doctor's appointment' every time I'd called within the past few months.

There had been a period lasting a year when I had no contact with Lyn because she showed up late or forgot to show up at all, one time too many. Could she purposely be ducking me, punishing me? 'Nah!' I thought, going home later that day, 'she's not like that; Marilyn's not vengeful.'

Curiously, the phone rang that very evening, sometime after dinner: 'Roger! I didn't recognize you; what a surprise! You *never* call—!' The absurdity of it hit me: 'What's wrong? Is it—*Lyn*?!' He answered in a loud, strange voice: 'If you want to come and see her, you better come now!'

'What? What?!,' I cried in agony, banging my head down on the kitchen table. And I ran where she lay alone, in-hospital, off a wing of the Sinai Medical Library; separated from her desk by a concrete slab, an obelisk of non-questioning, faceless windows, blindly blocking her access to—the very office!—that she would never use again.

Touching the moist coolness of her arm reclining, repining it's loss of life; wondering if I, too, on my trip to eternity, would be detained by the infernal 'beep' of the monitoring system: (beep) stay a while! (beep), the last sound heard, not the loving voice of a friend, the sigh of the wind or the trill of a bird, but that cold robotic chirp: flat-line.

And did she hear me? Did she hear me say to other friends that came in, 'What a swell lookin' chick she was, when first we met—knowing somehow she would like that—and them, agreeing? She stopped her silent struggling when I spoke, so I prayed she did, anyway; I always hope she did.

A woman I didn't know, stood by me, her eyes leaking tears: '*She kept it a secret that she had pancreatic cancer.*'

Like her, not to want anybody to suffer along with her; like me, not to realize how much I loved her till she left for good. I shall forever miss the lunches we shared and the blueberry blintzes at Jann's. Miss her company; her guiding strength. Miss her quiet self-reliance. This quiet, I cannot breech.

Lyn's sudden death had blindsided me and though I was still very much in love with Mack, it plunged me into a temporary blackness, not yet diffused by the softness of time. I plodded to work, thankful for its regularity, stunned by a different 'ache' than missing my children.

Soon afterward, I walked past the barbershop, just as the barber was swiveling Mack around, handing him a mirror to check the back of his neck. Our eyes met through the window: he looked shocked at my appearance. My shoulders were pitched so far forward as I walked, that a man could have been sitting on my back, knuckling me down.

'*Hey!*' Mack called to me hanging out from the doorway, still wearing the barber's cloth, 'You okay?' I rolled my eyes sideways, beseechingly at him; not answering, not even wanting his company, walking on. But he soon caught up with me: 'What is it?'

'Combination of various; don't worry about me.'

'But I *do* worry about you: look how you're walking!'

'It's how low I feel,' I shrugged, and didn't bother straightening up. 'It's—Groucho Marx!,' he said. 'Where were you *going*?'

'I was coming from *your* place: you weren't home,' I added, smiling a little bit. 'I'm sorry. It's everything; the kids, and now, her dying.'

'Marilyn?'

I was struck at his obtuseness—! He had to hand me his crumpled white handkerchief. 'Things have gotten hold of you, I know, but all life is a struggle. I only met her once. She seemed a nice girl—'

'No, she *didn't*,' I wailed, blowing my nose and trying to give him back his hanky. 'She was always frosty-cold when she first met a person! She was afraid of being hurt. Then, when she warmed *up* to you!!—then, you saw, if you—! *Then*, you saw; you *knew* what a great *heart*—!' I gasped, trying not to cry on the street; trying to walk away, to leave.

But love is a brilliant, blessedly enduring beacon, so I succumbed, thankfully, to Mack's blandishments. He took me home to hold and pamper me. He had met Marilyn only once, not enough to know her great heart, but he knew mine pretty well.

As he walked me later to the subway, I said, 'Mack is glad to see the *happy* package, not old me!' He squeezed me to him, 'Hush! I like everything about you; you know that. . . See that sunset?' He pointed at the ruddy glow back over the distant city buildings.

'It's going to be a beautiful day tomorrow. We'll plan some fun-time together, just you and me.'

That Wednesday morning, every bird in Central Park was singing a crazy, mixed-up tune. Daffodils and tulips stood tall on the slopes, bobbing their heads in a splendid acknowledgment of the breezy, sunny day. I spotted him leaning against a bench top, pushing his mailman's hat that looked like a chauffeur's cap, back on his forehead with his rugged right thumb, smiling broadly at me, as I walked up to him.

'I'm glad you could get the afternoon off. It's a grand day, isn't it?' I nodded, too buoyed up at first to speak. It had all worked out because I had delivered a letter uptown and my boss granted me the time.

'You said you wanted to show me something?'

'Won't take long,' he said. Holding hands, we walked along a broad, winding path, smiling at the passing people and a few frenetic squirrels, equally hyped up for Spring. He raised an arm, pointing outward like an Indian in a cowboy movie, at the dark wooden structure in the distance. As we got closer, we could see a smiling man loading kids up onto—?

'The carousel! Isn't it beautiful?' The man drew them up, little kids and 'big ones,' onto the polished, painted ponies, looking unblinkingly ahead, supremely confident under their different colors and coats of shellac. A sudden pang overtook me.

'Why don't you hop up and have a ride?'

'I will if you will,' I said. 'No.' (He pointed to his uniform by way of explanation.) 'You ride for both of us.' I shook my head, but he smiled enticingly: 'They're taking it down next year.' A tan stallion coasting by caught my eye, and in an instant, I was up on his gleaming back and away.

'Don't forget to grab the ring!' Mack yelled as we gained speed. '*Is* there one?' I called back, gaily laughing, as he shrugged—and trailed off behind me. In repeating circles, I anticipated: the flowered bush, the two laughing fathers, the mom eating her popcorn and waving at her child, and Mack! My guy! There he was, his hat shoved back on his head as handsome as Agent Double-Oh-Seven ever was, and he was smiling, enjoying and drinking me in as I whirled by, looking (almost *too* significantly) at me, Maura, under the blue-tarp Central Park Central-Casting sky.

It was the best merry-go-round ride of my life, and like all great rides, it was—over too soon.

'Macho-Macho-Man!' The young man bopped along Steinway as his shouldered boom-box blared, *'I just-want-to-be-a-macho-man!'*—so persuasively, that if there were any birds on the street (pigeons don't count) they would've sung right along. Wind chimes swayed in disco-chorus in the discount store fronts I passed, and all twenty-seven TV screens in the wide-open electronic store showed the dervish-dancing, maniacally-moving Village People.

I got a 'spinal rush,' then a flush of desire.

Why the blush of pride? That song came out the year before, the year we met, and if Mack wasn't the prototypical, biggest old Macho-man in the Universe—! Well, I didn't know who the heck was! Then, as I shivered, they followed it up with the boisterous 'WMCA,' giving me the same good vibrations. Indeed, I'd never be stupid enough to tell it to him, but he was '*it*' for me: Mack was my secret Macho-Man.

So that's how things stood, when I burst into his place that day, and there he was, working out; of course, wearing a frayed Tank-top and old shorts. His biceps, neck and chest were clearly visible and really something to see, I noticed, as he rolled the weights down and under his red workout bench. Mack grinned up at me: 'You're really early, aren't you? I've gotta have a sip of soda,' he sang out on his way to the kitchen, me after him, and popped open the lid on the can. As he held out the can to me—'Want some?'—I saw there was a cake-box on the table. 'You bought cake?'

'My Mom came by. She brought me a chicken for later on, too.'

'—How nice that she worries about you!'

'Oh, she *always* does that.' He swigged down some soda, wiping his lip with the back of his hand before continuing: 'She *cares* all right, but those chickens don't come free.' At the puzzled look on my face, he added, 'They usually come with a set of instructions on how to live my life!

'Come; come here. . . let's lie down for a while.' He led me off to bed. The world was right again, and I could now definitely hear those birds way down on Steinway.

I don't know what made me say it, because I was so happy in the moment. Maybe it was the challenge of the 'climb up Mt. Olympus,' or a challenge tossed in the faces of the Gods themselves, but as I sat there so sure of myself, looking down at him and his big chest, I chirped, 'Maybe we should see other people.'

'Yes,' he said, looking up at me very steadily, 'I think, maybe we should.' 'Then, let's!' I croaked, just before I fell down off the mountain.

We ate something later, I wasn't conscious of what, and—'Oh, before you go,' he said, 'I believe you have a few of your things in the closet.' Blindly, I poked through it and pushed my one or two dresses into a plastic bag, along with the tatters of my heart; spotting the gray dress with the coral flowers towards the back of the closet, I resolutely left it there.

'*Why had I spoken?*' I anguished, 'Why did I say what I said?'

Suddenly, it hit me! 'Oh! 'Remember? We have that fishing trip with your friends from work in two weeks!'

'Oh, we'll go to *that*," he assured me, 'I already *paid* for that. That's a date,' he promised, as I headed for the door and plunged off the edge of the planet.

The sinking sun and a chill wind had teamed up against me. People walked bowed forward, crowding, jostling their way down into the subway crypt.

Missed the train. Declined the next, as it was too crowded. Standing, staring, as the doors of the next packed 'G' train slid open and closed several

179

times, trying to slide shut over its burden of arms and legs, elbows and shoulder bags.

Someone within its crammed confines made eye contact with me before the door closed; the eyes, strange but familiar; the expression, tired, but truly kind. A tear formed, a frozen pea in the inner corner of my eye: I refused to release it, glancing away. The option to cry was not mine; not now.

Just a few weeks ago, I had tried to reach Marilyn, needed to hear the sound of her voice, hoping to release the burning pain somewhere near my heart. Now, I could never reach her.

'My friend,' I laughed, alone now, in the empty house on Spencer Hill, 'My friend!' I cried in the dark and put the heavy black receiver back onto its cradle. 'Where are you?' I took one or two sleeping pills a night. They helped. Of course, they couldn't erase the pain. It was always there, night or morning. It seemed it always would be.

But I hadn't counted on this. Somehow, I never saw this coming. 'It wasn't supposed to be this way!' I felt sure, inherently sure, that Mack and I were destined to be, well, forever, he and I. Captain Ahab of the Pequod: I felt like the last rat on a rapidly sinking ship.

Kim had gone to Houston to live with her new husband, Rod, who was an engineering student there, and her new family. Jay, still unsettled, lived mainly with pals or on the streets. We'd had a few issues over missing money, probably settling in some drug dealer's pocket. I hadn't even seen him in two weeks, and even though he was still a minor, and a baby by anyone's standards, he remained the 'Man of the House,' a house now, always in darkness.

My hope, to have a home and what might be called a 'normal existence,' was gone, now, completely gone.

The dog and I looked at each other with frightened eyes. I glanced over at the dust balls in the corners under all the desks, at the dingy drapes, the filthy floor, the sink-dishes—and back at the dog. 'I guess you're my only friend, Scotch.'

'Dusk now,' I said, 'Supper-time!'

I got up out of the capturing couch and heaped some dog food into her dish. She regarded me for a fond moment, gobbled it up and then walked over to the door. Clearly, she 'wanted out.' And Oh, Lord, so did I.

I took the damn bottle of sleeping pills, almost full, by my estimation, and slumped down onto the 'next-stop-the dump couch,' weighing the bottle in my hand. Took up the damn bottle of pills, uncapping them, putting them down on the end table; sat back on the lumpy couch and put my legs up on the saggy, straw-dispensing footstool. To the ripped and ratty curtains, ghostly, in the deepening gloom, I said, 'Now, why don't I do this? Why not?'

The house, in darkness, had no answer for a woman who had taken one blow too many in the houses of men.

It was so dark now, I could barely see. I cradled the pills in my hand, shaking, trying not to spill them, but just not brave enough to swallow them. There was an odd, shuffling sound that I took to be the dog, but when I looked up, there stood Jerry, swaying gently in front of me in street-worn blue jeans. He looked a little 'fuzzy,' but he took the scene in all at a glance.

'Oh, *Ma*,' he said, 'Oh, Ma, what're you *doing*?'
He switched on the lamp and pried the pills from my hand a bit too easily. I burst into tears. 'Ma, Ma,' he kept saying, his blue eyes a little red, but all reproachful; probably still high on reefers: 'You don't want to do this. Everybody needs you.'
'No, they don't! I've betrayed everybody.'
'—Stop it, Ma; it'll be all right.'
And then the truth came ripping out of me.
'Mack—left me! He doesn't *love* me anymore!' I sobbed. He sat next to me, patting my head and hugging me, kind of laughing, 'You'll see. He does. He cares about you. It'll be okay.'
He held my hand and I felt its warmth and comfort for a wonderful moment.

I sighed, 'What about you: will *you* be okay? I mean, about the drugs?'

'Yeah,' he lied, 'don't worry about it. Say, did Mack tell you I made the Air Force? I'm taking the oath in two weeks.'

'No, he didn't! Oh, that's wonderful! In two weeks??'

'Un-huh. That's when I'm being sworn in. . .

'Mom, why don't you go and *wash your face*? You'll feel better.'

I smiled as I walked to the bathroom, thinking of how many times I had told him to do that.

When I came out at last, he said, 'Feel better? Just so you *know*, I fed *the dog* for you!'

I laughed aloud, and then I sighed. 'Thanks, Jay. Yeah, I'll be okay.'

Probably, I was playing to the demons, the 'packed house' in the self-created nightmare that was my life. Probably, I could never have done it ('iced' myself). Those who have, provided they haven't taken anybody else along with them, have always had my pity and a twisted kind of respect.

When Jerry left, the warmth in my heart lingered. If Jerry could have a career in the Air Force; if Mack cared enough for Jay and for me; if the girls and I could go from trauma and despair to love and hope, and a happier life for them, then I would die in the innocence of my dreams. But not tonight.

Tonight, I would sleep.

'I'm in Jail, Mom.'

Before I could mumble 'Wrong number,' I recognized Jerry's soft voice. Whether you are coming out of a deep sleep or not, those four words are undoubtedly among the worst words a parent can ever hear, with the exception of, *'There's been an accident.'* I've heard both.

'Jerry?! Where *are* you?!
'Somers County Jail.'

'Where?? What did you *do*?!

'Nothing. I was just sitting in a car. I can't talk now. I go before the judge tomorrow morning—No, Tuesday!

'Can you be there?'

'Just a minute—'

'—Hurry!'

'—I have to get a pen!'

A stern voice spoke somewhere behind him.

'Just *come*, Mom!' The line went dead.

Driving up number 684 towards Somers, New York in the drizzling rain, sitting next to my brother, Tim, who was driving comparatively slowly, for him. The brother I swore I would never, ever, under any circumstances ride with again, kept his eyes on the white stripe and stared glumly dead ahead.

'We have to be there by nine,' I murmured. He gazed over at me as if I were a fly speck on the horizon.

'. . . He will be. . . in the docket. And we will be . . there. Don't worry. . . ' He went on a bit, perhaps sensing my fear. . . 'This is a first-time offense, right?'

'Well, I think so.'

'Hmph! I thought that this guy was going into the Air Force.'

'He was supposed to be sworn in the next morning at five o'clock—the night he got arrested.'

Tim sighed exasperatedly behind the wheel, and drove silently for a while. 'Well. . . he's young enough that it shouldn't go too bad for him. What's the charge, again?'

'Found sitting in a stolen vehicle,' *Jay* says.

'In the driver's seat?'

'No. Next to the driver. And two other guys in the back seat.'

'What ages?'

'Uh, they were all eighteen, I think. Maybe one, nineteen.'

'He could go to Spofford,' Tim muttered, mainly to himself, and said nothing more until we arrived at the Court.

183

As we sat through the morning's proceedings, I was glad I had heeded Mack's advice and called my brother: 'He knows the ropes: he's a cop. He's Jerry's uncle. He'd be more help to him than I could—I mean, I'll *go* with you, if you *want* me to, but I think you're better off going with your brother.'

Finally, Jerry and the others were led out into the docket. The others were wearing jackets. He was wearing a rumpled and dirty white shirt and jeans. He looked cold; he looked about thirteen years old.

He smiled an embarrassed smile when he saw us. Then, he did something I found disturbing.

I didn't understand what happened next, not at all. Jerry stood before the judge, words were said—and he was led off back through the doors—back to jail.

Directly after, in the hallway outside the courtroom, I looked up at my brother, puzzled. Before I had to ask, Tim explained, 'Listen. He goes before the court again in two week's time for sentencing. Now: You have the choice of having him released in your custody, or letting him stay here until adjudication.'

'You mean, he can come home with me—*today*?'

Tim nodded. 'Right now. Oh, but if you bring him *home*, you are responsible for him until his sentencing. . . Think it over.' He stepped back from me for a second.

'What kind of a jail is it?'

'Where he is? Not too terrible. But bad enough he won't want to go back in a hurry. So? What do ya think, Maura?'

'Tim, I don't know what to do. What should I do? I just don't know.'

'I can't tell you what to do.'

'I know, I know!' I moaned in anguish. 'Something—that he did in there disturbed me.'

'You mean, when he gave you the wink, and the thumbs-up?'

'Yes! That.'

'That's because he thinks you will always be there for him to bail him out if he screws up anytime; to pick up after his messes.

'But if you let him cool his heels up here, he'll have some time to think things over, about his actions.' A smile crossed his lips, 'and if he does *that*, then chances are good.'

'What chances?'

'That he'll stop screwing up! —Unless you *want* to keep bailing him out!?'

I let the kid sit 'in stir.'

On the way home, I had plenty of time to regret it, but I didn't regret asking for Tim's help.

'Don't worry,' Tim said, letting me out of the car. 'I'll check on him with the guys up there, and I'll be there for his release or his transfer. You don't even have to go along; give us some time to talk.'

'Thanks, Tim. . .'

'Good luck,' he said with his usual air of finality, and I knew that after this, I would be on my own with Jerry.

'Thanks, so much; I appreciate—' I was still talking as he drove away, full throttle.

After the sentencing, Tim told me, 'If the kid was just *two weeks* older, he'd be in jail right now!' he shook his head, 'He's one lucky—! Also, Spofford is overflowing right now. One lucky—!'

'—I hate to ask this!—What's his sentence?'

He handed me some papers. 'He has a parole officer he has to report to—*that's it!* The driver took the rap for 'borrowing' the car and had a previous charge,' he added grimly. 'He's doing time. So are the other two kids.

'Your son is a 'youthful offender,' but he better watch his ass. He's one lucky—!'

'Where is he now?'

'Down at Dunkin', getting some coffee and a donut, I think. I think he's bringin' you some, too.'

'You're a good brother,' I said and kissed him on the cheek.

'De Nada,' he grinned. 'But you better put some pressure on him. You can probably get him into the service, when this cools down. If he's smart, he can make the requirements.'

Not that the Demons of Loss had abandoned me: I was still that grinning skeleton jumping around, trying to shake them off as I wiped off tables in the fish restaurant.

I had taken a job as a waitress on weekends and some evenings in this new place, just blocks from home, at the suggestion of my friend and neighbor, Kara. After that appalling night when Jerry came and 'rescued me', I couldn't stand to be at home any more with the haunted, floating curtains; the huge black telephone that never rang.

'We'll train you,' said the wife of the owner, who knew I wanted to 'keep busy.' She made sure I did. I 'dervished' as a dishwasher-vacuumer-table-setter-waitress-hostess: I couldn't hold still—and always, with the rises death-grimace plastered on my face.

If I popped outside behind the restaurant for a smoke, I paced like a tiger—stopping once in a while spasmodically, saying suddenly, 'He misses me! He's *got* to! I know he's miserable, too!' I had lived for that fishing trip with Mack, just to see his face. And finally, though it seemed an eternity, it came—and went.

We went out on the boat (me, still wearing the demonic death-grin) and I caught a small striped bass. I took the fish to work with me later that day and the owner cleaned it.

As I stood with my order book, a luncheon party came in and like it was scripted, a lady asked, 'Is the striped bass fresh?' 'It ought to be,' I said, 'I caught it myself.' Well, no one thought it was very funny or laughed very much, especially not me. It had been our last official date, and that was no 'fish story,' either.

'Oh,' Mack had said at the end of our sun-bright day as the waves licked into the boat turning homeward, 'It was a great day, wasn't it?

'Before I forget, you still have a dress in my closet.'

'I do?' I said, acting surprised, 'What does it look like?'

'Gray, with flowers on it. I meant to bring it today. I'll mail it to you.'

'You don't have to bother, Mack,' I said, squinting into the sinking sun.

'It's no bother at all.'

13.

I was having coffee over at Kara's, who I had known for some years. A couple of years ago, she had married a handsome blonde Riker's Island sadist/guard named Rick. He worked out; kept fit, using, I am sure, prisoners, if no 'heavy-bag' was available to him and—he cheated on her. I know this because he once pinched my leg under the kitchen table, as we all sat around, and he made tongue-motions to me on one occasion when Kara looked away; oh, yes; he would've tongued me, if he could've. I didn't take it as a compliment; with Rick, I'm sure, it was any port in a storm, a 'no rules for us' policy.

We were in Kara's kitchen. 'The first part of my life must've been a coming attraction to the Horror Show I'm in now,' I was saying to Kara, as Rick walked in.

'What can I say to really hurt this guy?' I blurted.

'Whadee-_do_-taya?' Rick replied.

'He completely broke my heart. I just want something to say to him, should he ever call me again—On the off-chance!'

Rick looked puzzled at first, as to what I could possibly mean about a 'heart.' But then he shrugged, 'Okay,' and got down to the business he knew best, entering and breaking the human spirit.

'Any guy is all wrapped up in his Dick, see? You tell 'im he don't do it for you anymore, an' you found somebody else. You say it just like *dis*—!' (He gave me a few choice words to memorize and I did so, just in case I ever heard from McKenzie Jones again.)

'I really don't want to hurt him,' I qualified, 'I just want him to remember me and—!'

'—Hey Kara! More cawffee here! *Make it fast!*'

My Riker's consultation was over.

The memorized lines were all but forgotten. I kept running, from job to job; to the girls, and back again. Jerry had reapplied for the Air Force, thanks to Mack's earlier suggestion, and so my life ran along in those eddies; I kept running, from time to time, Rick of Riker's magic lines through my head, just in case Mack called—but he never did.

All this 'running' was getting confusing and I was half-incinerated with anxiety. I missed Mack. This was all I still knew clearly to be true.

One night, at perhaps three or four in the morning, the big clanging bell of the phone by my bed rang. I was not fully awake when I rolled over and picked it up. 'Hello,' said a slightly slushy whiskey-voice. Instantly, I knew the curtain was going up—and I didn't know my lines!

'Hello,' I said cheerfully, trying in vain to call up the speech Rick had given me. But, no: Head, vacant.

'How *are* you?' I stalled. There was a puzzled silence at his end.

'How are *you*?' he responded brilliantly, waiting. 'Like a sitting duck!,' I thought, *'ready to aim*, but where are those *words* I'd kept batting around in my brain for so long?!'

'How's your mother?' I asked charmingly.

'My—*mother*?!'

I was just about to hang up the receiver in desperation, when those words came flooding back to me.

'Oh, and one more thing—!' I said, and grimly proceeded to take apart his manhood, just as artificially as could be, but I recited the words as they had been given to me. Then, with an immense sigh of satisfaction, I uttered 'Good-bye!' and hung up.

In the morning, I was not even sure that Mack had called, but I awoke smiling, so he must have. That day and the day following went along as all the ones just before them, not good, but at least, consistently bad. I worked day and night.

A week passed. A Friday night passed. A long hot, busy Saturday passed, handing out fish dinners to the customers, trying to forget that the air conditioner in the restaurant was broken. I wiped my hands—and then my eyes—!

As I turned from the order window to view a table by the door, a tall man, dressed in what can only be called a 'smoking jacket,' was sitting there. He had a pipe in his hand and was far too elegantly turned out for this place. I realized it was Mack. As our eyes met, I recognized the gaffed look on his face. (The swordfish hanging on the wall over his head wore the same disbelieving expression—*'What am I doing here?'*)

'He's mine,' I thought, before I even went up to him, *'he's mine.'*

The owner's wife was staring hard at me from the kitchen door. I hesitated. Then I sat down across from him.
'I've missed you,' he said, and as we locked hands, love surged and flowed like silent gold through our bodies. It warmed us through. The sadness melted from his eyes, as it did from my soul. 'I missed you, too.'
I didn't know if I should come or not—after that— *telephone* call!'
'I'm glad that you did.'
'Everything's going to be all right, you'll see,' he said, squeezing my hands again.

As I hung up my apron that night, the owner's wife wore a wary look: she knew my days in the restaurant business were coming to a close. She'd have to advertise for a replacement 'Whirling Dervish.' There would always be those.

That formula worked. If I could only remember those words, I'd be a rich woman today.

It was his cousin, C.B, on the phone. *'What did you say to my cousin?!* I've never seen him so upset. He couldn't stop crying over you!'

'I really don't know,' I replied. She laughed a rich, hearty laugh. 'Well, good for you; I knew you two were meant for each other. And I'll be happy to be your Maid of Honor! When do you want City Hall?' She was the Assistant to the Chief Clerk.

'Sometime for the Fall?'

'Fine,' she said, 'I'll pencil you in! I loved C.B, and when she went to hang up, she said, chortling, 'Just let me know what you did to him! I have someone I'd like to try it on.'

(What were those words?!)

His cousin Vinnie, a black-haired, stocky Irishman full of ribaldry, was coarse in a wonderful way (maybe trying to live up to a future 'Cousin Vinnie' of future film-fame, ethnicity aside.)

'Vinnie will be the Best Man; is that okay with you?'

'Sure, that'll be fine. Vinnie was the first of your relatives that I met. . . Remember?'

It was all settled. We were sitting at his kitchen table in Astoria, happily planning that September wedding, twining our lives together.

Jerry had come to live with us, sleeping on the couch until his service term began. Mack had convinced me to take him in; I was doubtful, thinking he might be pulling a fast one.

190

One day in the car, Mack hopped out to get something at a store. Jer, 'riding shotgun,' turned around to me, and grinned: 'Hey, if I screw up, you're my *Mom*, right?'

'No, *not* right. It was *Mack* who wanted you to stay with us—not I!' The look on his face was priceless.

So things were going well. All of a sudden, it happened again: 'There's something I've got to tell you.' *('Oh, no!* That little voice within me! *Shut up! You're doing it again!')*

I tried, but I couldn't stop. I had to say it. 'Do you remember the time we were sitting in the Neptune Diner and you guessed my age at thirty-five?'

Protectively, Mack drew back in his chair, as he nodded.

'Well— well: by the time we marry in the Fall, I'll be—forty.'

'No!' he insisted. Then: 'So? You're two years older than I. That's nothing.'

'Yes, but those are big years, if you want to have a baby. Maybe I can't anymore. And I want you to be happy.'

He took a sip of tea. 'If you can't, then you can't. My first wife couldn't. We'll get a dog. How's that? And if you can, good.'

Even as I kissed him over the teacup, I proceeded, stubbornly determined to lose the one man I really, really loved: 'I know you love children, and so I'm going to go to a doctor to find out if I can still have a baby.'

'Do what you want to; you will, anyway.

'You know,' Mack added cautiously, 'my Mom had spoken to me about you before we broke up—not that she doesn't *like* you,' he added quickly, 'it's just that —!' here, he emitted a long sigh and looked down at his hands.

'Look, I don't blame her. You're her only son and she loves you. If it were *my* son who was dating a woman who had four kids and a crazy ex, I'd tell *him* to stay away from her, too!'

He looked up and cracked a smile: 'She's going to love you. And you'll love her and Dad.'

Doctor Haynes was a 'Fertility Doctor,' which sounded a lot like 'Witch Doctor.' However, he was soft-spoken and sweet and after the battery of tests concluded, he gently cleared his throat before explaining the results. After hearing 'amni' this and 'amnio' that, I wasn't at all sure of the direction his remarks were taking: 'Does this mean I can still get pregnant?'

He smiled: 'You go on and get married; yes, it is possible for you to become pregnant.' Even though I heard the words, I thought he was lying to me in the interest of true love. I was properly skeptical and probably honorable, at least in this instance, to a fault. Anyway, getting married was a '*Go.*'

It was Medieval-tournament weather, with the wind flapping the flags on the buildings in lower Manhattan like ties, perfect for a joust or pageantry, perfect for a wedding.

'There isn't a cloud in the sky,' Mack noted of the blue parapet above us, as we ducked into the 'Main Arena,' City Hall.

When we stepped off the elevator, a smiling C.B and Vinnie greeted us, everybody, smiling. We each leaned over her desk outside the City Clerk's Office and signed-off on the necessary forms.

'We'll put you in a little ahead of the mob,' she promised. 'I like your dress. Where'd you get it?

'Oh, it's just a plain old white day-dress my friend, Lorra gave me. I just sewed a blue flounce along the bottom.'

'Paisley. Nice. Is it borrowed? You know, something borrowed, something—?' '

Kind of,' I laughed nervously.

Winking at Mack, she handed me a small bouquet: 'Picked this up for you.'

'Thank you!'

'You look ecstatically happy.' 'I am; I feel like I'm walking on a carpet of clouds.'

Vinnie pinned a white carnation on Mack's lapel, saying in his brogue, 'An' what about Dooble-oh-seven, here?! The man in the tan gabardine suit?!'

'I'm happy as hell,' Mack said, his eyes crinkling as he laughed.

'Don't know if that sounds right,' said C.B agreeably, turning to me: '—Any of your family coming? Brother or sister?'

'No, my brother Timmy recently got separated. My sister, Cassie is shooting today. She's—'

'Oh, I know,' C.B said, 'Mack told me. She's in that soap. She's playing Mamie Wintour now, right? She's very good.'

'Yah. She loves it. She won't be here; she called me.'

'Well, that's okay; we have plenty of witnesses here. C'mon. I'll bring you to Noah's Ark.'

'What?' Mack asked, as we followed her. . . 'Everyone's two by two!' she laughed. 'It's Holding Pen 'A'. We're a bit backed up today.'

As we entered Room 'A,' we saw that it was filled with soon-to-be grooms and brides—some of whom were dangerously close to 'burgeoning.'

At the very least, we all had in common the unification factor. Otherwise, there were some curious combos: a pimply-faced sailor with a buxom lady of perhaps fifty years; an ancient man of ninety, accompanied by a gum-chewing gal who might have been a perfect 'match' for the sailor. Some men, especially those next to the immensely pregnant, seemed angry, scowling everywhere, but in between and all over the anteroom, as a 'softening agent,' were those C.B called, *'the lovey-doveys,'* wooing and kissing, oblivious to all but each other.

I stopped taking mental snapshots of those around me and with my heart pumping, questioned whether I truly belonged there, next to this man.

Swiftly, then, we were called in and after the rapid stream of amalgamating words flew past us and Mack bowed his head and kissed me, I knew I belonged with him. The pallid memory of my past two ceremonies to Devious Dick and Jealous Jason reared up for a half-second like ghosts—and were instantly mentally dispatched as affronts to all that was good, almost never to return.

We dined on a brunch of Eggs Benedict and Bloody Mary's—not 'quince with a runcible spoon,' though I felt Mack and I were very much the *'Owl and the Pussycat'*—and after our good-byes and thank-you's, took our first trip home to Astoria as husband and wife.

'I'm happy, but I don't feel there's any difference now.'

'That's because it was meant to be this way,' Mack replied, unlocking our door: We had come home.

Kim came home to New York for a visit to see Jerry before he went off into the service. She had done a little detective work and, unlike the FBI, had managed to locate Dick Earhart.

'He changed his name to Mike Smith and he owns a chemical company in Cleveland. He's remarried, and the father of—and he has two kids, a boy and a girl.'

'Michael Smith! How original!' scoffed Jay.

'But,' said Kay, 'even though he wouldn't come to the phone—he told his Uncle Herbert that it would be too *upsetting* to talk to me—he said he'll remember me in his Will!' She turned to me earnestly: 'Mom, do you think he will? Remember me in his Will?'

I smiled at her. 'Maybe. It would be nice. I hope we get to find out soon!'

The trips to Spencer Hill were over, with very little nostalgia, except that all the children's books were gone now; Jerry, gone now, to the Air Force; gone; Scotch, with a name-change to 'Cindy,' to friends of Mack's in Westchester, with a yard of her own (no dogs were allowed in our building); troubles, gone—some; just like that! Like nightmares, they pass—but new ones come along; thankfully, not yet; not right away.

Trips to the Fertility Doctor began.

'What do you mean, you can't move?' said Mack early one the morning.

'Not until I take my temperature! Hand me that Basal Thermometer?' This, inserted in the vaginal area, takes a core temperature to be registered on a chart. A (very!) slight increase in body temperature meant an egg had been released and was ready for fertilization. I was far too dull-witted and unscientific to carry this procedure very far, as was, apparently, my husband: 'Throw that thing out! If it'll be, it'll be!' No argument from me: I had to dress for work, too.

'The happiest day of my life' had flown. Enter 'Beyond my wildest dreams' (the way our union was going).

Mack was a relaxed and patient man, two long-missing components from my life. There was no bill-collector anxiety any more, no more sweet-talking the 'rental representative.' All of our bills were simply paid when due, *on time!*

To someone who had lived at the edge of a chasm of ruin for two decades, someone who couldn't even afford *bankruptcy* because she had nothing worth losing, this was a miracle. I still couldn't, wouldn't, buy anything for myself; that would take a lot more time. Earrings, make-up, pantyhose; things like that; lunches at work; these, I could get.

The one luxury I needed, peace of mind, I now owned. A dress here and there could come later. It's not that I was any angel, it was that piss-poor training period—my life—that put a crimp in my buying-style: I was a hair away from being a bag-lady and had nearly attained pack-rat status: I could throw nothing away. As a person without religion, I was pleased, at a later date, to meet my personal savior, the Microwave Oven, King of the Leftovers, God of Garbage Dinners: Nuke me now! But for the time being, I was content to cook, to reheat, to bag my lunches for work, with the occasional dinner out, of course.

One night, he had his hat on his head and his bowling bag in his hand, walking toward the door. A sudden feeling, an instinct, zapped over me: 'Where are you going?'

I was squatting down by the pots-and-pans cupboard.

'You know, *bowling* practice.' 'Don't,' I said, squinting up at him.

'*What?!*'

'Don't go. If you want to have a baby, don't go tonight. I have a feeling tonight's the night.' He hesitated, still leaning toward the doorway.

'Are you *sure?*' he said, 'because—!'

I shrugged, 'If you want to chance it, go to Sterling Lanes: *I* already *have* kids.'

He shook his head, slowly putting down his bag.

'There's something about you and bowling. I'd like to know what it is!' he muttered, hanging up his coat.

He found out nine months later—to the *day*, when our first child, a boy, was born. Don't ask me what that was all about. Like the Microwave Oven, I am just the vessel. Of course, the baby would be brought up not as a Casserole, but as a Catholic.

Very, very amusing, I am sure; but I was forty-three years old by then. Perhaps the climb up Mount Olympus had been worth it; still looked pretty good and no one had called me Grandma yet.

As for the Dad, he was higher than a helium balloon; unfortunately, I overheard him telling a visitor, 'It's the happiest day of my life!' ('*He can always remarry,*' I reminded myself, '*but he hadn't been sure he'd be a father. 'Kiss it up!'* as those who are inclined to say, do.)

His parents, in their 'seventies, were thrilled with the birth of a first grandchild.

Baby Peter John looked like he had been chiseled from stone into a miniature Mack, only his eyes were wider, like mine, staying 'capricious blue' till he was two, then turning that brilliant animal yellow-brown. He was two feet long at birth, and deadly calm. What would unfurl? Another picture-book— large, thoughtful, full of fears, introspections; loves, wanton disregarding; pride; a young man's fulfillments and failures—was about to be written with abandon, pleasure and pain.

Really, we were quite contented in our slightly larger Astoria apartment, just a stone's throw from the Kaufman Film Studios and a Yellow Cab Company lot, chock full of Checker Cabs, too, 'for da movies.'

While Mack pushed his mailman's cart in the city, I pushed Pete in his stroller far and wide—furthering my reputation, I guess, for giving all my kids 'the air'—as Pete stared with his golden orbs at the sea of Yellow Cabs before him.

Therefore, it was a shock when Mack's mom died, not only because we loved her, but because we moved to Rockaway to live with his Dad.

I fought the move, to no avail: the logistics of low rent, sentiment and the breadwinner's will prevailed. Our new home would be a well-kept three-story structure, off-white Cape Cod shingles, warm maroon trim, just a block from a big, sandy playground, the Atlantic Ocean.

However, floors two and three of the house were rented out, except for one small bedroom upstairs, so all of us and our combined furniture were shin-to-shin on Floor One.

'This is *turrible!*,' Big Pete wailed, inching between the furniture in the kitchen.

'I'll bet you're sorry we came, now,' I volunteered.

'I am!'

He was mourning, Mack was working and moving furniture around at night, and I was cooking and chasing around after little Peter, trying to quiet him, a sure recipe for domestic unrest. Overnight, I had gone from being Serene Queen of the Castle to Abject Slave of the Knavery.

'You can't cook under there! Katherine never did,' Pete admonished me when I tried to broil a steak. Nothing was done 'the way Katherine did it,' and I, even though I cooked him his big meal at noon ('the way 'Katherine did it') became a minor hell-cat of a daughter-in-law and a major one on the matrimonial scene.

There were sputters and spats aplenty, and one or two big fights, but gradually, they evened out, as things must.

'You two and the baby can take the big bedroom; the little one *oopstairs* is fine for just me.'

So said Pete, the softer, elder-version of Mack, and he now slept in the little room on the second floor, just off old George's studio apartment. Having George's apartment available to us would have made a huge difference in our lives, but how do you throw a ninety-two year old tenant, a working florist out on the street? (We had all stopped wondering when George's slippered foot would tread it's last.)

Daytimes in winter were the hardest, but that's a universal 'given.'

'Posie can sleep on the pull-out couch in the living room when she comes next month from California,' said Mack. I was really looking forward to her visit.

When we got to JFK to pick her up, I looked around anxiously for her, searching for the robust and hale waitress of yore, the electric blue spark charging the eye! I walked right by her.

'Allo?' a soft voice said quizzically, 'Maura?'

I hadn't seen her in years. Somewhere between then and now, Posie had melted down. In front of me stood a tiny gray dove, dressed (even though it was warm out) in a coat, little black hat and a ratty fox stole, tiredly tasting its own tail around her neck. Upon recognition, my face fell before I could stop it.

'Humph!,' she reacted, her face flushing, 'I think I look pretty *good*, for my age! It was a long *trip!*'

'You *do!*,' I insisted, hugging her carefully, 'You do! It's only that I haven't seen you in so long a while! Come on; Mack is over there.'

We went home. Candles flickered briefly in Big Pete's eyes; 'It's nice to have *company* for a change, eh, Pete?,' she laughed. He warmed right up to her, nodding: *'Adult* company!' Of course, she was 'no Katherine,' but he liked her.

'It's too hot to bake! Just relax, Posie; you don't have to do this!'

'No, I want to. I already bought everything I need. It won't take me long.'

Thus, one hot day in August, Rosie came to my kitchen by way of San Jose, California, and baked a perfectly vile lemon meringue pie. The crust was lead; the lemon, hot and sour and the meringue wheezled and drizzled all over it.

Some, as we perspired at the table and ate our dessert, pronounced it edible: 'Vuddy, vuddy good!' said Pete, my father-in-law. Others were not so kind.

Later, after we did the dishes and went out on the porch to cool off, she was still miffed at her pie being unappreciated. I smiled over at her on the porch swing.

'Did you know, Posie, you are the only one of my friends who knew all three of my husbands? What an *honor!*'

Pleased her, that did, and feelings mollified, she smiled back at me: 'Dick was like a horse that threw you as soon as you got on. The second one—that Jason! You never should have married him—! He *dragged* you—through the mud!'

'—For eleven long years!' I groaned. . .

We rocked together in the swing for a while.

'Prob'ly this last one; prob'ly, you'll ride off into the sunset with him.

'Probably.

'. . .I remember the time you and I sat on the Great Lawn, Posie. . .' *the dying sun, melting into the burnt pink water; the boats out there in silhouette, playing at being Clipper Ships, and the two kids, in silent awe, stopping their coloring to look at the grandeur and glow of that 'Seurat' moment: it was the poignancy of a personal Pointillism, one era hovering on the brink of the next.*

And suddenly, I smiled, aware that although time had passed, gold was also the color of sunrise, the wealth of hope and to some, the heavenly journey, the color of God.

'Do you remember that day on Acushnet Bay?'

She looked at me keenly for a moment. 'The kids were crayoning.'

'Yes. That's right. . . You know, I'm so glad you came to New York to see me.'

'It was on my way,' she shrugged, 'besides, how could I pass by 'my other daughter,' and not stop by for a little visit?'

The sun retreated.

Rosie went back to California and soon after her trip North, died at home in John's arms of a heart attack. It wasn't 'sposed' to be that way as she might have said. John, near ninety, was twenty years older than she was: I guess she pulled a 'Manny' on him.

But I can still taste that pie. . .

All recipes come to an end, the worst and the very best. Her quick death in San Jose set me up for the inevitability of my parents' deaths, but hardly prepared me for what lay ahead.

14.

If I *could* have; if I *would* have— Jumped ahead ten or more years into the future on some kind of super-shoes, I would have glimpsed the following later-life scenario; scenes that were going to be played out later on:

. . . The house was a shell, and had fallen into the quiet disrepair of the un-invested. A gentle tug on the tiny pull-chain— and the antiquated wall scone threw a pale halo of light upon the living room wall of their house in Queens.

Dad's old recliner chair faced the TV with, no doubt, remnants of old meals, cookie crumbs and small change intact therein.

Tim opened the front door, and as Cassie and I stepped over the threshold, there was nothing for me to fear. But fear, I did, in a great gulping downward spiral of remembrance—the same clutch of despair that always caught me by the throat when I came home, and made me into a cornered child again.

Tim ushered us past the decrepit living room and the tiny dining room, saddled with boxes to one side, the old dark wood table and bureaus, gone now; the telephone, on the floor; and we walked out into the kitchen.

'Need some air,' Tim said, propping open the old kitchen window with a can of dog food, glancing outside in back at the weedy garden. Cassie sat on a couple of cardboard boxes, stacked and corded for '*Good Will.*'

I sat in the lone kitchen chair; the small table stood facing me in the dinette area; underneath, Dilly the dog, eyed me with quiet suspicion.

'How's the family?'

I was taken aback. This was a question Cassie seldom asked me.

'Fine. Jerry's signed up for his second Air Force tour.

And Kim's divorced from Rod now.'

'So I heard.'

'But she seems to be doing all right.'

'That's good. I know Sally's with the UN, but what about Joy? Last time I heard, she was having some problems.'

'She still is. I don't know what's going to happen next for her. She says she's not on drugs, but—'

'—She was such a beautiful girl. And how's Jason? Does he still bother you?'

'No. He's still alive and fuming, but not at me, since I remarried.'

'Please. He's such a coward!. . . And, ah—Dick?'

(. . .Dick; the meaning of love is give it all, until that person breaks your heart?) 'No. I haven't. Never.'

'Do you realize they both died at exactly eighty-four and a half?'

'Yes, Timmy,' I said, 'but a year apart.'

'But both, after a protracted illness!'

Came the wisdom of Cassie: 'Yes. Compatible for once, in Death.'

It was strange, we (children, again!) being together in the old house without '*Them.*'

'Come on.' Tim began pacing and looked at the wall clock. 'If there's nothing you want down here, let's go upstairs to Mom's room.'

It was bereft of nearly everything. Her bed still stood, stripped of linens, a mute and poignant reminder of its recent occupant, and the little refrigerator that Tim got for her was still there. The one small closet door stood ajar. Once crammed with clothing, only a few outdated items of clothing hung on the rack.

Tim cleared his throat. 'Did you girls take whatever you needed?' He walked over to the window, facing the house with the Guyanese people living in it: 'She used to love to watch the birds and listen to them. Except for the Jays. Well, there're not too many of those now, for some reason; I don't know.

'Well?' He turned to face us. 'There are some perfumes and toilet articles on the bureau in the other room, and some gifts she never opened.' (That bureau was in the room she once shared with my father.)

'Well, what I could use, I took, Timmy. Maybe the rest of the things, since you *bought* her most of those things, Cassie—'

'Positively *not*!' She actually shuddered.

Luckily, before I spoke, I saw tears in her eyes, and kept silent.

We all stared at the ceiling for a moment. Tim sat on the mattress and curved his hands around his one good knee, chuckling to himself.

'Do you remember the story about her cutting the rubber sheets and packing parachutes during the war?'

'I *know* that story,' Cassie said. 'The only thing I want now is a cup of coffee.'

'Put on a pot,' Tim called out, as she walked back downstairs to the kitchen.

'Remember that?' I nodded.

'…She worked at Lord Manufacturing, in Erie: About the large scissors that left the red welts on her fingers? And no more wrapping parachutes, the toughest job of all. One night, she said—!'

'Tim, come on! I told _you_ this story: you were too little to know about—!'

'Yeah, yeah,' he said, waving me off with one hand. 'So she was all upset and said, 'Some of the women laugh and talk while they pack the chutes, and don't even look down at what they're doing. Some *smoke*. Never check their work!'

'*Yes, Timmy!* And when _I_ asked her why they *don't?*' she stared at me— with those eyes of hers—and said 'Maybe they don't care if a young body lies broken on the ground—*Maura!*'

'And she was proud that she made less money than they did; because she worked more slowly.'

'She had a conscience.'

'She told *me*, too! What do you think we *talked* about, Maura, while she was *dying* up here?! Did you think you were her only kid?!'

'What are you two talking about?, said Cassie, coming in with a tray. Here,' she said handing them off, 'two cups of black.'

'Yeah, talking *would* be the operative. Too bad Tim didn't talk like this when he was a kid!,' I said, blowing on the coffee. 'Remember those Christmas dinners? And the plays—'*Pull the plug?!* Everyone loved that play!'

'I noticed Barney Sweeney had no right thumb,' said Tim, changing the subject. 'I think he lost it in construction.'

'Of *course*, you both knew Grandma Connelly and Barney were lovers!' Cassie tossed off. Tim nodded and smiled.

This news struck me in the face. 'You've *got* to be kidding!'

'Mom told me, years ago! I thought you knew that.'

'Barney—_Sweeney!?_ Good God! Barney looked like—an Irish monkey— a *kindly* Irish monkey!' Tim and Cassie laughed.

'I mean, one can almost *see him*, grooming the back of another monkey!. . . *Can't* you?!'

In retrospect, the more I thought about it, I saw it, their liaison, as a probable fact. Grandma Kate's husband had died at age thirty-three of the Spanish Flu, when it wiped out half of New York City.

She was left with that sad, bemused expression, and three children under five—No funds or Social Security, back then.

So part of her mystique was cleared up, as some of her pain and loneliness must have been, but—

'Barney *Sweeney*?! How *could* she?'

Later, as Cassie and I headed downstairs, out the front door, and back to our respective lives, a shudder passed, and it passes again; only this time, I shrug and throw it onto the lazy wood-burner in the back of my mind.

Cassie had put together a successful local theatre group; she was doing very well playing the much despised and beloved Mamie Wintour, five days a week on TV.

Tim now lived in their old place with his black dog, Dilly, and assorted stacks of newspapers. The burden of caring for both Mom and Dad had fallen on him. Cassie sent regular checks and lovely presents (most of which still lay in their boxes). Through the years before Mom's Final 'Fall,' Cas had placed Mom in fancy 'spas'(actually, drying-out tanks) in Red Bank, New Jersey and one big famous place, out on Long Island, the name of which eludes me.

To me, had fallen the weekly or two-week superficial room-cleaning/cheer-up visits, extending over a five-year period. But it was Timmy who made sure their bills got paid, who argued vociferously with Dad, (bullying him back for all he had dished out to him!) and favoring Mom in all things; so Mom and Tim were the two upstairs Cohorts, Conspirators against the evil downstairs Gremlin.

And now, Tim lived alone, with their ghosts, hermit-happy: he had not shot himself, ate well, was even thinking of getting rid of The Van and buying a new car, without bullets. What's more, he had a new *girlfriend*— and with my brother's and my personal history of 'I'm *on*/you're *off*' romances, I immediately reevaluated the status of my still-young, 'solidasarock' marriage.

During their languishment, all the heavy money was on the Frail Finn to go first. But the Irish Tyrant was the upset factor in their grim final play-off game.

My parents were old, 'tireder' than ever, cognizant that duties, cares, the smallest of their chores were coming to an end, in preparation for, shall I say, the Dark Voyage; the Trip of Trips. How much do we know of ourselves? Even less, do we know our parents.

The Face was a mystery and remained so all his life to his family, expressing happiness or fierce anger, but divulging a true self to no one. One wondered if he <u>had</u> a true self.

Occasionally—a rupture. A glimpse was caught.

'What was it like when my father died?' He drew his head back in surprise at the question, both hands gripping the coffee cup like a shield: 'I remember my mother beckoning me into the room to kiss him goodbye; my brother waited at the door for his turn. My sister, only a babe in arms.' He measured, cup in hand, measuring out her size —'So big!

'As I crossed it, the room seemed so big. Five years old; I was five. I stood on tiptoe to reach up and kiss him on his forehead. And when I left—his eyes followed me back across the room.' He coughed a strange, little garble, looking down as he did, something wet on his cheek. 'I can still feel them on me, still see his eyes.'

'*Then* what happened?' (Of course, I had heard his story before.)

'Whad'you mean?'

'After he died.'

The shoulders came up straight, the answer, fast: 'My mother sent me away upstate, to stay at my Aunt's. For months, for a year, I don't know; I didn't know why. I went to find a rope.'. . 'A *rope?*'. . 'To hang myself. I thought nobody wanted me. So, I *found* a rope, but,' he chuckled softly, as when the joke is on yourself, 'I couldn't figure out how to do it. Too young! See, she had had some sort of nervous breakdown: three little kids, you know. Back in those days, they didn't know much about child psychology.'

'Did she finally come to get you?'

'To *visit*; just to visit. Then she'd sneak off without telling me she was leaving. I stayed with my Aunt Mary. Then they put me in the Seminary to study for the priesthood: the first son went to the priesthood, no question! And about that, about the Brothers—?! No. I won't talk about it!'

His mouth clamped shut in a grim line. He set his cup down into the sink abruptly. It was one of his last purposeful acts.

How much mystery? How much truth? And how much was just a goddamn lie?

The old man was going. When I went to their house to clean, I got the first clue.

'That book you brought me last time—'

'Oh? How did you like it?'

He half-rose from his chair, fixing me with an angry stare that must've come solely from the Christian Brothers: 'The last page was missing!'

'I'm so sorry! I never noticed,' I apologized as he handed it back to me.

'Don't bring me any old book like that again!' he said disdainfully.

It wasn't till I got home later and checked the book; that I found it was intact—last page? All there. It was Dad that wasn't all there. He sat in his recliner, staring out past the living room curtains with a far-reaching gaze that Cassie and I called, 'looking over the mountains.'

Pre-dementia, early senility or whatever that obstructed view of eternity is called, often begins with a series of set-backs: a fall, a trip to the hospital, a return home: The fall.

Actually, he was kind of funny in the hospital.

'Yes, Mortie, a pair of pants for each day of the week, seven! (*chuckle, chuckle, staring far-off*) You know I'm good for it. I always get my slacks from you. All the colors good? (*chuckling some more*) All right. Who do I make it out to—the check?'

As I stood by his bed, marveling at this conversation with his invisible clothier-buddy somewhere over my right shoulder, wondering what this 'apparel salesman' looked like, he suddenly drew his old white head back against the pillow, craning, trying to look around me.

'Maura, *move*! I can't *see* them!'

On a quieter day, I walked into his room unseen, as a smile was wreathing his face: 'Mom! I've been waiting to see you! . . . . . how *are* you? I've missed you. But *you* know!'

So, all of that. Then, before things got past Delirious and into Serious, he looked at me shamefacedly as I held his hand: 'Maura, I can't go. You know that *I can't pay the bill*.' I saw the terror and fear of his past misdeeds form in his eyes and wash over his face. 'I can't pay what I *owe*,' he whimpered sorrowfully, piercing into my eyes and into my ken: '*You* know!' he whispered, 'Is it all right?'

There it was. What a hush, as his meaning sunk in.

I was astounded that I felt sorry for him; I thought about this for a while before I replied, exhaling, 'It's all right, Dad. It's okay.'

'But—*you know!* Are you sure?'

'I'm sure. Your check cleared, Dad. You can go.' He fretted, still disquieted. 'I checked! The money is in there,' I squeezed his hand, 'I'm sure.' He drifted into a fitful sleep.

The next day, I didn't want to go back to the hospital. Mack—who really couldn't stand the old man—said 'You should go today.'

'We have too much to do today: we'll go tomorrow.' 'Today,' he said firmly.

His bed was empty when I got there. A rush of feeling overwhelmed me. I turned to go to the Nurses' Station, my legs practically wooden, when I saw him on a gurney, the attendant standing near him, drumming his fingers on the wall, as they waited for an elevator.

'Goin' up for some tests,' the aide said. But his eyes had a strange, a different look when he said it. Then I saw it: all Dad's tubing had been removed. Cassie's words leapt into my head. . . '*They let them go when the Medicaid runs out*'—which it just had. I looked down at the white head, the face fraught with care, the body tossing feebly, fighting hellfire and angels alike, no longer worrying whether they were real or not, just frightened.

'Don't be scared, Dad,' I said, 'I'm right here.' I took one curled claw of a hand, bent and kissed him on the forehead. The tension drained from his face for a second and as the elevator doors opened, I called, 'I'll be here, Dad.'

The doors slid shut, and that was it; that was the good-bye.

I walked back slowly toward the Waiting Area where Mack sat reading a magazine.

He looked up: 'Did you see him?' Tears wobbled in my eyes. I walked past him and rang for a down elevator. 'Thank you for making me come today, Mack.'

The telephone jangled just as we got inside the door at home; it was the hospital, just as I knew it would be.

So, in the end, she had outlived him; for, as Cassie said, 'With them, it was always some kind of a contest.'

Mom reigned happily upstairs in the catbird seat, her small fridge well-stocked by Timmy with food and non-alcoholic drinks (of which she seldom partook); reading the dailies as they passed like summer leaves; coolly appraising the 'Mets' or Judge Judy on her TV; a doctor or a home nurse popping in now and then—but, keeping their distance, which was how she liked it.

Yes, she had won. Or was it a draw? As Boom-Boom Mancini discovered (when he vanquished the courageous Korean boxer Kim Duc Soo with a last and lethal blow in a murderous exchange!) it is hard to win a contest with Death as the referee.

The mother had soft skin and angular features. Like most children, I didn't realize she had a face at all, knowing only that she was that warm presence that stood cooking at the stove, or tucking me into bed at night; until one day, a little playmate whispered, 'What's your mother *angry* about?'

'Angry?' I turned in surprise. 'My mother's not angry. She *always* looks like that!' I saw for the first time her facial expression, devoid of merriment, as others did.

Some years later, they had one of those *Dateline TV* shows and it showed all these Finns, dancing like crazy together on a crowded Dance Hall floor in Finland. As the camera panned, not one of them wore a smile. Except that their legs moved frenetically, they might've been dancing at their own funerals. We all howled, especially Mom, who had to wipe away her tears of laughter, gasping out, 'hot feet— cold faces!'

Certainly, she had not had much to smile about, living with Dad; she spoke not of her troubles, but she started to drink a hell of a lot by the time we were in our teens, and continued this outrageous pattern of escape. She became a silent and polite drunk, one that smirked, stumbled slightly and spoke a perilously-false 'French,' until the final escape.

For years, she had staggered under the burden of concealing what my father had done to me and to others; of his infidelities, plus the additional weight of what she had neglected to do, relieving it with drink, but never quite obliterating recall.

Timmy was her salvation. She never thought him caustic or selfish, though she knew he was sometimes both. When he tried to bully her in her bedridden days, she smiled and overlooked. He was her baby, her buddy; he who, as a tiny boy, crawled in the night to the foot of her bed, wiggling her big toe (to waken her, and not Dad) to let her know he was suffering. The childhood asthma he endured was unabated, un-medicated and unheeded by his father. Tim was the little soldier for whom she lovingly cared: in the final outcome, she knew she could count on him never to defect. She was right.

'Even the worse situation has a positive side,' Dad had asserted more than once.

When Mom fell in the kitchen, dead-drunk, breaking her pelvic-bone, that was a 'positive,' I later configured. Because after her hospital stay and once she was banked upstairs, she could no longer meet the liquor delivery guy at the front door. She could telephone, she could order her staples—vodka, vodka and vodka—but the Delivery Boy would be turned away when he got there.

With any drunk gone dry, there is initial anger, confusion and resentment, especially when it is enforced like that.

Eventually, the real person is forced to creep out, like a contentious small animal peering warily out of the cave of the inner self, its eyes adjusting to the light; peering this way and that, sure that no friendly face will be found. To the horror and utter dismay of all drunks, friendly people are all around, greeting them like returnees from a prison camp or a space ship: *'Hello! (Bright smile.) How are you?'*

How diabolical! How depraved! *How boring*!

Soon, the drunk, a little more comfortable in the skin that is not now too tight for its body, begins to un-tense—and smiles graciously. The 'other person' has emerged—leaving the cocoon of the empty vodka bottle behind, but not too far behind. It ever beckons. Come hither!

Well, the resultant dried-out period was always such a pleasure for us all. Ellen was then a delightful, witty, social being, a Queen Elizabeth, letting you in on her private jokes; her well-kept, well-tended inner-personality was, in the vernacular, 'a whole 'nother world.'

After she had won her 'victory' over Dad, I saw her sitting in her room, contented with Death, who had now become her quiet best friend, unseen, but tacitly acknowledged with a smile and a downward tilt of her head. I smiled when I saw her there.

'Oh, I meant to bring you some flowers today!'

'Why?' she replied, sweetly caustic, so I can smell them while I'm still alive?'

'It's preferable, but you do have your choice. . . next time I come, what'll it be?'

She smiled up at me, her eyes the soft color of cornflowers, a lilt in her voice.

'Oh, I don't know—violets, perhaps?'

211

'How Katherine Hepburn of you!' I replied. 'Violets, it is.'

After changing her sheets and doing a little dusting, I was on my way out the door, to go back home to Rockaway.

'Why not stay and watch Judge Judy with me?'

'Well, the traffic starts up in about—' I began my usual departure spiel, and then got a funny twinge.

'Why not?' I stretched out next to her on her bed and together, we laughed at all the litigants. I was glad I had stayed.

The reason this sticks in my mind, of course, is that she had a stroke later that evening.

Too late for the violets. . .

. . '*They come back every Spring, don't they!?*'. . .

Yes, Mother.

And the decision about scattering their ashes after the cremations at Jones Beach—which would parallel their lives together, 'forever at sea!'—to be grappled with at a later date, while they rested in two glassine bags, together but still separate, in my kitchen cupboard. . .

. . . All, all of this; their passing, the settlement of their house, the bumps in the road; still lay ahead like some large hairy creature hunkered down behind a rock, waiting to leap out at me 'on my way to market' later; a good ten to fifteen years later into my most fairy-tale future. . .

But for now, Posie went to her 'little rest,' and I, heedless of all that dying yet to come, went about enjoying the pleasures and the features of my new life.

15.

It was the last night for the bowling team, husband/wife partners' night and a final game for Mack, who had decided to quit company league-play as it was 'too much,' what with home and family duties.

'Too *much*? But you love it!'

'I just used it as a way to fill my lonely nights,' Mack replied—a little too loftily, and the lump his tongue made in his cheek too visible, to be sincere.

I had been coaxed into reluctant participation this night; a routinely bad player (I had broken a bone in my foot last year, jumping in the air at my sole strike) and was reassigned my role as Gutterball Gertie.

I did it to keep the peace, more than anything, and to have a night out with Mack.

I still had the writing addiction, and was 'writing with a vengeance'—probably the most accurate way to describe it!—amassing quite a collection of plays and stories along the way, and, certainly the world's worst poetry. '*But,*' I thought, '*I can leave it—and the two Pete's!—for one night!*'

Al and Mack were at the Bowlerama Front Desk. Mack turned to me: 'We've been switched from Lanes Three and Four to Lanes Twelve and Thirteen. Would you go down there and let anyone who's sitting down there on Three know about it?'

I went bobbing along on my rental shoes like I was on rocking-horse rails, down to Lane Three.

A lone woman sat there. She stood up and smiled at me as I approached.

Her eyes were dark brown and it struck me that she looked startlingly like my crazy friend, Lorra, from New Bedford. She wore a yellow sweater, brown slacks and loafers, and her hair was in a neat soft pouf, like Lorra's.

'You must be Al's wife.'

She nodded and smiled again. I looked down at her brown loafers. 'I see you didn't get your bowling shoes yet. I came to tell you they're meeting over on Lane Thirteen.'

'You just had a baby,' she said, coming closer to me.

'What? Oh. Almost a year ago.'

'There's more where *that* came from!'

I burst out laughing, showing her all of my teeth.

'I hardly *think* so! I'm forty-four years old. Well, then; I'll let you get your shoes now, and ah, we'll see you down there on— Thirteen.'

She kept smiling knowingly at me, soundless, and didn't seem to be moving any, so I turned to go. I'd walked only a few steps, when I heard her call something out.

'. . . Yes?' I turned back, and she was wagging a finger at me: '*Don't forget!* The best is yet to come!'

Back on Thirteen, Mack had his shoes on and was warming up.

'I told Al's wife we'd be over here.' He picked up his ball, looking quizzically at me.

'Al's wife didn't *come* tonight! He just went to try to find another partner! Must've been somebody else you saw.' I looked down to Lane Three. It was empty now.

'She's gone! Weird! She *said* she was Al's wife! At least, I *think* she did!'

'Well,' he said, hauling back, preparing to throw a vicious hook ball down the alley, 'You must have misunderstood her.'

Yes, Mack threw strikes all of that night: One of them—portentously enough, was—another baby boy.

. . . *'What is it, with you and bowling!?!'*

All Hell broke loose that particular day, some nine months later. It was the anniversary of Katherine's death and Pete was in a bad mood.

I had been cooking—at the stove all day, making four main courses, two pies and one cake. Pete walked back and forth, eyeing me skeptically, muttering, 'Enough food to feed a *camp fulla lumberjacks*!' and comments like that.

I was famished, and just about to dig into a huge dinner, when—

'I can't eat!' I cried, putting down my fork, 'I think—I think I'm having the baby!'

'Hmmph!,' snorted Pete. *'Thought* so!'

Totally carried, feet dragging, into the hospital, supported between two men, Mack and his cousin, my only thought at age forty-five and a half was, *'Will I die?'*

Some long hours later, after a lot of huffing and puffing, little Pete had a baby brother. I was happy to see him—happy to *see, period*!

At home, Old Pete was happy again. Young Pete was perplexed, fixing this newby intruder with a baleful amber eye, unsure whether to strike out at him, or recoil into his den; instead, he later called him Sonny; the old parents, siblings, and pals, too, called him Sonny; later still, skinny, a grin, freckles sprinkled across his nose; now, a young lad headed for pleasure and pain; headed one day, for a home of his own.

As prophesied, the best indeed had come. Winter or summer, sunshine or rain, flawed only occasionally by the ordinary, my life is a combining harvest of all that is wholesome and good and home is my haven.

When the sun stretches up over the Atlantic, I feel that its warmth touches me first; that the friends who've known and loved me are with me still; lucky, is how I feel, as if I've won the Lottery. Like the Ancient Greeks, I am nearing the end of my 'sky-path' journey, riding along in the Sun-chariot with the God Apollo. I am bliss.

LaVergne, TN USA
19 October 2009
161378LV00001B/68/P